"Colleen Coble is my go-to author for the best romantic suspense today. *Three Missing Days* is now my favorite in the series, and I adored the other two. A stay-up-all-night page turning story!"

—Carrie Stuart Parks, bestselling and award-winning author of *Relative Silence*

"You can't go wrong with a Colleen Coble novel. She always brings readers great characters and edgy, intense story lines."

—BestInSuspense.com on *Two Reasons to Run*

"Colleen Coble's latest has it all: characters to root for, a sinister villain, and a story that just won't stop."

—Siri Mitchell, author of *State of Lies*, on *Two Reasons to Run*

"Colleen Coble's superpower is transporting her readers into beautiful settings in vivid detail. *Two Reasons to Run* is no exception. Add to that the suspense that keeps you wanting to know more, and characters that pull at your heart. These are the ingredients of a fun read!"

—Terri Blackstock, bestselling author of *If I Run, If I'm Found*, and *If I Live*

"This is a romantic suspense novel that will be a surprise when the last page reveals all of the secrets."

—*The Parkersburg News and Sentinel* on *One Little Lie*

"There are just enough threads left dangling at the end of this well-crafted romantic suspense to leave fans hungrily awaiting the next installment."

—*Publishers Weekly* on *One Little Lie*

"Colleen Coble once again proves she is at the pinnacle of Christian romantic suspense. Filled with characters you'll come to love, faith lost and found, and scenes that will have you holding your breath, Jane Hardy's story deftly follows the complex and tangled web that can be woven by one little lie."

—Lisa Wingate, #1 *New York Times* bestselling author
of *Before We Were Yours*, on *One Little Lie*

"Colleen Coble always raises the notch on romantic suspense, and *One Little Lie* is my favorite yet! The story took me on a wild and wonderful ride."

—DiAnn Mills, bestselling author

"Coble's latest, *One Little Lie*, is a powerful read . . . one of her absolute best. I stayed up way too late finishing this book because I literally couldn't go to sleep without knowing what happened. This is a must read! Highly recommend!"

—Robin Caroll, bestselling author of the Darkwater Inn saga

"I always look forward to Colleen Coble's new releases. *One Little Lie* is One Phenomenal Read. I don't know how she does it, but she just keeps getting better. Be sure to have plenty of time to flip the pages in this one because you won't want to put it down. I devoured it! Thank you, Colleen, for more hours of edge-of-the-seat entertainment. I'm already looking forward to the next one!"

—Lynette Eason, award-winning and bestselling
author of the Blue Justice series

"In *One Little Lie* the repercussions of one lie skid through the town of Pelican Harbor, creating ripples of chaos and suspense. Who will survive the questions? *One Little Lie* is the latest page-turner from Colleen Coble. Set on the Gulf coast of Alabama, Jane Hardy is the new police chief who is fighting to clear her father. Reid Dixon has secrets of his own as he follows Jane around town for a documentary. Together they must face their secrets and decide when a secret becomes a lie. And when does it become too much to forgive?"

—Cara Putman, bestselling and award-winning author

"Coble wows with this suspense-filled inspirational . . . With startling twists and endearing characters, Coble's engrossing story explores the tragedy, betrayal, and redemption of faithful people all searching to reclaim their sense of identity."

—*Publishers Weekly* on *Strands of Truth*

"Just when I think Colleen Coble's stories can't get any better, she proves me wrong. In *Strands of Truth*, I couldn't turn the pages fast enough. The characterization of Ridge and Harper and their relationship pulled me immediately into the story. Fast-paced, with so many unexpected twists and turns, I read this book in one sitting. Coble has pushed the bar higher than I'd imagined. This book is one not to be missed. Highly recommend!"

—Robin Caroll, bestselling author of the Darkwater Inn series

"Free-dive into a romantic suspense that will leave you breathless and craving for more."

—DiAnn Mills, bestselling author, on *Strands of Truth*

"Colleen Coble's latest book, *Strands of Truth*, grips you on page one with a heart-pounding opening and doesn't let go until the last satisfying word. I love her skill in pulling the reader in with believable, likable characters, interesting locations, and a mystery just waiting to be untangled. Highly recommended."

—Carrie Stuart Parks, author of *Fragments of Fear*

"It's in her blood! Colleen Coble once again shows her suspense prowess with a thriller as intricate and beautiful as a strand of DNA. *Strands of Truth* dives into an unusual profession involving mollusks and shell beds that weaves a unique, silky thread throughout the story. So fascinating I couldn't stop reading!"

—Ronie Kendig, bestselling author of the Tox Files series

"Once again, Colleen Coble delivers an intriguing, suspenseful tale in *Strands of Truth*. The mystery and tension mount toward an explosive and satisfying finish. Well done."

—Creston Mapes, bestselling author

"*Secrets at Cedar Cabin* is filled with twists and turns that will keep readers turning the pages as they plunge into the horrific world of sex trafficking where they come face-to-face with evil. Colleen Coble delivers a fast-paced story with a strong, lovable ensemble cast and a sweet, heaping helping of romance."

—Kelly Irvin, author of *Tell Her No Lies*

"Coble . . . weaves a suspense-filled romance set during the Revolutionary War. Coble's fine historical novel introduces a strong heroine—both in faith and character—that will appeal deeply to readers."

—*Publishers Weekly* on *Freedom's Light*

"This follow-up to *The View from Rainshadow Bay* features delightful characters and an evocative, atmospheric setting. Ideal for fans of romantic suspense and authors Dani Pettrey, Dee Henderson, and Brandilyn Collins."

—*Library Journal* on *The House at Saltwater Point*

"*The View from Rainshadow Bay* opens with a heart-pounding, run-for-your-life chase. This book will stay with you for a long time, long after you flip to the last page."

—*RT Book Reviews*, 4 stars

"Set on Washington State's Olympic Peninsula, this first volume of Coble's new suspense series is a tensely plotted and harrowing tale of murder, corporate greed, and family secrets. Devotees of Dani Pettrey, Brenda Novak, and Allison Brennan will find a new favorite here."

—*Library Journal* on *The View from Rainshadow Bay*

"Coble (*Twilight at Blueberry Barrens*) keeps the tension tight and the action moving in this gripping tale, the first in her Lavender Tides series set in the Pacific Northwest."

—*Publishers Weekly* on *The View from Rainshadow Bay*

"Filled with the suspense for which Coble is known, the novel is rich in detail with a healthy dose of romance, allowing readers to bask in the beauty of Washington State's lavender fields, lush forests, and jagged coastline."

—*BookPage* on *The View from Rainshadow Bay*

"Prepare to stay up all night with Colleen Coble. Coble's beautiful, emotional prose coupled with her keen sense of pacing, escalating danger, and very real characters place her firmly at the top of the suspense genre. I could not put this book down."

—Allison Brennan, *New York Times* bestselling author of *Shattered*, on *The View from Rainshadow Bay*

"Colleen is a master storyteller."

—Karen Kingsbury, bestselling author

THREE MISSING DAYS

ALSO BY COLLEEN COBLE

THREE MISSING DAYS

THE PELICAN HARBOR SERIES

COLLEEN COBLE

THOMAS NELSON

Since 1798

Three Missing Days

Published in Nashville, Tennessee, by Thomas Nelson. Thomas Nelson is a registered trademark of HarperCollins Christian Publishing, Inc.

Thomas Nelson titles may be purchased in bulk for educational, business, fundraising, or sales promotional use. For information, please e-mail SpecialMarkets@ThomasNelson.com.

Quotes in chapters 12 and 22 are from *The Screwtape Letters* by C. S. Lewis. First published in 1942.

Quote in chapter 11 from *Mere Christianity* by C. S. Lewis. First published in 1952.

Publisher's Note: This novel is a work of fiction. Names, characters, places, and incidents are either products of the author's imagination or used fictitiously. All characters are fictional, and any similarity to people living or dead is purely coincidental.

ISBN 978-0-7852-2852-3 (trade paper)
ISBN 978-0-7852-2853-0 (e-book)
ISBN 978-0-7852-2854-7 (library edition)
ISBN 978-0-7852-2855-4 (downloadable audio)

Library of Congress Cataloging-in-Publication Data

Names: Coble, Colleen, author.
Title: Three missing days : a Pelican Harbor novel / Colleen Coble.
Description: Nashville, Tennessee : Thomas Nelson, [2021] | Series: Pelican Harbor ; 3 | Summary: "The third book in a riveting new series from USA TODAY bestselling romantic suspense author Colleen Coble"-- Provided by publisher.
Identifiers: LCCN 2020044576 (print) | LCCN 2020044577 (ebook) | ISBN 9780785228523 (paperback) | ISBN 9780785228547 (library edition) | ISBN 9780785228554 (downloadable audio) | ISBN 9780785228530 (epub)
Subjects: GSAFD: Christian fiction. | Romantic suspense fiction.
Classification: LCC PS3553.O2285 T49 2021 (print) | LCC PS3553.O2285 (ebook) | DDC 813/.54--dc23
LC record available at https://lccn.loc.gov/2020044576
LC ebook record available at https://lccn.loc.gov/2020044577

Printed in the United States of America
HB 04.04.2024

For my cousin Mike Fordyce
Thanks for all the help with nuclear material—you rock!

ONE

I know what you did."

The muffled voice on her phone raised the hair on the back of Gail Briscoe's head, and she swiped the perspiration from her forehead with the back of her hand. "Look, I've reported these calls. Don't call me again."

She ended the call with a hard finger punch on the screen and stepped onto her front porch. The late-May Alabama air wrapped her in a blanket of heat and humidity, and she couldn't wait to wash it off. She should have left the light on before she went for her predawn run. The darkness pressing against her isolated home sent a shudder down her back, and she fumbled her way inside. Welcome light flooded the entry, and she locked the door and the dead bolt with a decisive click that lifted her confidence.

She stared at the number on the now-silent phone. The drugstore again. Though there weren't many pay phones around anymore, the old soda shop and drugstore still boasted a heavy black phone installed back in the sixties. The caller always used it, and so far, no one had seen who was making the calls. The pay phone was located off an alley behind the store by a Dumpster so it was out of sight.

The guy's accusation was getting old. Counting today, this made seven calls with the same message. Could he possibly know about the investigation? She rejected the thought before it had a chance to grow. It wasn't public knowledge, and it would be over soon. She clenched her hands and chewed on her bottom lip. She had to be vindicated.

But who could it be, and what did he want?

Leaving a trail of sweaty yoga shorts and a tee behind her, she marched to the bathroom and turned the spray to lukewarm before she stepped into the shower. The temperature shocked her over-heated skin in a pleasant way, and within moments she was cooled down. She increased the temperature a bit and let the water sluice over her hair.

As she washed, she watched several long strands of brown hair swirl down the drain as she considered the caller's accusation. The police had promised to put a wiretap on her phone, but so far the guy hadn't stayed on the phone long enough for a trace to work. And it was Gail's own fault. She should have talked with him more to string out the time.

She dried off and wrapped her hair in a turban, then pulled on capris and a top. Her phone vibrated again. She snatched it up and glanced at the screen. Augusta Richards.

"I got another call, Detective. Same phone at the drugstore. Could you set up a camera there?"

"I hope I'm not calling too early, and I don't think that's neces-sary. The owner just told me that old pay phone is being removed later today. Maybe that will deter the guy. It's the only pay phone in town. He'll have to use something else if he calls again."

"He could get a burner phone."

"He might," the detective admitted. "What did he say?"

"The same thing—'I know what you did.'"

"Do you have any idea what it means?"

Gail flicked her gaze away to look out the window, where the first colors of the sunrise limned the trees. "Not a clue."

"Make sure you lock your doors and windows. You're all alone out there."

"Already locked. Thanks, Detective." Gail ended the call.

Ever since Nicole Pearson's body had been found a couple of months ago, no one needed to remind Gail she lived down a dirt road with no next-door neighbors. No one wanted to buy the neighboring place after such a lurid death, so the area remained secluded other than a couple of houses about a mile away and out closer to the main road.

She stood back from the window. It was still too dark to see. Was someone out there?

Pull back the reins on your imagination. But once the shudders started, they wouldn't stop. Her hands shaking, she left her bedroom and went to pour herself a cup of coffee with a generous splash of half-and-half from the fridge. She had a stack of lab orders to process, and she couldn't let her nerves derail her work.

The cups rattled as she snatched one from the cupboard. The coffee sloshed over the rim when she poured it, then she took a big gulp of coffee. It burned all the way down her throat, and tears stung her eyes as she sputtered. The heat settled her though, and she checked the locks again before she headed to her home office with her coffee.

No one could see in this tiny cubicle with no window, but she rubbed the back of her neck and shivered. She'd work for an hour, then go into the lab. The familiar ranges and numbers comforted her. She sipped her coffee and began to plow through the stack of papers. Her eyes kept getting heavy. Weird. Normally she woke raring to go every morning.

Maybe she needed more coffee. She stretched out her neck and back and picked up the empty coffee cup.

Gail touched the doorknob and cried out. She stuck her first two fingers in her mouth. *What on earth?*

The door radiated heat. She took a step back as she tried to puzzle out what was happening, but her brain couldn't process it at first. Then tendrils of smoke oozed from under the door in a deadly fog.

Fire. The house was on fire.

She spun back toward the desk, but there was nothing she could use to protect herself. There was no way of egress except through that door.

If she wanted to escape, she'd have to face the inferno on the other side.

She snatched a throw blanket from the chair and threw it over her head, then ran for the door before she lost her courage. When she yanked it open, a wall of flames greeted her, but she spied a pathway down the hall to her bedroom. Ducking her head, she screamed out a war cry and plowed through the flames.

In moments she was in the hall where the smoke wasn't so thick. She pulled in a deep breath as she ran for her bedroom. She felt the cool air as soon as she stepped inside and shut the door behind her. Too late she realized the window was open, and a figure stepped from the closet.

Something hard came down on her head, and darkness descended.

"I want you to leave my husband alone."

Chief of Police Jane Hardy turned toward the snippy female voice that carried over the sound of the milk frother and blew away the good feelings induced by the aroma of coffee. The vitriol belonged to Lauren Dixon.

And was directed at *her.*

Her police dog, Parker, heard the note of aggression too and stepped in front of her with a soft growl. The ruff of his red fur stood at attention, and Jane put her hand on his head to calm him.

Dressed in a baby-blue shirt and tight jeans, the blonde exuded sex appeal. Her confidence was as compelling as her silky locks and sinuous long legs.

Lauren jabbed a finger toward Jane. "I'm talking to you, *Chief* Hardy. Defender of justice and keeper of the peace. You're not doing a very good job of it in the personal arena."

A wave of heat surged up Jane's neck, and she glanced around to see several Pelican Brews patrons standing nearby and listening with avid expressions. The wail of a fire engine rose above the din in the room. She snatched her coffee and beignet off the high bar and exited the coffee shop with Parker on her heels.

Her forehead beaded with perspiration from the early morning sunlight before she reached the shade of the park down the street. She found an outdoor café table far away from any other people.

Lauren followed as Jane had hoped. If they had to have this conversation, she would rather it be in private. Jane plunked her breakfast onto the small black wrought-iron table and turned to face Lauren again. Parker stepped between them.

Jane tipped up her chin. "I have nothing to say to you, Lauren. Your fight with Reid has nothing to do with me."

But they both knew it did. Lauren's ex-husband, Reid Dixon, was the father of Jane's fifteen-year-old son. Their past was murky and convoluted, and Jane wished they could find their way without entangling themselves in Lauren's machinations.

Lauren had disappeared eight years ago, and after seven years, Reid had her declared legally dead. Her appearance had upended everything. Something Lauren clearly liked doing.

Lauren tossed her blonde head and stared at Jane through narrowed green eyes. "Reid is still married to me."

"You're legally dead, Lauren. It was what you wanted. You walked away from Reid and Will without a thought. You haven't so much as called to check on either of them. Not even Will."

The glint in the woman's eyes dimmed a bit. "There were circumstances that prevented me."

"You were tied up in a cabin with no phone for almost eight years? In a place with no internet? Out of the country?"

Lauren's gaze didn't flicker this time, and she tucked a strand of hair behind her ear. "It's something Reid and I will have to work out and has nothing to do with you."

"Will is *my* son."

"He's legally mine. I adopted him."

While Jane wasn't sure yet if she'd fight for Reid, she'd do battle with her last breath for the son she'd thought was dead for fifteen years. "He doesn't want to see you, Lauren, and can you blame him? He was devastated by your abandonment."

"I can make it up to him if you step out of the picture."

"Step out of the picture? He's *my son*! I carried him in my body for nine months while you ran off at the first opportunity."

"Oh, you're the perfect mother, aren't you? Yet you had no contact with him for most of his life."

Jane flinched. "You have no idea what happened all those years ago. Reid never told you."

This time Lauren flinched. "I'll admit your ghost was always between us. Reid didn't like to talk about the past and never even told me your name. If you have any morals at all, you'll give us space to work out our differences."

Jane gasped. "The marriage is over. Your lies are easy to spot. All you want is Reid's money."

Lauren's smirk held all the confidence in the world. "That's not what my attorney says. I came back in time to set aside the decree. Check out Chapter 156 in Nevada law if you don't believe me. It means we're still married, and I still own half of Reid's property. It's like he never filed that paper at all. I only want what is due to me."

The blood drained from Jane's face, and she shook her head. "That's not true."

"Reid knows. My attorney filled his lawyer in two weeks ago. Looks like he's keeping secrets from more than just me."

Lauren spun on her high heels and walked away with her head high. The appreciative stares of every male from fifteen to sixty followed her down the street to her car.

The strength went out of Jane's legs, and she sank onto the chair. While she wanted to deny what Lauren said with every fiber of her being, Reid had been odd the last couple of weeks, and she'd been so restless trying to figure out what was going on. She chalked it up to the pain of his recovery. She hadn't been herself either with the nagging pain of being shot still lingering in her shoulder. And things had been hectic at the station, tying up loose ends after the thwarted attack on the oil platform.

Even as she ran through the litany of reasons for Reid's reserve, her eyes blurred with moisture. He wouldn't keep something like

7

that from her, would he? He'd promised to be truthful ever since she found out Will was alive.

Still stunned and numb, she gathered her coffee and beignet and stumbled toward her car. She hurried for her SUV and let Parker into the backseat before she headed straight for the marina.

They'd already decided to go out with Alfie Smith, a local shrimper, but Reid needed to tell her the truth.

Her radio sprang to life with the dispatcher's voice. "Chief, there's a fire fatality. Augusta spoke to the vic before she died after a threatening call." She gave the address.

"On my way." Talking to Reid would have to wait.

8

TWO

The Bon Secour River flowed sluggishly off to the left side of the yard as Reid and Will Dixon headed to their SUV. Reid waved away a horde of mosquitoes buzzing his head. The bull alligator Will had named Brutus roared somewhere off to their right.

Reid caught a glimpse of his reflection in the rearview mirror as he slid behind the wheel for a fishing trip with Will. Short black hairs were beginning to fill in the smoothness on Reid's head. He actually was sporting a thatch.

He touched it, and his son caught the gesture. "Takes getting used to. Why are you growing it out anyway?"

Will wasn't a kid who liked change, especially when it came to his dad, who had been the one steady support in his fifteen years.

Reid rolled down his window to breathe in the scent of early morning dew and newly mown grass. He started the car and pulled out of the drive while he thought about his answer. "I shaved it the day after we left the compound. I wanted to be a new person, the dad you needed. I wasn't proud of my past and wanted to make a fresh start. It's time to move beyond the guilt and shame."

Will was sprouting like crazy, nearly Reid's height now, and his muscles had filled out in the past two months. It would take a while for Reid's hair growth to match his boy's shaggy black mane.

"What did you have to be ashamed of, Dad? Your parents were the ones who took you into the cult. It wasn't your choice."

A complex question that had no easy answers. "I think back at how gullible I was and I'm ashamed, but I also deserted everything my dad worked for, and I'm not proud of that either."

"But he killed your mom when you were ten."

"No one ever said our emotions were easy."

Will looked up from perusing his phone. "I got a text from Mom. She said to go fishing without her. She's at a crime scene."

Reid pulled into a parking spot by the Pelican Harbor marina. The first beams of daylight lit the bobbing boats with golden rays. Only a couple of months ago he'd owned one of the boats docked at a slip, but it had burned after an explosion meant to kill Jane. By the time the insurance came through, Lauren was skulking around demanding money, and he hadn't dared spend a penny more than he had to.

He stepped out into the aroma of salt air mixed with freshly made beignets and lifted a hand in greeting to Alfie Smith, an old shrimper who had offered to take them out on his trawler today. Alfie was out on the pier fiddling with his boat. They'd thought to have a fun adventure on Jane's day off, but plans for a law enforcement officer in a small town often ended up changed at the last minute.

"Cool, Alfie brought Isaac with him. Grandpa got a new drone, and I thought I'd see if Isaac wanted to come fly it with me." Will slammed the truck door behind him. "Do you see Megan?"

Jane's best friend and office dispatcher, Olivia Davis, had a pretty daughter a year younger than Will, and the two were as tight as clamshells. Alfie's assistant, Isaac, was a handsome young man, and Reid would have thought Will wouldn't want to share Megan's attention.

Reid waved to the girl cutting through an alley toward them. "Here she comes." He reached back inside the truck to grab the half bun of a sandwich he'd kept for the gulls.

The sun lit Megan's brown ponytail with gold, and her smile was bright as she spotted Will. He walked over to meet her, but they didn't touch. Reid grinned at the yearning on Will's face. He knew the feeling well himself. A new relationship was as fragile as sea foam and just as beautiful.

He tossed bread crumbs to the gulls who squawked and hopped after them. "How's your mom?"

Olivia had ALS, and her condition varied from day to day. Jane had hoped the disease was Lyme or something else, but those other tests had come back negative.

"She worked today. Did you hear about the fire?"

Will shook his head. "What fire?"

"Just out of town. I think there's a fatality."

"That's probably where Mom is then."

They were all part of the coconut telephone. One little snippet of information built on another until the whole town knew everyone else's business. At least partly.

Reid dusted the crumbs from his fingers. "Do you know who died?"

"No, but it was at Gail Briscoe's house."

"I know that name," Reid said. "She's the one who found Nicole Pearson's body."

Had it only been a little over two months ago? It felt like an eternity since he'd come here to Pelican Harbor and made himself known to Jane. Since Will had met his mother. Since Reid had realized his feelings for Jane had never died.

Life would never be the same again.

"I think Alfie has *Seacow* ready to go out." He led the way out to the old trawler.

Alfie had plied these waters over sixty years on his old boat, and the vessel looked its age in the same way the old man did with weathering from the constant exposure to sun and water. The hull boasted a fresh coat of paint, though the masts still creaked with age.

But it was a seaworthy vessel and a common sight in these waters. Everyone knew Alfie was the greatest shrimper ever to set sail from this port.

Reid clapped the old man on the shoulder. "Thanks for letting us tag along, Alfie."

Alfie wore his long pants tucked into boots that used to be white. "It's not going to be a picnic, son. I'll expect you to work those muscles. You sure you're up to it?"

He nodded. "I'm thirty-five, not a hundred. My ankle is healing, and I can work without injuring it more. It will be good for me."

Alfie usually went out at night, but he'd made an exception for his passengers. He fixed his rheumy blue eyes on Reid, then motioned for them to come aboard. Once they were on deck, he stepped to the beam and loosened *Seacow* from her slip. She glided out into the bay's smooth water.

A curl of smoke to the north as they exited the mouth of the river caught his attention. "I didn't think camping was allowed there." The small island was a wildlife habitat.

"Some folks got permission," Alfie said. "Way I heard it, some survivalist group is staying out there."

Reid's breath caught in his lungs. "Know who they are?"

Alfie shrugged his shrunken shoulders. "Nope."

It couldn't be Liberty's Children, could it? Reid wouldn't put it past Gabriel to bring his hate to Reid's doorstep. He had to find out.

Jane loved the little town under her protection. She drove along Oyster Bay Road past its quaint French Quarter–style buildings with lacy black railings. Apartments like hers were above the shops lining the brick sidewalks. Colorful flowers swayed in the hot breeze, and magnolia trees provided shade here and there in green spaces.

Once she hit the edge of town, she saw the smoke in the distance and headed that way. She parked behind her detective's car and got out by a crape myrtle tree, blooming with profuse pink blossoms.

As she neared the smoldering ruins of a house, the stench of fire and smoke burned Jane's lungs, and she coughed into the crook of her arm. The sun blazed down, turning the dew on the roof to mist. The heat from the fire tightened the skin on her face. She felt older than thirty this morning.

Her detective, Augusta Richards, exited the building, and Jane hurried to join her.

"What do we have, Augusta?"

Augusta had been part of the department a month, and she was married with two school-age kids. Augusta's husband opened a sporting goods store downtown after they'd moved here from Mobile. The family had all taken to small-town life with gusto. Her tall, lanky figure was as placid as her soft brown eyes that missed nothing. Jane thanked God for her every day.

Augusta pulled off the respirator she wore. "Two bodies, Chief." She reeked of smoke fumes.

"*Two* bodies?" Jane looked toward the low country shotgun house. She'd never been inside this one, but all those houses were the same—one room opened to the next and the next, right to the back of the house.

"We've got a dead firefighter as well as the owner, Gail Briscoe. An anonymous caller summoned the firefighters. They'd retrieved Gail's body, then one of the firefighters rushed back inside without a word."

"Who was it?"

"Finn Presley."

Jane winced. Everyone liked Finn. About thirty and divorced, the young fireman could often be found at the hospital with his yellow Labs visiting the elderly and children. His loss would be felt by the whole town.

"Any idea who called it in?"

"Said he was a passerby and hadn't seen anything. Just reporting the fire. I guess he didn't want to get delayed with questions."

"She'd been getting threatening calls, right?"

Augusta nodded. "And she had another one this morning. I talked to her right after it came through. This morning the caller said his usual, 'I know what you did.'"

"What does that mean?"

"Gail claimed she didn't know, but she was in such a panic, I suspect she just didn't want to tell me."

"I don't like it. This could have been a homicide."

"I think so too."

Jane studied the house. A large V-shaped hole marked where the fire had been the hottest, and tendrils of smoke rose into the sky. The wind carried the strong stench of burned plastics, carpet, and any number of other items in the house. It was a smell not easily mistaken for any other kind of fire.

Movement caught her attention as two firemen exited with a

gurney between them. The black body bag was a stark reminder of the tragedy.

Jane averted her gaze to gather her composure. "Finn?"

"Yes. Gail's body is already en route to the morgue."

They fell silent as the men loaded the body into the back of the ambulance. It pulled away silent and dark, with no urgency. No fast arrival at the hospital could save the young man.

The fire chief, Wayne Gardner, approached them. Jane jerked her head at the departing ambulance. "How'd he die?"

"A burning rafter fell on him. It broke his back, and he died instantly, as near as we can tell. Thank God."

The crash of more falling timbers made Jane jump and take a step back. The crushing weight of two untimely deaths pressed down on her. This was her town and these were her people. Telling the loved ones was always hard.

Jane reached for her detective's discarded respirator. "I'm going in."

The fire chief stopped her. "It's not safe, Chief. Overhead beams are still coming down. One barely missed me. The inside is still smoldering in places. I can't allow anyone else to go inside until the fire is totally out. You'll have to wait until tomorrow to investigate."

"A top arson investigator will be arriving in the morning from Mobile," Augusta said.

Jane had been so used to doing everything on her own that she was still getting used to having quality help. "You're good, Augusta."

"Thank you, Chief. I didn't want to take the chance of missing something important."

"Signs of arson?"

"Burn patterns and an incendiary fluid of some kind. Smelled like kerosene to me, but the investigator will know for sure."

Jane nodded. "Anything else?"

"Tire tracks in the dirt road to the house. Luckily, we'd had some rain before the fire, so we should be able to get good casts. Could be Gail's vehicle, but could also be the arsonist's."

"Do we have next-of-kin information?"

Augusta shook her head. "Jackson's working on it."

Jackson Brown was Jane's other new hire, an eager young black man just out of the academy. "I'll head to the office and see what he's found out."

Augusta put her hand on Jane's forearm. "It's your day off, Chief. Let us do our job. When we have more information, I'll call you. You work too much. Take advantage of your awesome officers." She flashed a wide smile.

Jane glanced at her watch. If she hurried, she might catch the boat yet. After seeing the devastation here, she wanted to look at her son and revel in being with him. But being with Will meant facing what Lauren had told her.

Was she ready to hear that Reid had lied to her—again?

THREE

R eid planted his feet on the boat rocking in the waves and shooed away a gull trying to land on his head. He turned to watch a pod of dolphins begging for fish just off the starboard side. Dolphins often followed shrimp boats since any catch other than shrimp had to be thrown overboard. They knew how to find a free meal.

"Hold the boat," Will called, holding up his phone. "Mom is coming after all. Can we go get her?"

Reid squinted through the bright sun bouncing off the brilliant blue water and stared toward shore. "What's her ETA?"

Will pointed at a small figure jogging down the boardwalk in the distance. "There she is."

Alfie spun the wheel and the trawler banked. "Won't take but a minute to pick her up. Have her wait at the end of the dock. You can get her in the dinghy."

The boat reversed course back to the marina, and Jane's figure grew closer. Reid's pulse kicked when he recognized her wind-tousled light-brown hair. It had grown out a bit, just like his, and now brushed the collar of her shirt. She wasn't in uniform, though she'd been called to a scene. She wore white shorts and a red tank top that showed off her tanned skin and stood with her head high. He'd always loved her I-can-do-it attitude. People said she resembled

Reese Witherspoon, but he didn't think anyone could be as beautiful as Jane.

"I'll get her," Will said.

Reid helped him lower the inflated dinghy and watched as he rowed toward shore. Parker gave a happy bark when he caught Will's scent, and the golden retriever leaped aboard the dinghy when it reached the dock. Jane followed, and Will rowed them back to the trawler.

Smiling, Reid moved to the rail and reached out to help her aboard. His smile faded when she ignored his extended hand and clambered onto the boat without assistance. She didn't look at him and didn't smile. It must have been a bad murder scene. But if it was only work, why was she acting so cold?

She brushed past him and even the smile she sent Will's way was tight. "Sorry I was so late. Augusta is taking over since it's my day off. I feel guilty leaving it all to her though."

"That's why you hired her," Reid said.

He frowned when she still didn't acknowledge him. Her stiff back indicated anger or displeasure with him, but he couldn't think of anything he'd done.

Alfie waved to her. "'Bout missed us, Janey-girl."

Pete, the pelican Jane had rescued as a fledgling, flapped down to perch on the boat's railing. If he knew Jane, she had some fish in the small cooler she carried. Sure enough, she opened it and tossed Pete some fish.

Reid grabbed the halyards and hoisted his sail. The wind filled the canvas, and the old vessel creaked as it plied the waves out on Bon Secour Bay. The scent of the sea lifted on the breeze. No one spoke as they tended to their duties guiding the old boat out to the shrimping grounds, but Reid kept stealing glances at Jane's set face. The gold flecks in her hazel eyes seemed to spark with fury, and dread curled in his belly. What could have happened to make her so aloof? She hadn't even cracked a genuine smile Will's direction.

"Drop the nets," Alfie shouted.

Isaac and Will tossed out the shrimp nets, and they sank into the blue waters. Megan hovered nearby, and her gaze never left Will's broad shoulders.

Will turned and approached Jane. "You okay, Mom?"

The answering grimace could only be called a smile by someone who didn't know her. "Fine, honey. Just a lot on my mind."

Will gave her a doubtful glance, then shrugged. "Wanna swim with us?"

"I didn't bring my suit. You kids go ahead."

Jane turned away and walked to the bow and stared off into the horizon. Will lifted his brows at Reid and jerked his chin her direction.

The kid was throwing him to the sharks. Reid nodded, and the boy turned away to jump off the stern with Parker, Isaac, and Megan. Reid made his way to where Jane stood and waited until she noticed his presence.

When she gave no sign that she wanted to talk, he nearly retreated, but he squared his shoulders and stepped closer. "I can see you're upset, Jane. Want to talk? Was the murder scene bad?"

His gut told him her demeanor had nothing to do with the murder scene and everything to do with him.

Her knuckles went white with her grip on the railing. She turned her head and narrowed her eyes on him. "Are you still married to Lauren?"

He held her disdainful gaze. "I don't know. It's something the court will have to decide. Scott thinks a case could be made either way, but no one has tested the Nevada law."

"And how long have you known this?"

He flinched. "A couple of weeks. Scott isn't sure what to do, and I was waiting for more direction from him before I talked to you about it. I didn't want to worry you if he was able to find out a clear ruling."

"You should have told me right away."

"Maybe so. I thought I was doing the right thing for you. Filing for divorce for abandonment seemed a waste of time when I'd already had her declared legally dead."

"But she had a year to contest that death ruling, and now everything is up in the air," Jane said.

How did she know all this? Did Scott tell her? "Scott doesn't think I should run the risk of going before the court with this. He says it would cost more than paying her off."

She winced. "Where does that leave you if you pay her and she drops the lawsuit?"

"I don't know. To assure my status, I might have to file for divorce."

"Which she might contest and ask for even more money."

The horrible thought had kept him up at night, but he didn't look away and gave a short nod. "Lauren is unpredictable. Scott wants to tie any settlement to a binding agreement so she will not contest it again."

"But your marital status would be very ambiguous."

"It could be. Scott says the whole thing is a mess and could go either way. What do you want me to do?"

Her chin came up, and she tucked strands of hair behind her ears. "It's not my decision, Reid. The whole situation is more than

I can wrap my head around. You let me find this out from Lauren instead of telling me yourself."

"You spoke to Lauren? When?"

"This morning. She asked me to stay away from you and said I should give the two of you space to work out your marriage." Her voice wobbled, and she turned away as if to hide the pain in her eyes.

Reid set his hand on her forearm. "I wouldn't stay with her for any amount of money. She abandoned Will. She hurt him. The pain she caused me isn't nearly as important as the way she destroyed Will's confidence. Would you step back away from him and let her have your spot?" He saw her recoil. "And your reaction is exactly how I feel. Don't let her do this to us, Jane."

She still wouldn't look at him. "I'll have to think about it."

Jane's eyes burned after talking to Reid. She didn't know how to process the reality that Reid might still be married, but for now, she planned to stay far away from him until she sorted out her feelings.

The kids, glistening like playful seals, emerged from their dip in the water with the pod of dolphins. Pete fluttered down to perch on a rail, and several other pelicans dove to the water and came up with wriggling fish.

Will shot her several anxious glances as she sat in the bow. She snatched up her phone with something akin to relief when Augusta called.

"You notify next of kin yet?" Jane asked.

"Jackson did. I'm set to interview Gail's ex-husband in about two hours."

Conventional wisdom indicated the murderer was generally known to the victim. "Anything from the coroner?"

"Nothing yet, but I still suspect foul play. We'll know more after the autopsy."

Jane stared at the shoreline. They were only about half a mile out. "I think I'll go along on that interview."

"I can handle it, Chief."

"I know you can." Jane shot a glance Reid's way. "I'll be there in an hour."

"If you insist."

The tightness in Augusta's words gave Jane pause, but only for a moment. Her hair still stank of smoke, and she wouldn't be able to loosen the muscles in her shoulders until she had answers to at least something she could control. The situation here was impossible. She ended the call and went to tell Alfie she needed to put ashore.

"Hold your horses." The old man blinked faded blue eyes and gave a shrug. "Got binoculars on you?"

"No, should I?"

"Yer man didn't tell you about them survivalist types camping over yonder?" He waved a wrinkled hand toward smoke rising from the treetops on a small, unnamed island filled with impenetrable forest.

"He's not my man." She turned and shaded her eyes with her hand to peer through the sunshine at the location. "Survivalists? Any idea who they are?"

"Coconut telegraph hasn't sussed it out yet. Their boat's called *Westwind*. That's all I know."

The smoke seemed ominous after the fire, especially when she caught a whiff of it, but her nerves were playing tricks on her. This group was unlikely to have anything to do with Liberty's Children or even the fire this morning.

She lowered her hand. "Have any of them been to town yet?"

"Ain't seen anyone but tourists."

Jane glanced at her watch. "We've got time to stop by and see what's going on. I can make a friendly official call and make sure they are legally allowed to be there." The location was outside her jurisdiction, but the campers were unlikely to know that.

The Liberty's Children cult was an offshoot from Mount Sinai, a survivalist group Jane and her father had fled when she was a teenager. She and Reid had confronted the group a few weeks ago and learned the leader hated her mother. And Reid. She had to know for sure if there was any connection with that curl of smoke to the dangerous group.

Alfie gave the order to haul up the nets, which dripped water and little else other than a bit of trash and debris onto the deck. In minutes they were underway to the island.

Jane had never set foot on the island, and she didn't know many people who had. First of all, access was difficult. There was no pier and no protected bay to find anchorage. The people there would have needed to use rowboats to ferry themselves and their belongings ashore, and even then, landing was tricky. A small spot without vegetation existed on the eastern side of the island, and she trained Alfie's binoculars on it.

"See anything?"

Her gut clenched at Reid's deep voice. His voice always reached in and held her in a spot she hadn't known existed until he'd come back into her life. His tanned, muscular arm brushed hers, and she moved away just a bit.

She swallowed and nodded. "Looks like they landed there." She handed him the binoculars and pointed it out. "There are marks in the sand and mud. And you can see several inflatable boats through the bushes farther up."

"I see them." He lowered the binoculars. "You're suspicious it could be Liberty's Children?"

"Aren't you? Gabriel knows where you are now. And where I am. He could have come after us or sent a group to be a thorn in our sides."

"For what purpose?"

"I don't know. The hatred he showed toward my mother had me wondering what she'd done to him. What if he thinks I can lead him to her?"

Reid raised a brow. "You're stretching."

"Am I? I'm not so sure."

Isaac lowered the anchor, and she moved toward the inflatable rowboat.

Reid followed her. "I'll come with you."

"I can handle it alone."

"While you *can*, the question is, should you? If you really think these people could be part of Liberty's Children, they might be dangerous."

"Then the kids need you to stay here and protect them."

His expression sobered, and his mouth twisted. "Fine." He bent down and helped her get the craft over the side of the old shrimping vessel.

She clambered down toward the whitecaps rolling atop the blue water. The sea spray hit her in the face, and she was wet by the time she hopped into the dinghy. The tide helped her as she rowed toward shore, and the bottom scraped sand more quickly than she'd expected. The sea soaked her legs to the knees when she climbed over the side and hauled the craft to the shore.

Though careful to watch for snakes, she forced her way through the marsh toward the sound of voices. Her feet sank into the soft, wet ground and made sucking sounds when she pulled them free. A marsh was never her favorite place to be. Mosquitoes buzzed her head, and she waved them away. She reached drier ground where briars tore at her clothing. Water oak trees reared into the blue sky, and she found a newly trodden path to the clearing.

She didn't have to see any people to realize she'd been right. Gabriel's voice carried to her ears on the wind, and she had to hide her dismay before she stepped into the space filled with tents and camp stools.

Gabriel spotted her the moment she stepped out of the shadows. A slow smile stretched across his face. "It's the pretty little police-woman, Button. Didn't take you long to come looking for me. I didn't think it would."

She hated that old nickname from the cult, and he probably knew it. His face was a map of intent, and Jane wasn't sure she wanted to know his plan. In his forties, he was built like a tank, and she would have trouble fighting him. But whatever it was, it involved her family.

FOUR

Gabriel had an agenda.

The scent of smoke from the wood fire added to Jane's unease, but she lifted her chin and stepped closer to him. "This is a protected area. Who gave you permission to camp here?"

His balding blond hair was a little longer than it had been a few weeks ago, but it framed hard eyes that contrasted with the soft curls around his ears. Ten other men were with him—no women that Jane saw, unless there were some out of the campsite.

One of the men seemed familiar, and she could tell by his expression he recognized her too. He must have been a member of Mount Sinai.

Gabriel grabbed a sausage from the fire and bit into it. Juices ran down his face and dripped to the red dirt, but he didn't seem to notice.

Jane gave him a minute before she repeated her question.

Gabriel swallowed the mouthful of food. "You didn't think you could drop a bombshell and disappear, did you? You had to know we'd come looking for you."

"I don't know what you're talking about. What bombshell?"

"Your mom. You didn't know she'd left, did you? You were with her those last three days, and I would have thought she'd have talked to you about what she did."

"What last three days? What she did? I have no idea what you're talking about." Jane narrowed her eyes. "You made me believe she was dead. You knew all along she was alive. Why did you lie?"

He tipped his head to one side, and his cold blue eyes swept over her. "I said she was in hell. There's a difference, don't you think?"

"I don't have time to decipher your cryptic comments. Why are you here?"

He stepped closer, and she gritted her teeth and made herself stand still despite the sweaty stench of his skin and the menace in his eyes. He had to weigh three times what she did, and she fought the urge to order him to back off. Showing fear would be an aphrodisiac to a man like him.

When she didn't recoil, a grin spread across his face. "I like you, Chief. Little thing like you ought to be screaming and running for the boat, but you're standing here like a she-bear defending her cubs." His hand gestured to the barren area. "This place isn't much to defend."

"I don't let vermin scare me. What do you want? It can't be coincidence that you're here."

"I want you to call your mom and tell her to come here and face me."

"Even if I agreed to do that, why would she listen? She's never contacted me."

"Because she has something I want. And she won't want you involved."

She was done playing games and backed up a step. "Then tell her yourself. She doesn't care anything about me."

"Where'd she put the stuff? You have to know."

"What stuff? You're not making any sense. I wasn't with her all that much. She was always with Moses helping to manage the camp."

Gabriel's hands clenched. "You're just playing dumb. I've gone over and over what happened, and those three days were the only time she was unaccounted for. You were with her. Where'd she take you?"

Jane shook her head. "I never spent three days away with her. You've got your facts wrong."

"Lies. Always lies." His face reddened. "I'll show you." He stalked off to a red tent and ducked inside, then returned moments later with several pictures in his hand. He thrust them at her. "That's you right there. Driving off in the Jeep with your mother. You didn't come back for three days. Now tell me another bald-faced lie."

Jane took the pictures and leafed through them. She was clearly pregnant and looking at the vegetation and the skiff of snow. The pictures were likely taken about a month before Will was born. A month before the attack on the compound when she fled with her father, believing her son was dead.

A month before her life changed forever.

She had no memory of a day like the one in the photo though. Her mother had always busy, and Jane had often longed for even an undisturbed afternoon with her. Something that had never happened. The top picture showed her face turned toward her mother and the camera. Jane winced at her own expression of pure joy.

How could she forget something that would have been so important to her? She spied a duffel bag in the back of the topless Jeep, so they did appear to be going somewhere.

She clutched the pictures. "I'll keep these."

"Those are mine."

"I don't have many pictures of my mom, and they're mine now."

His eyes narrowed, but he didn't make a move to take them back. "So where did you put the stuff?"

"I have no idea. I don't remember anything like this. Maybe someone altered the photo and made it look like we'd left together. We didn't."

"I took these photos myself. I watched you leave, and I saw you come back." His gaze went shifty.

He was hiding something. Gabriel wouldn't reveal anything unless he was ready.

He poked a finger at the top picture. "The picture in the rain with the top up is the day the two of you came back. These are authentic, and you're just stalling."

Jane couldn't process this information with his eyes boring into her. She would have her forensic tech, Nora Craft, analyze them. Gabriel wasn't the trustworthy sort, and Jane *knew* she'd never gone away with her mother for three days. Which meant these pictures were fake.

"You never answered my question about who gave you permission to camp here," she said.

He folded meaty arms over his chest. "Out of your jurisdiction, Chief. I don't answer to you."

She shrugged. "Fine. I'll make a few calls and find out if you're here illegally. If you are, you can expect a visit from the authorities. So get packed up and ready to leave." His smirk told her he had permission from someone.

When she turned to retrace her footsteps, he called after her, "This isn't over, Jane Hardy. You'll tell me what I want to know. One way or another."

Her throat tightened at the menace in his words, but she stalked back to the inflatable craft without giving him the satisfaction of seeing her unease. He had no power here. This was her turf now.

———

Terns and gulls swooped overhead as Reid and the kids helped Alfie throw fish from the net overboard. The birds vied with dolphins and pelicans for the discarded catch, and Reid straightened when he saw Jane approaching in the inflatable boat.

Her eyes were narrowed and her mouth was pinched when she climbed aboard. It must not have been a good visit.

"Who was there?" he asked.

Her hazel eyes were stormy, and she began to haul up the dinghy. "Gabriel and several other men."

His pulse kicked up, and he grabbed the rope to help her. "He had to have followed us here."

"He did." Jane went past him to speak to Alfie.

The wind snatched most of her words away, but the way she gestured to the shore indicated she was in a hurry to get back. Alfie barked out orders to the boys, and the old shrimper turned his trawler toward land.

Reid followed her to the bow of the boat where she stood tapping out a message on her phone. When she didn't look at him, he dove in anyway. "Did he say why he's here?"

She lowered her phone and glanced his way. "He says my mother hid something. He called it 'stuff,' so I have no idea what he means. Items belonging to the cult? Money?" She shrugged. "He wants me to tell her to come here and face him. Like she'd listen to me anyway. He's delusional. You were there for a while after Dad and I left. Did you hear any scuttlebutt about Mom stealing something?"

He shook his head. "But you have to remember, so many people died the day of the police raid. My dad would have known, but he was one of the first ones killed. I wandered over to Liberty's Children but didn't know all that many people."

"I had to ask."

The boat slowed, and Reid went to help the boys dock the boat into its slip. It was nearly lunchtime, and Pelican Harbor residents milled the grassy areas and picnic table with sacks of food and cups of sweet tea. A vendor sold raw and grilled oysters from a food truck, and the aroma of beignets wafted from another vendor on the other side of the street.

Jane stepped onto the dock. "Have Will take care of Parker." She hurried toward her SUV. She slammed her door and accelerated away in her vehicle.

Will joined him with Parker at his side. "What's up with Mom?"

"I think she had to go to the crime scene again. She wants you to take care of Parker for her."

The boy had been through a lot in the past couple of months and, at fifteen, was nearly a man now, but Reid didn't want to hurt him with the knowledge of how Lauren was trying to destroy them all.

"I think it's more than the murder." Will glanced over at Isaac and Megan, who waved him over. "We're going for ice cream. Wanna join us?"

Reid recognized the reluctance in the invitation and grinned. "I've got some stuff to do, but have fun."

He stepped off the boat rocking in the waves and walked through the shimmering heat toward his attorney's office. Without an appointment, he didn't know if Scott could see him—or if he was even in on a Saturday—but Lauren's new attack merited alarm.

The brick sidewalks buzzed with activity, and he nodded to

several acquaintances who were shopping or eating on busy Oyster Bay Road. He spared a glance at Jane's French Quarter–style apartment above Petit Charms. He and Will had played dominoes with her there over pizza on Tuesday. After the day's events, it seemed like an eternity ago.

The door to Scott's office opened when he pulled on it. The air-conditioning was a relief from the humidity, and Scott's receptionist smiled when she saw him. "Going to hit ninety-five today, Reid. I don't have you down for an appointment though."

"Sorry. I'm surprised you're open on a Saturday, but I took a chance."

"He's taking off a few days next week so we scheduled a few clients for today."

She was in her forties and always wore a smile, but he didn't know her name. He looked past her to Scott's closed door. "Is there any chance I could talk to Scott for a few minutes? It's important."

"It depends on how long his current client takes. I might be able to squeeze you in for fifteen minutes." She gestured to the bank of chairs. "Have a seat."

He dropped into a chair and watched the news flashing across the television screen on the wall, though he didn't have enough of an attention span to name what new disaster was playing out. News these days was a constant play on people's fears, and he seldom watched it.

Scott's door opened, and Reid stood as a man dressed in a gray suit walked out. The guy smiled and nodded at the receptionist, then exited the office.

She lifted the phone and spoke too softly for Reid to hear before she gave him a nod. "Scott has about twenty minutes before his next appointment."

"I appreciate it." Reid hustled back to Scott's office and closed the door behind him. "Sorry to bust in on you this way."

"Not a problem."

Scott Foster always reminded him of a woodpecker with his fading reddish-brown hair and thin neck. He had been Charles Hardy's best friend for years, and Reid had found him very calming and knowledgeable.

Reid dropped into a chair in front of the desk. "Lauren tracked down Jane this morning. She's claiming we're still married."

Scott pursed his thin lips. "I got the papers today, but I haven't had a chance to read them yet. Her attorney hinted there might be a big surprise in the lawsuit she'd filed. And I warned you we might not prevail in court."

"How do we make sure I'm not tied to her? I don't trust her to take any money I give her and leave me alone in the future."

"Getting her to sign paperwork promising not to sue for more money won't necessarily ensure that she won't ignore it and sue you anyway. I'm afraid the only way to be certain you're not married is to file for divorce."

Reid slumped in his seat. "That's not what I wanted to hear."

Scott tapped his pen against a pad of paper. "I'm sorry, but I don't believe there's any other solid way to handle this, Reid. The Nevada law isn't clear. She seems to want to test it."

"Wouldn't she have a right to more money if I divorce her?"

"She deserted you and Will and hadn't been heard from in almost eight years. I think it's likely an Alabama judge would take that into consideration. For a divorce, we wouldn't have to go to Nevada and see how it all turns out."

Jane wouldn't like a divorce proceeding any more than Reid

did. "What about Will? She legally adopted him. Can she sue for visitation even though his real mother is here?"

"It's a crazy, mixed-up mess, but yes, it's possible. Do I think the judge would lean her way? No. Will is a teenager, and any judge is going to take his preferences into consideration. I think that's a meaningless threat. The property and money issues are the only things you have to deal with. And honestly, that's all she's interested in. If she sued to see Will, it would only be to annoy you."

Reid exhaled a long sigh. "Can we file for divorce and invalidate the suit she's filing for money?"

"I think I can get that dismissed since it will be dealt with in the divorce."

Reid stood. "I guess I have to do it then."

"I'll draw up the papers. Stop by at the end of the week to sign them. I'll be back in the office on Thursday. My assistant will get them done before then."

"I'll do that."

But the thought left him feeling dirty and stained. He'd tried to do right by Will, and this would drag his son into court too.

FIVE

Gail Briscoe's ex-husband was the type of man Jane detested—dismissive and full of himself. When Drew's secretary ushered them back, he looked her and Augusta over through furrowed black brows, his lips curled.

He didn't stand. "Have a seat."

Drew Briscoe was the VP of a seafood processing plant that employed a large number of the town's residents, and his office was a testament to the way he liked to demonstrate his importance. Pictures of him accepting awards hung on one wall, and photos of his escapades on the ski slopes covered another wall. His thick brown hair was precisely coiffed in every photo, and in every smile he displayed teeth too perfect to be real.

The furniture in his office clearly cost a lot of money, and even the carpet was thick and luxurious. According to scuttlebutt around town, Drew hadn't been willing to share any of his wealth with his ex-wife, and she'd finally given up in disgust just to be rid of him.

Jane didn't sit. "We have a few questions."

His glower deepened. "I don't have much time, especially when you didn't give me the courtesy of making an appointment for whatever this is about."

Augusta took out her notepad. "Where were you last night?"

His brown eyes widened in the first show of emotion. "I'm under suspicion for something?"

"I'm asking a simple question."

He looked to Jane as if to bypass her underling. "What's this all about?"

"Please answer Detective Richards's question, Mr. Briscoe."

He shrugged. "I was home all night."

"Any witnesses?" Augusta asked.

He folded his arms over his chest. "I'm not answering any more questions until you explain."

"Your ex-wife died last night," Augusta said.

"Murder?" He sat back in his chair and a *whoosh* of air went out of him. "I wasn't expecting that. Look, Gail and I haven't even spoken in well over a year. Our relationship ended a long time before our marriage terminated officially. I can't even tell you who she was dating now or anything about her private life."

Jane took advantage of Augusta's skillful questioning to watch the man closely for evidence of lying. He kept staring down at his hands and didn't meet their gazes directly. And he kept fingering a pen.

Augusta scribbled something on her paper. "Your divorce was hostile."

"As is every divorce. But once it was over, it was done. I didn't look back."

"How about Gail? Did she look back and wish things were different?"

"She held more hostility than me and called me every name in the book. She wanted more money than had been awarded to her."

Jane tried to remember the different rumors swirling around town at the time of the divorce. Something underhanded. What was it? She gazed over his shoulder to the workmen milling around the plant's interior, and the answer came.

"I heard one of your employees claimed to have had an affair with Gail, but it was later proven he'd lied. Did you pay him to derail Gail's attempt for a fair division of property?"

His face reddened, and he stood with fisted hands at his sides. "I'm done talking without an attorney. I know how the police work—you always assume a person is killed by someone known to them. Officers railroad people all the time, but I won't let you do it to me. Her murder has nothing to do with me."

He strode to the door and threw it open. "I want you to leave now."

Augusta started for the door, and Jane paused to slip a card into Drew's hand. "If you think of anything, call Augusta or me. Thank you for your time." She kept her tone light. Might as well keep the doors of communication open and not put his back up.

They exited into the heat and humidity of the Alabama afternoon and hurried to Jane's SUV.

She started the engine and turned the air on full blast. "He's lying."

Augusta nodded. "Lots of 'tells' in his behavior. I think we'd better dig into their relationship a little deeper. I'll talk to his neighbors."

"I think I'll go see her brother myself. He's only up in Mobile, so close enough."

Augusta buckled her seat belt. "I'll call the parents once I verify they've been notified. Gail might have mentioned something to a family member."

"We can talk to her employees too. Her murder could have been work related."

The investigation would consume much of Jane's time, and though she itched to talk to her dad about Gabriel's appearance, it would have to wait. Gail's death took precedence over Jane's personal troubles.

Reid settled on the sofa beside Will and clicked on the video. Images of the concrete structures built during the ancient Roman Empire began to flicker across his computer screen.

"What's this?" Will asked.

"My next project. Did you know the technology the Roman Empire used to create concrete was lost? I want to highlight the architecture and talk to scientists who think they've discovered the formula. It should be interesting."

"Will you have to go to Italy?"

"Oh sure. And before you ask, I intend on taking you."

Will grinned. "And what about Mom? You know how much she loves anything to do with Rome. She'd love walking through the old buildings and seeing the Colosseum."

"The thought had entered my mind. I might be able to wait on this project until she solves this latest murder."

"That might be months! I bet she'd take a vacation if she got to go to Rome."

"You might be right. I'll talk to her about it."

What if he waited until things were fully settled between them? They might make it a honeymoon trip. Even if they had their son along, it would be a trip to remember.

A hard knot curled in Jane's stomach as she parked on the street by a water oak tree in front of a modest home in an established Mobile neighborhood. Splashes of color from the bed of geraniums added curb appeal to the plain gray 1970s-era one-story house.

Notifying the next of kin was always the worst job, but it was possible Gail's parents had already called her brother, Ned Berry. She got out and skirted a shiny new Harley-Davidson parked in the driveway. Several lizards dashed across the sidewalk to get out of her way as she approached the door. She pressed the doorbell, and a Garth Brooks tune blared from somewhere inside.

Heavy footsteps approached the entry, and she had her ID ready. A slightly built man in his forties peered through the storm door's glass. His light-brown hair was mussed from a helmet, and he still wore his leather and boots.

Jane held up her badge. "Ned Berry?"

"Yeah." He glanced from the badge to her face. "What do you want? Someone's house get broken into?"

"No, sir. I need to talk to you. May I come in?"

He stepped aside, and she entered a small foyer area that smelled of fresh paint. The homey touches around the space made Jane think a woman lived here too. "Are you married, Mr. Berry?"

His pale-blue eyes blinked rapidly behind rimless glasses. "Yeah, but she's not home from work yet."

Jane would have preferred to deliver the news when he had someone to turn to, but it couldn't be helped. "I'm afraid I have bad news, Mr. Berry. It's about your sister, Gail."

He stiffened. "That lousy ex of hers finally cave her head in?"

39

Jane kept her face impassive, though his comment was way too close for comfort. "Gail was found dead in a fire this morning."

His eyes widened, and his Adam's apple worked. "A fire? But she's a stickler for fire alarms and security. Are you sure it's Gail?"

"I'm afraid so. Is there someone I could call for you?"

He shook his head and wandered past the foyer into the living room. Jane followed and sat opposite him when he sank into a recliner.

"I can't believe it." He raked his hand through his hair.

"You mentioned her ex-husband. Did you fear for Gail's safety?"

He looked up from his clenched hands. "If she died in a fire, why are you asking about Drew?"

"Your sister had some threatening phone calls, so we're investigating as we wait on the autopsy results."

He slumped back in the chair. "She was taking him back to court, you know. She got a new attorney who said she'd been robbed in the settlement. Gail hoped to at least get some alimony out of the bum."

"We're reviewing all possibilities. When did you last speak to your sister?"

"We only have contact by email. I don't want the EMF pollution from the phones in my house, and I only have wired internet, no Wi-Fi. I got an email from her a couple of days ago. She asked me for money."

"She was in financial trouble?"

"Yeah. That's why she wanted to try to get alimony. She was being investigated for reporting false blood test results."

"I'm a little vague on her business. She owned a lab, correct?"

Ned nodded. "Most of her clientele was the government, mostly drug testing for custody cases."

"Did she say if she was afraid of Drew?"

"She'd always been afraid of him. That's why she divorced him. The man had a mean temper."

"Was he ever physically abusive?"

"He sent her to the hospital several times. After he broke her jaw the last time, she finally left him."

"Did she ever file a restraining order or call the police?"

Ned's color was beginning to come back. "No. I tried to convince her to throw him in jail, but she claimed to love him. I thought she'd go back to him when she left, but she found out he was seeing someone else. That was the final straw. And she thought she'd get half the property. He weaseled out of that somehow. Her attorney was lousy, and Drew had a whole team on his side. The judge was a golfing buddy too. Justice doesn't work for everyone."

"And then the investigation on top of things made Gail's life miserable. Would you forward me a copy of her emails?" Jane passed her card to Ned. "And if you know the name of her attorney, that might be helpful as well."

He fingered the card. "I'll forward you what I have right away."

Jane rose and put her hand on the man's shoulder. "I'm very sorry for your loss, Mr. Berry. Thank you for your help."

He looked up with wet eyes. "Thank you. Do you know yet how she died?"

"The autopsy isn't back yet. I'll let you know what we discover."

"And our parents. Have they been notified?"

"If they haven't, it should be any time."

"There might be an email from them." He heaved himself out of the chair and went to a desk in the corner where he flipped on a computer. It dinged a few moments later. "There's an email from them. Maybe I'd better call them. The phone is upstairs."

She held out her cell. "You're welcome to use my phone."

"No cell phones. They are the worst about RF radiation." The color drained back out of his face. "I think I'll wait for my wife to get home. Please see yourself out." He pulled out the desk chair and clicked on an email.

Jane shut the door behind her and went to her SUV. She was supposed to meet Reid for dinner tonight, but she wasn't sure she was up for another battle.

SIX

Would Jane even show up?

Reid sat at a back table in Jesse's Restaurant in Magnolia Springs and listened to the low murmur of people enjoying dinner together. The aroma of seafood and Angus beef made his mouth water, but he wasn't positive he'd get to eat anything on the menu. If Jane stood him up, his appetite would vanish as well as his hopes for the future.

He checked his phone again. No message, and she was fifteen minutes late. He reached across the white tablecloth and buttered a piece of bread. The ice in the sweet tea he'd ordered for them both was melting. Should he message her?

No, not yet.

When Jane stepped into view, he finally relaxed. She'd taken the time to change into a turquoise dress that skimmed her slim figure and highlighted her hazel eyes. That had to mean something, didn't it?

He lifted a smile her way as he rose to pull out her chair, but his spirits plummeted when she didn't return it. He tucked her chair in as she settled.

"Does Will still have Parker?" she asked.

"He does. They were going frog hunting along the Bon Secour. Rough day?"

43

She finally met his gaze. "Very. I wasn't sure I was coming tonight."

He scooted in his chair. "I wasn't sure you were either, not after being verbally attacked by Lauren. I'm sorry you had to learn about it that way."

Her eyes were shadowed. "And why did I, Reid? You should have told me as soon as you knew."

"I didn't want to believe she'd go that far. I saw Scott today, and he again said there is no way of knowing how a judge would rule in a case like this. The law has never been tested."

"I think it's obvious how a judge would rule. If the law reads that the death ruling is set aside, it makes sense every *result* of a death ruling would be set aside. Including the validity of the marriage. We already know she'd get her property back. I think that would likely include you."

"I'm not her property!" He picked up a menu to try to calm himself enough to lower his voice. How could she be so callous about something this important? She'd tossed that remark out as if it didn't cause a seismic shift under all of them.

She reached for a piece of bread. "I didn't mean it quite like that. But if you think it through logically, a judge isn't going to set aside only part of the ramifications of her being declared dead. It's not realistic, Reid."

"Scott thinks I should file for divorce and do the property split all at one time. Do you have any idea how I feel knowing I'll have to agree to give her money I've worked hard for all by myself?"

"But would you have to give her much? Yes, she was techni-cally still married to you, but she deserted you. I think she's in a worse situation than either of you suspect. You'll be able to show how she left you and Will without a word. That she paid nothing to help support Will all those years. Maybe she'll be ordered to pay you."

"I should be so lucky. I told Scott to proceed with filing the divorce papers. She won't expect me to act so quickly."

Jane nodded. "She expects you to cave and offer her a bunch of money."

"If I thought that would make it all go away, I'd do it. But it would still leave my neck on her chopping block."

Jane wasn't giving Reid any hint of their future. They both believed in the sanctity of marriage.

He buttered his bread. "Are you ready to tell me the rest of what Gabriel said to you? You were white and shaken when you got back on the boat. More so than him just saying he's looking for something your mother hid."

She sipped her sweet tea and eyed him over the rim of her glass for a long moment before she set it down. "Do you remember me disappearing with my mom for three days? It would have been about a month before Will was born."

Reid didn't have to think about it. "Sure, I remember. I worried about you the whole time you were gone. The two of you rolled off in the Jeep down a trail known for having rock slips. I kept imagining you and our baby buried by mud and debris."

The color drained from her face, and she sat back in her chair. "Reid, I have no memory of that time at all. None. Gabriel mentioned the trip, but I thought he was trying to rattle me. Why wouldn't I remember it?"

"Maybe your mother didn't want you to remember. She might have given you drugs. It was a favorite tactic my dad used with people."

She gasped. "But I was pregnant! Surely she wouldn't have endangered the baby."

He didn't want to remind her how little her mother seemed to value her or her baby, but he didn't have to bring it up. The pain in her eyes told him she knew full well where her mother's loyalties had been.

"Why take me if she didn't want me to remember? Where was my dad? And your dad?"

"They both went to Detroit to get supplies. They planned to be gone for a week, though they got home a day early."

"Did they know we'd been gone?"

"I don't know. I didn't tell them. Dad wouldn't have liked it, and I didn't want to get you in trouble."

"Someone else might have told them."

"I don't think anyone paid much attention. A lot was going on at the time. Was that all Gabriel said?"

"He wanted me to contact my mother and have her come here. When I said she was unlikely to listen, he said she wouldn't want me involved. He clearly doesn't care about me in any way."

"Why does he want to see her?"

"He wants to know where she hid something. He was very cryptic."

The conversation ended when the server approached to take their order. Jane wanted the diver scallops, and he ordered his favorite shrimp and grits. But even as he smiled and chatted with the friendly server, his mind wouldn't let go of the Gabriel problem. His appearance here couldn't be anything but ominous.

———

The scent of tonight's seafood dinner still in her hair, Jane disarmed the alarm and walked into her dad's house without knocking.

Reid's presence gave her the courage to face whatever she might find out. How did his broad shoulders and steady manner give her so much confidence? He'd be wealthy if he could bottle that.

The flicker of blue light from the large TV screen mounted on the wall illuminated the dark living room and revealed her father sleeping in the recliner. He wore his usual sleeping attire of running shorts and a T-shirt. Though white-headed, his knotty muscles and top-notch fitness would have fooled anyone who didn't know he was in his early sixties.

He startled awake when she muted the television. "Jane?" He slammed the footrest down and stood. "What's wrong?"

She walked deeper into the living room and dropped onto the leather sofa. "You're slipping, Dad. You didn't even budge when I opened the door." Reid followed and sat beside her with his arm up on the back of the sofa as if to cradle her a bit.

Her prepper dad had more security than the White House, and he could usually tell if a cricket crossed the front porch.

She eyed his flushed face. "You feeling okay?"

"A bit of a cold," he said in a raspy voice. "Want some tea or something?"

"We just finished dinner." She lifted a takeout box. "I brought you the leftover scallops."

"I didn't eat dinner."

"I'll warm it up a bit."

"I don't mind it lukewarm." He held out his hand, and she passed over the box and a packet of plastic tableware. He settled back in his chair and opened the box, smiling as the aroma of garlic and seafood hit his nose. "You were at Jesse's."

"Guilty as charged."

He wolfed down the food that comprised more than half of her meal. Her appetite had vanished as she'd faced the situation she and Reid found themselves in. Lauren would be a thorn in their side for months yet.

And she was still wrestling with the thought of Reid getting a divorce.

Her dad wiped his mouth with a napkin. "You didn't come to bring me dinner. What's up?"

"Gabriel is in town, Dad."

She watched the realization hit his eyes, though his jaw didn't flicker. "He didn't waste any time following us once we met him. He says Mom hid something that he wants back. He called it 'stuff.' Any idea what he's talking about?"

Though she itched to ask him about the missing three days, she'd take it one question at a time.

Her dad said nothing for a long moment. "I thought it was a rumor."

"What was a rumor?"

"There was talk around the camp of a stash of guns and other weapons. Even a bunker-busting bomb." He tossed out the word like it was nothing.

Guns and bombs sounded far-fetched to her too. "What else could it be? Drugs?"

His hazel eyes sharpened. "Why would you think that?"

"He said Mom and I disappeared for three days. It was when you went to Detroit for supplies about a month before Will was born. I don't remember it at all. How could it be erased completely from my memory?"

"I didn't know about it. Maybe your mom drugged you."

She nodded. "I hate to think she would have risked the life of my baby that way, but what other explanation could there be?"

A frown darkened his eyes. "Your mother hated drugs. She wouldn't even consider the idea of giving you pain medication for childbirth. That would be so out of character for her. But then, I didn't know her as well as I thought I did. Obviously."

"So you never heard that we went off somewhere?"

He shook his head. "She was different when I got back from the trip to town though. Quiet, almost secretive. Several times she disappeared into the woods and wouldn't tell me what she was doing."

"Did you ever follow her?"

A tide of color washed up his neck. "Yeah. Not proud of it, but I followed her. I thought maybe she was meeting a man."

"And was she?"

"No. She went to an old cabin. The second time I marched to the door and threw it open. She was sitting in an old rocker reading a book. A novel." He spat out the word like it was dung.

"I've never understood why you hate novels so much."

"It's what weak-willed people do to escape life. I should know. My mother always had her nose stuck in a book and ignored me and my brother. We pretty much raised ourselves thanks to her obsession with romance novels."

"It's not the book's fault. Maybe she was unhappy."

"Then she should have changed things. Instead, she let our dad beat us while she pretended it wasn't happening."

He'd never talked much about his childhood, but the revelation explained so much about his hardness and self-reliance. He'd found out early on that he couldn't depend on anyone but himself.

"I'm sorry, Dad."

He shrugged. "Water under the bridge. The lessons taught me well."

"What did you do when you found her in the cabin?"

"I grabbed the book and ripped it to shreds, then tossed the pages in the fire. I told her to get home. She gave me a look I'll never forget. Like she hated me."

Reid lowered his arm from the top of the sofa. "You're an idiot, Charles. She wasn't a child. She was an adult woman and could make her own decisions about what to do in life. What to read, who to befriend. You had no right to do that."

"As her husband, I had every right."

"You might as well save your breath," Jane muttered. "No woman wants to be treated like a child. Or a possession."

A wave of love swept over her as she took in Reid's narrowed eyes and clenched fists. His respect for other people was one of the many things she loved about him.

She rose. "If you think of anything else, let me know."

"What about Gabriel?"

"He wants me to contact Mom." Her laugh sounded bitter to her ears. "He has the insane idea that she'd come here if I asked. He clearly doesn't know her."

Reid passed a beignet over to Jane in the next chair and flicked powdered sugar off his fingers. Parker sniffed the white stuff and licked it up. Lights lit the street below her balcony, and jazz music floated on the night air. The scent of jasmine mingled with the scent of grilling shrimp—not exactly a pleasant combination.

In a parking lot below, Will was skateboarding with some local kids, and the laughter lifted Reid's spirits.

"Any progress on the arson investigation?" he asked her.

She licked powdered sugar off her fingers and shook her head.

"Nothing concrete. Still waiting on the autopsy. I spoke with her brother and ex. I didn't much care for Drew Briscoe. Pompous and arrogant. He didn't show an ounce of regret for her death."

"Did her brother have anything to add?"

"He told me Drew was abusive, so that's a definite red flag. I'll interview him again when he's had a chance to recover from the shock."

"What will you do about your mother?"

She looked down at her hands in her lap. "Nothing right now. My personal problems can't take precedence over my job. If a killer's out there, I have to bring him to justice."

"While you're waiting to find out if it's even murder, we could go talk to your mom."

"I should have the autopsy on Monday, and I want to hit the ground running."

"We could leave tomorrow, talk to her the same day, and fly back on Monday. Augusta could handle things until we arrive back in the afternoon."

He held his breath as she fidgeted and stared out at the street-lights and neon shining in the dark night. She had to be afraid, and he tried to put himself in her place. He'd never doubted that his mother loved him, but facing his father was a different story. If the situation were reversed and he had to confront his father, he wouldn't want to do it either.

She shook her head. "It can wait. And why do you care anyway?"

"Because I love you, and I want you to have some peace and resolution about all this."

"What if she won't talk to me? What if it makes the situation even worse?"

She hadn't responded to his comment about loving her, and he didn't blame her. They had a lot of garbage to get past, but he knew she loved him too. It was hard for her to trust.

He rubbed his forehead. "I understand, honey, but you have so many questions. Answers are never bad."

Parker lifted his head and rose to press against her leg. She petted him. "I'm okay, boy." She stared at Reid. "I'm not sure I want to hear them when I can't know if she's telling me the truth."

What could he even say to truth like that? He nodded and let it drop.

SEVEN

The foam-tipped waves deposited seashells on the sand before rolling back out. Gulls fought over food scraps and stared at Reid with beady black eyes. Several oil platforms rose in the distance out in the Gulf as Reid walked through the churning waves to the beach.

A decent number of beachgoers milled about on this Memorial Day weekend, and Will had found other teenagers to coax into volleyball in the thick sand. Megan and Olivia should arrive anytime.

With water streaming from his skin after his swim, Reid flopped on his back next to Jane and lifted his face to the hot sun. Jane's very wet, sandy dog stretched out on the sand beside him. "I meant to ask you last night if you believed what your dad said about those missing three days."

She clutched her knees to her chest and shook her head. "I don't know what to think. It's disconcerting to be forced to accept the fact that I lost three days of my life. And it sounds like they might have been an important time."

"At least Will didn't have any effects from whatever drug she gave you. He's perfect."

A proud smile lifted her lips. "In every way."

He still felt he was wading through quicksand with her. Ever since Lauren cornered her, he'd felt Jane holding him at arm's length, and he wasn't sure how to break through it. He might not be able to until he managed to resolve his situation with Lauren.

He lifted the cooler's lid and extracted a cold, wet bottle of sweet tea. Jane already had one beside her. "Did you think any more about what I said last night? About your mom?"

"I barely slept for thinking about it." She reached down and picked up a handful of fine sand that she let sift through her fingers. "I think maybe you're right. I'll have to talk to my mother."

"Face-to-face or a phone call?"

The wind blew her light-brown hair into her eyes, and she swiped it away. "What do you think I should do?"

It was a step in the right direction that she cared enough to ask him. "You already know how I feel—talk to her face-to-face. She might not answer a phone call. Caller ID would tip her off that it's you, and I doubt she'll answer."

Before Jane could reply, Megan, dressed in a white cover-up over her bathing suit, called to them as she and her mother came their way across the sand. Her mom, Olivia, wore a navy top over white capris, and she looked almost normal until Reid noticed her stiff gait.

She made slow progress across the uneven ground. He should have suggested they meet somewhere else.

He rose and helped her to a waiting camp chair. "Thirsty? We've got sweet tea and lemonade."

Olivia lowered herself onto the chair. "Tea would be great."

He exchanged a quick look with Jane at how slurred Olivia's words were. So far her weakness and speech issues were the main symptoms.

Megan rushed past them to join in the volleyball game with

Will, and the sounds of teenagers' shouts mingled with the roar of the surf. Reid dug out a dripping bottle of cold sweet tea and uncapped it for Olivia.

She took a swig, then choked on it. Her face went red, and he patted her on the back. "You okay?"

After she took a few breaths, Olivia nodded. "I've been having some trouble swallowing." Her hand shook as she set the bottle into the chair's cup holder. "You two looked very serious. Is it the murder?"

Jane shook her head. "Augusta is handling that. It's a situation involving my mother." She ran through the details of yesterday and what Gabriel had said.

Olivia listened without interruption. "You're going to contact your mom?"

"I think I have to. I thought about calling her."

"She won't answer. You're afraid to see her, aren't you?" Olivia brushed a few windblown strands of brown hair away from her face. "You have to go in person, Jane."

Jane looked away to stare at the waves. "Seriously, I'm confident it will be a total disaster. She's known where I was all along, and she told Dad not to tell me her location. That says a lot about what kind of reception I can expect."

"Anyone would be terrified." Olivia nodded.

"Reid also said I should fly over to see her. But as good as Augusta is, the homicide investigation is my responsibility."

Reid dropped back down onto the blanket. "I'll go with you. Like I said last night, we can make it a two-day trip. Over one day, back the next."

Jane's gaze flitted to the whitecaps rolling to the shore. "You don't have to get involved in this, Reid. It's not your fight."

"Anything that involves you matters to me. I wouldn't want you to go alone."

Olivia's smile of approval emerged. "You're a keeper, Reid Dixon."

He only hoped Jane thought so. "What if you asked your dad to call her? She might talk to him."

"I don't think he's had contact with her in some years."

Olivia leaned back in the chair. "Wait. What if you gave her number to Gabriel? Even if she didn't answer, he could leave the message he wanted her to have."

Reid hated to burst their bubble. "I don't see your mom responding to Gabriel. She hasn't had contact with him in over fifteen years."

Jane rubbed her forehead. "You're probably right. I'll probably have to show up on her doorstep."

Reid could imagine that scene, and it wasn't pretty. There had to be a better way to get in touch with Jane's mother. Did he have any contacts in Maine he could send over and impress on her how important it was that they talk? He'd had an intern from Bangor. He reached for his phone and looked at the map. It wasn't that far from Folly Shoals. And if that didn't work, he could try calling himself.

He placed the call and spoke to his friend only to find out the guy was on temporary assignment in California. He ended the call. "No go. My friend won't be back in Maine for another month."

"I appreciate the effort." She gazed out toward the water. "I can do whatever I have to do."

He'd never doubted it. She was the little engine that could.

———

Jane's team sat at the front table of the war room when she entered into the Monday morning scents of coffee and beignets. Augusta's brown eyes were alert and eager beneath her fringe of short brown hair. Jackson sat at one end of the table, twiddling a pencil between his fingers, and the forensic tech, Nora Craft, had her nose in her computer at the other end.

Jane ordered Parker to lie down as she stepped to the front by the whiteboard and picked up the marker. "I hope the atmosphere in here means you have leads on Saturday's homicide. Nora, you go first. What have you gleaned from the crime scene?"

Nora looked up from her laptop screen. In her late twenties, she was a no-nonsense type of woman who always turned up something important to the team.

She tucked a strand of brunette hair behind her ear. "No prints other than the deceased's and family we've been able to identify. The back door lock was broken, so it's likely the arsonist entered that way. The arson investigator determined the accelerant used for the fire was kerosene, so it's going to be impossible to track. There was a trail of kerosene from the back door to the bedroom."

Nothing Jane didn't already know or suspect. "Any sign her ex-husband has been in the house lately?"

"I have her computer, and she's had some nasty emails from him, but I found nothing in the house. That doesn't mean anything though. He could have worn gloves, and the fire would have destroyed hair and fiber evidence."

"Her phone records?"

"Got 'em. Multiple calls to Drew, but he doesn't seem to have picked up. The messages were short, like she left messages on his voice mail."

Jane's phone vibrated as she turned to Augusta, who was looking at her laptop. "Any word on the autopsies?"

"Downloading Gail's right now. Give me a second."

Jane reached for her phone, then left it where it was. "I think I just got it too, but it will be hard to read on my phone."

A frown crouched between Augusta's eyes. "I didn't expect this. The autopsy found traces of Rohypnol in her stomach."

Roofies. "Someone drugged her?"

"Looks like it," Augusta said. "Official cause of death was smoke inhalation, but someone drugged her so she slept through it."

"Do you know if she'd been at a bar or anything like that on Friday, the night before the attack? The drug could have been left over from the night before."

Augusta shook her head. "Her neighbor at the crossroad reported she saw her come home from work at seven, and she didn't leave until an early morning run at six."

"Homicide," Jane said.

"Looks that way to me," Augusta said.

Nora pursed her lips. "I'll get the contents of the fridge and see if anything's there. Takeout maybe?"

"I can canvas the delivery places," Augusta said. "And I'm talking to anyone who might have seen someone on the pay phone."

The marker squeaked under Jane's fingers as she wrote down suspects. "We haven't narrowed down our suspect list. Could have been the caller, could have been her ex-husband, or someone else entirely."

"That's about it," Augusta said. "We don't have a prime suspect yet."

"I've got the names of both attorneys working on the alimony case. And any complaints against her business in case it's a disgruntled client who's been calling."

Augusta smiled at the rookie. "Good work, Jackson. See what you can find out about the whereabouts of those affected by the falsified tests."

Though he was fresh out of police academy, the young man was an excellent officer. His southern drawl masked the sharp intellect in his black eyes. But he'd grown up with police work in his blood. His daddy was one of the best officers around, and his marksman scores were impressive.

"You got it."

Jane jotted down the words *disgruntled clients* on the list of possible suspects. "A felon would have had access to roofies or anything else he wanted. And according to her brother, Gail was demanding a lot of money. I want Drew's finances. Would paying her have taken him down too? Or was he just greedy and didn't want to pay up? Does he have a girlfriend who might have decided to intervene? This case could go in a lot of different directions."

Augusta went back to her computer. "We have Finn Presley's autopsy now too. A timber fell on him. He died instantly."

"That's a blessing at least," Jane said. "No other surprises."

Jackson cleared his throat. "This probably doesn't mean anything, but there was no pet in the house. Never has been according to neighbors. Yet there was a sticker on the window. And that sticker was what drove Finn back inside even after they retrieved Gail's body. He was a huge dog lover, and his fire chief told me he ignored orders to stay out of the house because he was afraid a trapped pet was in there."

Jane remembered. "'Save My Pet.' A sticker left over from a previous owner?"

"Gail and Drew had the house built," Jackson said.

"Maybe Drew had the pets, and the sticker stayed even after he moved out," Augusta said.

Jane wrote *Save My Pet* on the board. "Talk to Drew and see if that's the case. It's probably nothing important."

She took a snapshot of the board with her phone and uploaded it to the files for the rest of them. "Good work, everyone. Let's get out there and find that killer. Gail deserves justice."

EIGHT

Reid crossed the street and dodged a speeding car. He barely missed hitting his thigh on the guy's bumper. Reckless kid. He batted some hanging moss from a cypress tree out of his way when he stepped onto the curb and reached Scott's office.

The receptionist looked up with a smile when he yanked open the door. "I only called fifteen minutes ago."

"I couldn't believe the papers were ready. You're fast."

"Scott wanted them at the top of my to-do list." She slid the stack across the table to him. "Let me put you in a conference room so you can read them. I've got stickers where I need your signature."

His gut was tense as he followed her down the carpeted hall to a small room containing only a table and chairs. "Thanks."

"Bring them out when you're done." She shut the door behind her.

Reid stared at the papers. They wouldn't sign themselves. Divorce. Such an ugly word. But their marriage had been over long ago. Lauren's own choice, not his at the time.

He read through the legalese and jotted his initials on every page where indicated. There was no settlement amount offered to Lauren in the documents, and he was asking for $25,000 in past child support. It wasn't nearly as much as anyone would have paid, but it was bound to enrage her.

Reid signed his name with a flourish at the final sticker and stood. Even though this wasn't a done deal yet, he felt a weight lift. His decision felt good.

On his way out, he handed the papers to the receptionist and thanked her again before he stepped out into fresh air scented with roses from a bank of flowers in the lawn. He spotted Officer Jackson Brown exiting a sandwich shop and waved to him.

Jackson waited for Reid to join him. "You looking for the chief?"

"Maybe. Depends on what kind of mood she's in." Reid grinned to show he was kidding.

"You've got a woman with a one-track mind. Delivering justice is never far from her thoughts. Just finished up a meeting with her and got my marching orders." He held up his big drink. "After lunch, of course. A big guy like me has to keep up his strength."

Jackson's gaze went over Reid's shoulder, and his smile vanished. He stepped past Reid and handed his sandwich bag and drink to a homeless woman curled against a tree trunk in a small patch of shade.

"Here, ma'am. It's turkey and salami on rye. And sweet tea with lots of ice."

The woman appeared to be in her fifties and wore several layers of dresses. A backpack, ratty and dirty, lay propped against the tree trunk beside her.

Her brown eyes widened, and she took Jackson's offered food hesitantly. "You're sure?"

"Oh yes. I bought it before realizing I'm not really that hungry."

She took a long slurp of sweet tea and gave a heartfelt sigh. "That's good. Thank you, young man."

"You're welcome. Is there anything else I can do for you, ma'am?"

Her gaze lifted to his face again. "Your mama raised you right, son. This is all I need right here." She opened the bag and pulled out the sandwich.

Jackson watched her eat for a moment before he rejoined Reid.

"Nice thing to do," Reid said.

"Her name is Millie. Her husband died several years ago, and she has no family. When her house in Pensacola was repossessed, she found her way here and has been living on the streets. Mostly she sleeps in the park."

Just the kind of guy Reid would like to know better. He clapped him on the shoulder. "Want to share a pizza for lunch?"

Jackson consulted the time on his phone. "If we do by-the-slice so I don't have to wait, I can squeeze that in."

The aroma of crawfish étouffée filled Olivia's small house, and the taste lingered on Jane's tongue. She put down her napkin. "That was delicious, Megan. I can't believe you made it by yourself."

Megan rose and put her plate in the sink. "Thanks, Jane. Mom helped too. I'll go grab my stuff, and we can get going."

Jane smiled at the girl's eagerness to see Will. "I'll be ready in fifteen minutes or so." She reached for Olivia's plate, then drew back when she saw her friend hadn't finished. "You didn't like it?"

"You know I love étouffée, but I-I was having trouble swallowing." Olivia's hand trembled as she reached over and grasped Jane's forearm. "Would you bring me the manila envelope in the drawer to the left of the sink?"

"Sure." Jane retrieved it and noticed Scott Foster's firm's address in the upper left corner.

Olivia had trouble pulling the papers out and shredded the

envelope in the process. "You have to see how much I'm deteriorating. I expect the doctor to give me bad news tomorrow, and I want to be prepared for it. I asked Scott to draw up guardianship papers for Megan." Olivia's brows drew together over dark-blue eyes. "You're still willing to care for her?"

Jane's chest pinched, and she swallowed hard. "Of course, Olivia. You know I love her. But you're still in the early stages of ALS."

"Thirty percent die in a year, and 50 percent die in two to five years. This thing seems to be racing right through me. I need to have all my ducks in a row so I can rest in God's provision for me."

"I don't like the way this conversation is going. It sounds like you're giving up."

Olivia's eyes filled with tears. "I don't think I'm going to beat this, Jane. You like to fix things, but sometimes outcomes can't be changed."

It was all Jane could do to stay in her chair. She wanted to pace, wave her hands, and shout. She inhaled and let out a slow breath to calm herself. "I want you to fight, Olivia! Some people live decades with ALS."

"A few. But I feel myself slipping daily. I've lost twenty pounds, and I'm having trouble doing a lot of things that used to be so easy." She held out the papers for Jane to take. "If you're willing, please sign these before Megan comes out. I don't want to worry her."

Jane took the sheaf of papers and scribbled her name at the marked spots without reading through them. "You know I'd do anything to help. You can both move in with me. I'll help take care of you."

"And where would you put us? Your place just has one bedroom."

"You and Megan could have the bedroom, and I'll sleep on the sofa." But even as she made the offer, Jane knew it would never work.

"I guess you'd have trouble climbing the stairs. I could come here then. I could sleep on the sofa."

Olivia shook her head. "Let's not get ahead of ourselves. If we need to make changes, we can do that, but I wanted to make sure Megan is taken care of first. This sets my mind at ease, so thank you. I don't want to leave Megan, but if that's God's will, we have no choice."

"How could God do that? I don't understand why he'd be so cruel." Her voice wobbled as she tried to imagine a world without Olivia in it.

Olivia was one of the good ones. Always willing to extend a helping hand. Always thinking of other people. Even more importantly, she never seemed to lose her trust in God. She was an inspiration Jane had always looked to for grounding and comfort. A mother figure, really.

Olivia patted Jane's hand. "God is never cruel. He always has a plan, and he sees beyond this temporal life. It might not be what we'd have chosen, but he always works things together for our good."

"There can be nothing good in this, Olivia. Nothing." Jane shoved the papers across the table to her friend and paced the tiny kitchen. "We have to do something."

Before Olivia answered, Megan came bouncing into the kitchen. "I'm ready."

Jane exchanged a long look with Olivia and turned toward the girl. "We'll shove off then, Olivia. Get some rest and let me know if you need anything. I'll have her back by ten."

Megan bent down to brush a kiss across Olivia's cheek. "Bye, Mom. Thanks for letting me go."

"Have fun, honey."

A shudder rippled down Jane's back as she noticed how gaunt

Olivia appeared. How pale and frail. She couldn't bear to lose her, but she felt so helpless.

And what would they do if Olivia died?

———

Reid's eyes burned from working on the computer all day. He was attempting to do his own editing, and it wasn't going well. He wasn't as fast as Elliot, though he knew his way around the software. Reid sighed with satisfaction as he closed his laptop and watched the sun set through his window.

He'd heard the faint strains of video games coming from Will's room most of the afternoon, and he went down the hall to roust the teenager away from the screen for the rest of the night.

Will's door stood open a crack, and Reid swung it back against the wall.

Reid stepped into the room. "Whoa, what happened here?" It still smelled like a teenage boy's smelly athletic socks. That wouldn't change for years yet. But the room was unexpectedly clean. Not even a sock lay on the tan carpet.

Will rose and stretched out his back. His tanned legs looked impossibly long in his gym shorts. The kid was shooting up by the day.

Will swiped a rag along the top of his dresser. "Megan is coming by later. I didn't want her to think I was a pig."

"I should have known. Do I need to pick her up? Her mom didn't seem very steady yesterday."

"No, Mom was stopping by to eat crawfish étouffée with them for dinner, then she'll bring Megan over for a while. That's okay, isn't it? I asked you, but you were deep in editing mode and only mumbled. I didn't think you really heard me."

Reid vaguely remembered the boy stopping by his desk when an important part of the documentary had seemingly disappeared into the laptop's black hole, and it hadn't penetrated his head. "Sorry. It's fine, of course."

"Because anything Mom does is fine?" Will's brown eyes held a twinkle.

Reid gave his son a small shove. "Well, there's that."

Will's grin faded. "Are you guys okay? It seemed like she was mad at you on Saturday."

How much should he tell him? Will was nearly an adult now, but it felt weird to talk about his relationship to a fifteen-year-old. And Reid had been treading lightly when it came to mentioning Lauren. Though Will adored his real mother, Lauren's abandonment had brought a lot of pain.

Will tossed the disposable dust cloth into the trash. "It's about Lauren, isn't it? I'm not stupid, Dad. Rumors are flying around town that she's trying to take you to the cleaners. I figured out a long time ago that she didn't love me and never had. And that's okay. I have you and Mom and Grandpa. My other grandparents now too. I don't need her. She'd be the last person on earth I'd go to if I was in trouble."

"Lauren confronted your mom and asked her to back off so our marriage could be repaired."

Will's brows shot up. "You've got to be kidding! You'd never go back to her, would you? And you're not really married."

"We might be." Reid told him what he knew about the Nevada law.

"Wow, Mom wouldn't like to think she broke up a marriage."

"And she hasn't. Even if I'd never found your mom again, I'd never live with Lauren. That leopard hasn't changed her spots. She only wants money."

"She'd never live here either. We've only been here a few months, but I already feel more at home here than anywhere we've ever lived. Don't you feel that way too? These people are our friends. I never want to leave Pelican Harbor."

"Me neither."

Their lives had changed so dramatically since they drove into the city limits of this place. It was more than a new start—it was the beginning of a new life mixed with the ashes of an old life he'd thought had totally burned to the ground.

But it hadn't. The embers were still smoldering, and life would never be the same.

NINE

Jane kept her distance from Reid in the kitchen as she loaded the dishwasher. An action movie for the kids blared on the TV in the living room, and the ambient noise quelled the agitation she'd been battling. She pulled out a chair at the table and lowered herself into it.

"What's bothering you?" Reid asked.

His brown eyes seemed to search her soul, and she couldn't look away. All her fears trembled, ready to be spilled on the tip of her tongue. How did he do that? No one else seemed to really *see* her the way Reid did.

"Olivia thinks she's going to die." Tears filled her eyes when the words erupted from her mouth. "I haven't wanted to voice that feeling because it might make it come true." Her voice wobbled.

He reached across the table and took her hand. "Some people live many years with ALS. Stephen Hawking lived over fifty years with the disease."

"But 50 percent die in two to five years."

"She said something to you today?"

Jane took comfort from the warmth of his hand on hers. "She told me she's having trouble breathing and will see the doctor tomorrow. And she's the one who told me about the statistic. She asked me to sign on as Megan's guardian."

"Right on the spot?"

"She had the papers all drawn up and asked me to sign them before Megan came out of her room. Of course I said yes. We'd talked about it when she first got sick."

She saw the wheels turning behind his eyes. "You think I shouldn't have agreed?"

"No, that's not it. I was just thinking through logistics. If we end up with Megan and Will in the same house, we might have to be uber careful about leaving them alone. Young love and all that."

Her breath hitched in her chest. "You're assuming we'll be in the same house."

His gaze held her captive. "I love you, Jane. We're meant to be together, and I think you know it too. No matter what is going on with Lauren, we'll have to figure it out. It might take a few months, but so what? We have a lifetime ahead of us."

She squeezed his fingers as she battled the lump in her throat and her burning eyes. "Do we? I thought Olivia had many more years ahead of her until this ALS diagnosis. Life is unpredictable."

"All the more reason to live each day to the fullest. You can't let fear of loss keep you from moving forward with life."

"Is that what you think I'm doing?"

"Aren't you? You thought you lost everything when you were fifteen, and that experience has colored everything you do. You're afraid to let yourself truly love me because of it. You've never been in a real relationship since, have you?" A slight smile lifted his lips. "Not that I'm complaining. I don't know what I would've done if you'd married someone else."

Her chest squeezed at his admission. "Maybe I always knew you were out there somewhere."

And she was only half teasing. Hadn't he always been in the back of her mind and her thoughts? Will's sweet baby scent had followed her everywhere too. Some things change you forever, as much as you don't want to admit it.

"I wish I could believe that's the reason you hold back so much of yourself."

She pulled her hand back. "I give everything in me to Will."

He gave a grudging nod. "True enough. One thing you need to know, Jane—I'm not going anywhere. I'm patient, and I'll be here when you realize it's safe to tear down that wall."

With his words she felt a small crack develop in that very wall. How could she tear it down all the way? And did she even want to yet?

He picked up the iPad and slid it across the table to her. "I booked two flights to Folly Shoals for tomorrow morning, and we'll come back on Wednesday. Your dad is going to take care of Will while we're gone. I've reserved a rental car."

She should have been angry he'd done it without consulting her, but his tender care for her overwhelmed her pride. "What time?"

"Just before ten out of Mobile. We get into Bangor around four. It's about an hour by car to the ferry stop out to Folly Shoals from there. We can be on her doorstep by dinnertime."

She squeezed her eyes shut. The thought of facing her mother made her pulse wonky, but why was she so fearful? She already knew her mother didn't love her, so there would be no surprises. All Jane needed to do was deliver Gabriel's message and find out from her mother what he was doing in Alabama.

She was on the cusp of finding out the last pieces of what

happened so many years ago. The knowledge might finally blow up the wall Reid had mentioned. She might be able to step out of the shadows and into the bright light of a new life.

The sun had barely poked a few rays through Jane's office window at the station when Augusta opened the door and stepped inside, bringing the scent of early morning dew with her. Parker raised his head, then plopped back down to resume his nap.

Jane looked up from skimming the progress report from yesterday. "Thanks for meeting me so early."

Augusta's brown eyes were alert. "Not a problem. You saw the update?"

"Traces of roofies in Gail's coffeepot. So we're definitely investigating a murder. Any new prints?"

"Nothing new, but she was clearly drugged at home."

"What about Drew? Anything new there?"

Augusta smiled. "Oh yeah. Nora found a treasure trove on Gail's hard drive. He told her she'd better drop the suit for more money or he'd make sure she lost everything."

"No threat of personal injury?"

"Not a direct threat, but his rage was clear. I posted them in the file a few minutes ago, and you should be able to access them now."

"I'll be back in town tomorrow night, and I'll check them out then."

"I had Jackson follow up on that Gabriel fellow and his cohorts, and I put out some feelers. Several people spoke to them in the hardware store when they picked up supplies. They were warned not to go out to the island but clearly didn't listen."

"I'm not surprised."

"Your dad is still mum about what he knows?"

"He claims he doesn't know what Gabriel is talking about. Which is why I'm going to go see my mother. We wouldn't want a firestorm here like the one that went down in Michigan fifteen years ago."

Jane glanced at her watch. "I'd better drop the dog at my dad's. I'm meeting Reid there. Keep me posted."

As Jane hurried to her SUV with Parker, she tried to quell the nervous shiver running down her spine. Meeting with her mother after all these years was enough to make her want to run, but she had to face this. And Reid's presence would bolster her courage.

TEN

Parker ran to sniff Reid's tires when he parked in front of Charles's big two-story brick farmhouse behind Jane's SUV and got out. Will tossed a ball to the dog as soon he got out of the backseat, and Parker chased it with his tail wagging. Jane wasn't in her SUV, so Reid went up the steps to the front door. When he entered, he heard raised voices from the living room. Was that food burning?

Uh-oh.

He found Jane standing toe-to-toe with her father. Fists clenched, chin up, and eyes flashing, she was madder than he'd ever seen her. Smoke roiled from the kitchen, and Reid rushed past them to turn off the skillet of bacon.

Reid opened a window and the back door, then returned to the living room. "Whoa, what's going on?"

Spatula in hand, Charles whirled to face him. "This is all your doing! Buying a ticket to go see her mother. Are you insane or just stupid?"

Reid exhaled and relaxed his fingers. He took a stance of non-aggression and prayed his own anger wouldn't spike. "She needs answers, Charles. You aren't giving them to her, so we'll go see what Kim has to say."

"You're just like your father. Always meddling, poking your nose into my business."

"I've always wondered if you blamed me for who my dad was. I guess you do." It shouldn't have hurt Reid, and he couldn't let Jane see how it stabbed him. "You want to tell Jane what she needs to know? If so, I can cancel the tickets."

Charles swiped his hand over his bushy white hair. "Her mother will hurt her more. Don't you understand? The woman should never have been a mother."

"She has two other daughters," Jane said.

Charles whipped around to glare at her. "And maybe she neglects them like she did you."

Jane winced and took a step back. "For someone who doesn't want to see me hurt, you're twisting the knife, Dad. This is something I have to do. I don't trust Gabriel, and I need to find out what he wants before he hurts someone here. I always knew I'd face my mother someday. It might as well be today."

"When you asked me to watch Will, I had no idea it was for a harebrained scheme like this." Charles tossed the spatula on the end table. "I'm not going to help you."

"Fine. He can stay with a friend. You're not stopping me, Dad. I'm doing this."

More red spread across Charles's cheeks in ugly splotches. "You're a pigheaded fool."

Reid clapped his hand on the man's shoulder. "Charles, calm down. You want to hurt Will as well as Jane? You and our boy have a wonderful relationship. Don't spoil it like this. He'll be inside any minute. You don't want him to see you angry."

Charles took several deep breaths, then snatched up the spatula and strode to the kitchen where he banged around the skillet and other pots.

Jane took Reid's hand. "Thank you."

"Want to change your mind?"

"Yes, but I'm not going to. I'm terrified of seeing her, but it's time. Past time. I'm trying to prepare myself for her rejection, but I'm not sure how I'll take it. I'm glad we're not bringing Will. It would be hard on him." She nodded toward the door. "Here he comes now. Don't say anything."

"Of course not." Reid forced a smile and turned to greet his son and rub Parker's head. "You hungry? Your grandpa is fixing breakfast."

The boy sniffed. "Smells burned. Grandpa, what'd you do?" He joined Charles in the kitchen to inspect the bacon. "I don't mind burned bacon. Nothing ruins bacon." He popped several charred pieces into his mouth. "Can you make me an omelet? One of your hot ones with the peppers? I brought a new game for us to play."

As Will chattered on, the color in Charles's face receded. He was nodding and smiling by the time Reid brought in Will's backpack and computer.

He touched Jane's hand. "Let's get out of here while we can."

They hugged Will but skirted any more conversation with Charles before they headed for the door. Parker followed them with a mournful expression.

At the door Jane rubbed her dog's ears. "You have to stay here, boy. We'll be back in a couple of days."

Reid shut the door behind them. "In spite of everything, I'm looking forward to having you to myself. Does that make me a terrible person?"

Her smile reached all the way to her eyes. "Being with you is the only thing that will make it bearable."

"Careful. Words like that just might go to my head."

She laughed, and the sound kick-started his anticipation. There might be some time for a little romance in Maine. He could hope.

———

Reid's shoulder brushed Jane's as they stood at the bow of the ferry and watched Folly Shoals draw near. The sea spray hit him in the face, and he licked the salt off his lips. In spite of being early June, the air was crisp with the wind. It was supposed to be near sixty but it felt more like forty. "Glad we brought jackets."

She nodded and pulled the hood up on her navy windbreaker. "And jeans. I'd be freezing in shorts."

He zipped up his jacket and rubbed his cold ears. "I'll be ready for coffee when we land."

He tried not to worry about what she was facing, but it was nearly impossible not to imagine the look on her face if her mother rejected her. And that scenario was very likely.

The ferry engine puttered down, and they watched the island draw nearer. He'd never been to Maine, and the remoteness surprised him.

Jane pointed. "Look at that hotel and the gorgeous watermelon tourmaline inset in the stonework around the entry door. We're staying there?"

"Yep. Got us two rooms."

Like the masthead of a great ship, the stone walls and mullioned windows of Hotel Tourmaline surveyed its island location of wind-tossed waves and craggy rocks. The island of Folly Shoals sat just northeast of the Schoodic Peninsula, and the five-story hotel dominated the landscape atop its pink granite cliffs.

"You still scared or did the flight calm you down?"

Jane tucked a loose strand of light-brown hair back into the hood of her jacket. "Petrified." Her hazel eyes were more green today in the sunlight as she turned her gaze up to his. "If I didn't have to do this, I wouldn't."

"I know. I wish I could carry the burden for you, but it's something you have to face yourself."

Her gaze flickered. "You are carrying more of the weight than you know. I think I would have procrastinated if you hadn't taken charge. I don't really want to hear her excuses."

He slipped his hand around her waist and pulled her against his side to shelter her from the stiff breeze. "Maybe your dad hasn't told you the whole truth. He's not exactly forthcoming."

She didn't pull away, which encouraged him, and he rested his chin atop her hair and breathed in the vanilla aroma of her hair mixed with the scent of the ocean. Sometimes he wished he could take her away from the stressful job of police chief. Just the three of them off on an adventure together. Maybe Hawaii or Alaska. But she'd never go for it. She had a streak of responsibility as wide as the Atlantic Ocean foaming around them.

The ferry bumped as it docked, and the throng of people began to move toward the gateway. She straightened but didn't move until most of the passengers disembarked. "It's showtime."

"I know. Let's get our car. I've got the location to your mom's house already in the GPS. I think it's about five minutes from the hotel."

Her hand felt clammy in his, and he detected a bit of a tremble as he led her to the car he'd rented in Bangor, a bright-blue convertible.

After shutting the door behind her, he went around and got in, then put down the top in spite of the chill. It was warmer here off the water with the buildings breaking the wind. Maybe the sunshine would lift the pall surrounding both of them. He drove off the ferry onto the island and turned to drive to town.

He drove past the lavish hotel and along the streets of Folly Shoals. The quaint town was a fishing village straight out of a Norman Rockwell painting. Lobster traps lay heaped in the yards. Boats of all sizes and conditions, from pleasure boats to fishing boats, bobbed in the waves at their moorings in Sunset Cove. Bigger, nicer homes with manicured lawns sandwiched the older homes occupied by fishermen. People with coolers awaited the fishing and lobster boats chugging toward the pier.

Jane craned her neck. "No wonder my mom moved here. What a darling town." She consulted her phone. "I think our turn is up ahead."

The GPS confirmed it, and he swung the car around the corner onto a narrow street lined with shingle and clapboard cottages in pastels of blue, yellow, and white that stairstepped the hillside.

"You have reached your destination," the GPS intoned.

Reid parked in front of the address. They fell silent and surveyed the pale-yellow clapboard cottage. Colorful flowers lined the stone walk, and a bright-red door beckoned them to approach. It looked safe and friendly, but what awaited was anything but what it seemed.

Jane inhaled and opened her door. "Let's beard the lioness in her den."

He followed her to the door and stood back as she pressed the doorbell. It rang from inside the house, but no one came. Jane tried again with the same result, and her shoulders slumped.

He pressed her arm. "Maybe she's at work."

"Or maybe she knows it's me and isn't answering."

"How would she know?"

"Dad might have called to warn her."

He started to reply, then closed his mouth. While he would like to think Charles wouldn't sabotage her like that, the man had already proven he liked to keep secrets. Who knew what kind of machinations he might try to orchestrate behind the scenes?

A young woman from the next house stepped out of her blue door and glanced their way. "You looking for Kim or Jason? He's away on a trip and not due back until tomorrow morning, but I think Kim is down by the water." She gestured to the back of the house. "That way."

"Thanks." Reid felt the tremor in Jane's hand as they went that way.

Showtime.

ELEVEN

Jane's heart felt like it would bounce out of her chest. The late-afternoon sunshine warmed her arms, but fear was a cold blanket enveloping her with its chill. This was a moment she'd dreamed of and longed for, but now that it was here, it took all of her strength not to turn and run. She might have done just that except for the steadying touch of Reid's fingers on her elbow.

They rounded the side of the house, and her breath seized at the scene of incredibly blue water rolling to a beach of boulders and sparkling sea glass. Movement in a gazebo caught her attention, and she stared transfixed at the woman who stepped into a patch of sunlight. Her mother. The scent of patchouli floated in Jane's memory, though all she smelled now was the scent of the sea, teeming with life.

When she'd last seen Kim Hardy fifteen years ago, she'd been thin, almost gaunt. She looked . . . different . . . almost too good to be true. She exuded good health and happiness. Her mother's unsophisticated blonde hair had been replaced with a hairdresser's attention to detail, with lowlights and an expert cut that just brushed her jawline. Her curves had filled out, and she was beautiful in stylish capris and a sleeveless top. A smile stretched across her face as she threw a ball for the eager German shepherd dancing around her feet.

Jane must have made an involuntary movement because her mother's smile faded, and she shaded her eyes with her hand to look their direction.

Reid took Jane's hand. "Steady."

Jane inhaled and let it out in a slow exhale. "Thank you." She released his hand and took a step forward. "Kim Hardy?"

Her mother took a step back. "Kim Wilkinson. You must have the wrong address." Her voice trembled, and she cleared her throat.

Jane had interrogated enough people to recognize the note of panic in her mother's voice.

Her father had been telling the truth.

Jane stepped out of the house's shadow and lifted her face to the sunlight. She'd been a girl, only fifteen, but surely a mother would recognize her own daughter. She couldn't have changed that much.

Her mother stood staring at her, and Jane registered the moment recognition dawned on her face. Her lips parted, and her hazel eyes widened. Jane clenched her fists and held her breath as she waited.

A small gasp escaped her mother's lips. "Jane." It wasn't a question but a statement of fact.

Jane wanted to run, but she forced herself to step closer. Reid's presence by her side gave her courage. "Hello, Mom. You've hidden well for a lot of years."

Her mother shot a glance toward the house, and she clenched her hands in front of her. "What are you doing here?"

That was it? No welcoming smile, just fear? Jane's eyes burned, but she swallowed down her dismay and forced her face muscles not to reveal how much she was hurting inside. What good would it do? Her mother obviously didn't care.

Her mother wet her lips. "Well?" Her challenging tone was a contrast to the wobble in her voice. "You shouldn't have come. I told Charles never to tell you where I was. My girls will be home soon. I want you gone by then."

My girls. No mention of missing her. No fierce hug that told her never to go away again. Jane inhaled past the stab of pain to her heart. Even faced with her past, her mother wanted her out of the way before anyone knew she'd come.

"Dad didn't tell me. I discovered your whereabouts without his help." She forced a carefree tone. "Believe me, Dad made sure I knew you didn't want to see me. What did I ever do that made you cut me off so completely? What went on at Mount Sinai that made you separate yourself from your family? I'm here for answers. You took something from Liberty's Children, and Gabriel wants it back."

Her mother's gaze darted to the left and right, and she took a step back. "You've talked to Gabriel? He knows where I am?" Her voice rose.

"He doesn't know where you are, but he showed up in Pelican Harbor looking for you. He's threatened me and my family if you don't give back what you stole. I realize that our well-being means nothing to you, but Will is everything to me, and I'm not leaving here without whatever it was you took. So if you want your past to remain secret, you'd better start talking."

"I don't know what you're talking about."

"Then why are you twisting your hands together? Why do you seem so terrified? Are you afraid I'll tell your so-called husband you're not really married? He doesn't know you're still married to Dad, does he? How would it look for the world to know he's married to a bigamist?"

Her mother held out a pleading hand. "Look, you need to get

out of here. Please. I can't talk to you now." Tears tracked down her cheeks.

Jane didn't want to have any sympathy for her, but she couldn't stop the traitorous stab of pity. "You have to give me some answers, Mom. I can't leave town without them."

"The girls will need dinner, and I'll get them settled doing homework. Are you staying at the hotel?" When Jane nodded, she rushed on. "What's your room number? I'll meet you there at eight."

"I don't have it yet, but I can text it to you. If you don't show up, I'll come back here. I won't be put off."

"Fine, fine. Please, just get out of here before the girls get home."

Jane gave a jerky nod and turned back toward the house.

"They're home," her mother hissed. "Walk along the water like you're on a stroll."

Reid took Jane's hand and tugged her to the water's edge. Jane heard the sound of teenage laughter and saw two girls, chattering excitedly, hurry toward her mother. She drank in their faces and fixed them in her memory. The oldest one resembled their mother. And Jane. The youngest must have taken after her attorney father. She had dark hair and a taller build than Jane and her mother.

Jane's knees trembled, and she clung to Reid's hand as he helped her walk along the shale and rocks until the sound of the waves drowned out the young voices. She'd probably never even get to meet her half sisters, though everything in her made her want to turn and proclaim the truth. What right did Kim have to live a lie—to deprive Jane of a real relationship? She'd hated the lies told to her by her father, and yet here she was letting her mother continue them.

Who was she to judge what Reid and her father had done? She was doing the exact same thing by walking away.

The brutal confrontation with Jane's mother had taken its toll. Reid eyed Jane over the rim of his water glass and wished he could take the shadows from her hazel eyes. How hard it must have been to realize Kim cared nothing about seeing her firstborn daughter.

He watched Jane aimlessly smooth the white linen tablecloth as she stared out the large windows facing Sunset Cove. The waitstaff buzzed through the Sea Room's full tables with smiles and courteous service, but Reid's attention was fixed on Jane's face. They'd both ordered scallops, but he knew she'd have trouble eating. Food was the last thing on her mind.

She checked her watch for the third time in five minutes. "She won't come, and I'm not sure what to do when she doesn't show up."

"We're here for the truth, and I don't think we should leave without it."

She held his gaze. "Even if it destroys her family?"

"Does truth ever really destroy more than it gives? Would you rather not have learned that your dad lied to you?"

She bit her lip. "Of course not. Knowing Will has been my greatest joy in life. But the truth might destroy life for my mom."

"It might. Does that make the truth wrong?"

"I know it's wrong to want revenge, but I'd be lying if I didn't admit part of me wants her to suffer the way I have." She ducked her head and reached for her crystal water glass.

"You wouldn't be human if you didn't feel that way. We have to find what she took and why. That's the only way to get to the bottom of what's going on."

"I can't see her being honest about it. Her whole life has been spent covering up her past. Getting her to open up will be hard. Maybe impossible."

"And if she refuses? Are you going to go back and tell her husband she's a bigamist?"

She raised her gaze to lock with his. "I don't know. What would you do?"

He winced. "I didn't do a very good job of handling things with you. I wish I'd been honest right from the start. But there's a lot to consider here. Those teenage girls, for one thing. You're a good police chief and a good detective. You can find the truth no matter what she does or says. So if you want to wait, I wouldn't judge you for it."

Her gaze softened. "You sound like you have a lot of confidence in me."

"I do."

Their server, a perky twenty-something brunette, delivered their food, and Reid said nothing more for several minutes. He wasn't sure what to advise her. What good would it do now to demolish her mother's house of lies? It wouldn't change anything. Jane's half sisters were too young to be allowed to have a relationship with her. Their father wouldn't welcome finding out he'd been "married" to someone who already had a husband. It would be a huge mess that might be impossible to unravel. On the other hand, the truth was never wrong, and he'd regretted not being honest when he first came to Pelican Harbor. What to do?

"You're thinking dark thoughts," Jane said.

"Just considering all the possible outcomes."

She put down her fork. "I'm not going to blow up her life. I can't do that to her girls. There would be no advantage for them to learn about me. I can wait if I have to. I'll figure out what Gabriel wants some other way."

"You could always meet your sisters when they're older."

She nodded. "While I've decided not to tell her family, Kim doesn't have to know that yet. If she doesn't show up tonight, I'll go back there after the girls are in bed. If she thinks her present life is in jeopardy, maybe I can pressure her into telling me the truth."

Reid nodded and tucked into his steaming pile of sautéed scallops. "Yum, this is good."

Jane pushed her food around before she took a reluctant bite. Her eyes widened. "It's delicious."

He watched her eat a few bites, then his phone dinged with a message from Will. He read it aloud. "'Hey, parents, hope you're having fun. Gramps and I went fishing today, and I caught a shark. It bit my arm as I was hauling it in. Ten stitches, but I'm doing okay.'"

His pulse stuttered, and Reid looked up in time to catch Jane's gasp as she grabbed for her phone.

Her message alert came, and she frowned. "That brat. It's a joke. He went fishing at the lake and caught trout."

"Nothing like getting our heart rates up without having to jog."

She shook her head and put her phone down. "That boy of ours is a handful. But I wouldn't trade him for anything."

"What about us? Would you trade us?"

She caught her lower lip between her teeth and shook her head. "I don't know what it'll take for us to be together, but I can't see life without you and Will in it."

His breath caught at her admission. "It's about time you said that. I wouldn't want to turn into a stalker."

"It's hard to walk away from someone with as much heart as you."

Her chuckle lifted his heart. "I'm the steady sort."

Her smile faded. "When will Lauren be served with divorce papers?"

"This week sometime, I think. I signed them yesterday. I'm praying she doesn't put up too much of a fight."

"Not going to happen, Reid. She wouldn't have stuck around this long if she didn't intend to fleece you for all you're worth."

"I have to admit, I sometimes wish she'd get hit by a truck or something. Poof, she'd be gone." Her eyes widened and he knew he shouldn't have said it. "That's wrong of me, I know. I shouldn't want revenge, but she's still hurting Will."

Jane reached across the table to take his hand. "Things will work out. C. S. Lewis said, 'We all agree that forgiveness is a beautiful idea until we have to practice it,' and I guess it's true. I keep stumbling over that whole forgiveness thing. It's harder than I ever dreamed."

"Before Lauren showed up, I would have said I was good at forgiveness, but I was wrong. It's easier to let go of what she did to me than it is to know she's hurt Will. And you. If she hadn't shown up, I would already have a ring on your finger."

A teasing light flashed in her eyes as they crinkled into a smile. "You're awfully confident, Mr. Dixon. I might not be that easy to catch."

"Will did most of the work."

Her fingers tightened on his. "I think you did it all by yourself. I could have Will without taking you. Divorced parents do it every day. But I don't think I can live without you now."

While they were words he'd longed to hear, a dark foreboding warned that things couldn't be that easy.

TWELVE

Jane flipped on a light, more to drive away her own dark thoughts than the murky shadows that descended with the sunset. She arranged the desk chair opposite the sofa in the hotel suite's sitting room, but she still wasn't sure her mother would show up. Reid had opened the sliding door to the balcony, and the roar of the waves pounding the rocks seemed to deepen her trepidation.

She inhaled the water's salty scent and checked her watch. "Any minute now. If she even comes."

Reid was on the brown tweed sofa, and he crossed his legs as he leaned back. "You were pretty fierce. She won't dare to ignore you—not if she wants to convince you to stay away."

At the knock on the door, Jane's chest squeezed, and her heart rate accelerated. "There she is."

"I'll get it. We'll play good cop, bad cop." He rose and stepped over to open the door.

Her mother's face was pale and pinched, and she'd changed into jeans and a long-sleeved top. "Let's get this over with."

She brushed past Reid, and he shut the door behind her. Tension and anger vibrated off of her like the scent of patchouli that wafted in her wake.

So that was how Kim wanted to play it.

Jane steeled herself to stand up to the rage that had replaced her mother's original fear. If she sensed Jane would temper what she'd threatened, Kim would be like a shark smelling blood.

When her mother stopped to face her with her hands on her hips, Jane squared her shoulders and stared her down. "Did you bring what you stole?"

Her mother flinched at the word *stole*. "You don't know what you're messing with, Jane. You're opening a huge can of worms." Her mother glanced at Reid. "Who's your friend? You didn't introduce him."

"You would have known him at Mount Sinai as Moose, Will's father."

Her mother swayed, and Reid grabbed her forearm. "Are you okay?"

Her mother's gaze never left Jane's, and she shook off Reid's grip. "You never should have come here." Her bloodless lips barely moved. "You need to leave and forget you ever saw me. I stayed away for your own good. You've got to get out of here."

"Stayed away for me? That doesn't make any sense."

"That's because you don't realize the danger you're in." Her words took on an edge of desperation, and she caught at Jane's hand. "You have to believe me. You don't want to get involved in this."

It was the first time her mother had touched her, and it broke Jane's heart that it wasn't inspired by some kind of love.

She pulled her hand away. "It's too late. Gabriel threatened my family. He doesn't seem the type to pack up and leave because I ask him to. I nearly lost Will and Reid a few weeks ago, and I won't ignore a threat now."

"If he thinks you couldn't find me, he'll leave."

The hopelessness in her mother's voice stirred Jane's compassion. "What are you afraid of?"

When her mother swayed, Reid took her arm again and guided her to a seat on the sofa. "You want some water?"

Kim shook her head. "Powerful people are associated with that group who will stop at nothing to make sure what they did is never discovered."

"What did they do?"

Her mother stared at Jane. "You really don't remember?"

Jane curled her fingers into her palms. "Was it when we went off to a cabin?"

"You *do* remember."

"I have no memory of going anywhere with you, but Gabriel mentioned it. Did you drug me?"

Kim's reluctant nod came. "I didn't really think it would work though. I thought you'd eventually remember."

Jane's heart was trying to beat right out of her chest, and she felt a little woozy. She sank onto the desk chair opposite the sofa. "What could have been so bad that you'd drug your pregnant daughter? Dad said you hated even regular medicine. What could be so bad that you'd run that risk?"

Her mother clenched her hands together in her lap. "Murder, Jane." She jerked her chin toward Reid. "His mother's murder. You helped me bury the body."

Jane's vision darkened, and she heard a faint scream from somewhere in her memory. She smelled moist, fecund soil and could almost feel the hard shaft of a shovel in her hand.

"No," she whispered. She leaned her head in her hands.

"You didn't want to do it, but I made you. You were screaming for Moose and begging me to call a doctor."

Jane couldn't take it in, but it was all so hauntingly familiar, like a melody she used to know but couldn't quite remember. Clearly she hadn't *wanted* to remember something so horrendous.

"You killed my mother?" Reid's voice was a strangled whisper. He darted a glance at Jane, as if to question whether she'd taken part in the murder too.

She hadn't—had she? Everything was turned upside down by her mother's words. What had happened in that woods so many years ago?

Jane blinked the darkness and questions away. "You killed her?"

"Oh no, Denise was my friend. Moses killed her when she objected to his taking another wife. Gabriel helped. They didn't know we were there, and once they left her for the animals, I made you help me bury her."

"If they didn't see you, then why is Gabriel searching for you?"

Her mother sighed and rubbed her head. "Because I was stupid. After everything collapsed following the police raid and the fire, I told Gabriel I had proof of what he did. I promised to turn it over to him if his father made me one of Liberty's Children's leaders. He agreed, then tried to have me killed. I escaped and never looked back."

Jane moistened her dry lips. "What proof?"

Her mother reached into the pocket of her capris and withdrew a brass key. "In the safe-deposit box you'll find pictures of Moses and Gabriel with bloody knives standing over her body. It's all in the box. Give it back to him and let it be over, Jane. Leave me to live out the happy life I've made for myself here."

A bitter taste settled on Jane's tongue and made her shudder. "This was never about protecting me. It was about protecting your life. Your power. If your husband finds out you never divorced Dad, it's all over, isn't it?"

Kim wasn't stupid. She'd know Gabriel wouldn't truly rest. He'd never stop. Jane took the key. "What bank?"

"Pelican Harbor Bank and Trust."

"My town? You've been to Pelican Harbor?"

Her mother shrugged. "Once. Long enough to take a look at you and your dad. Charles never knew I was there, and neither did you." She paused as tears pooled in her eyes. "I'm sorry. I knew I couldn't stay with you and your father because Gabriel would eventually track me down. The best thing was simply to disappear."

"Is that all you took?" Reid asked in a quiet voice.

The older woman sighed. "Money. A lot of money. But it's all gone, and I can't give it back."

A burning question Jane had for years erupted. "How did Dad get so much money?"

Her mother stared at her. "He never told you? He was the treasurer for Mount Sinai. When he left with you, he took it. I would assume he invested it wisely. He's that kind of man." She shook her head. "That's not important though, and I need to get home. The pictures are really what Gabriel wants. Give them back, and this will all be over."

Jane's gaze settled on Reid's anguished face. The fallout of this would never be over, and she'd played a part in hurting him.

───

Jane's mother fidgeted on the sofa, but Jane wasn't about to let her leave yet. She still had too many questions without answers. "Why didn't you go with me and Dad?"

Kim stared at the carpet. "Charles was a hard man to love. There's always been a wall around him, probably because his dad was such a stern, unbending man. I had hoped Mount Sinai would be better for him than the Divine Rights compound, but your dad just couldn't settle, no matter what. He found fault in everything."

Wait, what? "Divine Rights compound? Was that another place like Mount Sinai?"

"You don't remember? We were there until you were five. Your grandfather Mitchell started it. All of the Hardys were part of it in the early days. It was in Kentucky, the Cumberland area."

Jane exchanged glances with Reid. That was where they'd first seen Gabriel. "I don't remember it at all. Did they own a lot of land?"

"It was quite large. Money wasn't a problem. Your uncle Edward put the squeeze on businesses around town to provide 'protection.' He filled the coffers with a lot of money, which made your grandfather happy, but your dad's puritanical streak couldn't handle it. He always had a lawman's heart."

"Is Dad's father dead? He always said he was dead," Jane said.

"Mitchell is dead to your dad for all intents and purposes. When we left Divine Rights, he swore all of us would face retribution. If that sounds extreme, think of the movie *Deliverance*." Jane's mother hugged herself. "They are scary, scary people. I was so glad to leave there."

"Did he ever try to hurt you or Dad?"

Her mom shook her head. "But I still look over my shoulder." She shuddered and clenched her hands together. "He mostly hates your dad, and I don't think he knows where I am."

"Does he know where Dad is?"

"I doubt it. He would have already taken revenge if he did.

Maybe he's dead, though even if he is, Edward hates your father even more than Mitchell did."

"But they're brothers!"

"Which made our leaving even more of a betrayal."

Jane digested her mother's revelations. "Are there more family members?"

"Edward was your dad's only sibling. He had four kids when we left. Mitchell's two brothers and three sisters were there too, and they all had kids. I think there were about seventy-five or a hundred at the compound when we left."

"We found Gabriel in the Cumberland area."

"I heard the two groups merged. Gabriel never was strong enough or smart enough to lead for long. He's a better enforcer than a leader."

Jane bit back a gasp. "Gabriel is with Dad's brother now?"

"He was a few months ago. I try to keep tabs on what's going on. I always expected Gabriel to show up looking for me."

Jane should have been used to finding out secrets about her dad, but this still hurt. She'd grown up with a dearth of family, and she would give her right arm for more contact with aunts, uncles, and cousins.

Her mother rose. "I've given you what you wanted, and I need to get home to check on my girls." She took a step toward Jane, then seemed to think better of it. "I'm sorry this visit hurt you, Jane."

"Did you ever really love me, Mom?"

"I still love you, Jane. I know it doesn't seem like it, but sometimes absence is better."

Jane struggled to keep tears from falling. "For whom? Not for me. I never got over not having you around. I doubt I ever will."

Kim's expression didn't change, and she brushed past without a word, then closed the door softly behind her.

Jane curled her fingers into her palms and willed herself not to run after her mother. It would change nothing and would just ramp up the anguish in her chest from painful to agonizing.

He'd always known his mother was dead . . . but why did it hurt so much to hear confirmation? Reid threw a pebble into the waves glimmering white from the moonlight. The pink granite walls rose behind him, and he could hear the dim tinkle of piano music from the hotel. The scent of seaweed and saltwater swirled around him with the water surging against the rock where he stood. If it came any higher, he'd have wet shoes.

Jane had wandered off, lost in her own thoughts, down along the water's edge somewhere, and he resisted the urge to go find her. They each had to come to grips with what they'd learned tonight. If he could, he'd board a plane this minute and search for his mother's remains. She didn't deserve to be left in that cold dirt where no one visited but forest animals.

"Reid?"

He turned at Jane's soft voice. "I'm here."

Pebbles and sand crunched under her sandals, and he reached out to help her up onto the boulder where he stood. Her fingers were damp and chilly, as if she'd dipped them in the ocean.

She released his hand and slipped her hands into the pockets of her capris. "A rogue wave got me. I'm a little wet. Are you okay?"

"I'm not sure yet." He crossed his arms over his chest and turned to stare out over the waves. A boat chugged past, and he caught a whiff of lobster. "Do you remember anything from those days with your mom?"

"When she was telling me about it, I had the sensation of a shovel in my hands. And the smell of dirt." Her voice went higher and trembled. "I don't think I really want to remember. I'm so sorry, Reid."

He turned back toward her. "Maybe it's better if you don't think about it."

"I should have remembered it. I should have told you when it happened."

"You didn't even see me between that trip and when Will was born."

She gave a small huff of displeasure. "I could have sought you out."

"My dad might have killed you. Me too, for that matter. If he could murder Mom in cold blood, he was capable of anything. He'd just kidnapped a woman when the raid went down. He was evil."

She stepped close and wrapped her arms around his waist. "It's a miracle you're such a good man."

He hugged her close. "I had Mom. She taught me what love and honor looked like. I was remembering the last few weeks before she died. I'm pretty sure she had been thinking about leaving. She mentioned her parents a few times and asked if I remembered them and if I would like to see them in Indiana. I brushed off her questions because I knew I wouldn't leave you and the baby. I wish I'd talked to her." His voice wobbled. "I wish I'd been more receptive to her fears."

"You didn't know."

"No. I was a kid and consumed with my own life. I wish I could go back and change things."

She rubbed his back. "Regrets can wreck us if we let them. That's what I was thinking about as I walked along the water's edge. I knew you were feeling regret too, and something I read in *The Screwtape Letters* hit me. C. S. Lewis said, 'For the Present is the point at which time touches eternity.' Today is all we have, Reid. I realized I have to forgive my mom. I have to let go of the pain I feel from the past."

"Sounds like you had a reckoning with God."

She nodded against his chest. "It's been a long time coming, and I finally realized he has forgiven all my mistakes and sins. I can only take today and do all I can with it to walk as a Christian. That has to be enough. When you see me not acting right, help me remember what I just said."

He hugged her tightly and rested his chin on top of her head. "You do the same for me. Following God is a journey, not a destination."

She drew back and looked up at him. "What do you think about going to Kentucky from here instead of back home? I checked in with Augusta, and she doesn't need me. It would add a day to our journey."

"I'm game, but what do you hope to find?"

"My uncle Edward. Maybe we can get him to tell us what Gabriel is really doing in Pelican Harbor."

"Let me change our flight." He dropped a kiss on her forehead and pulled out his phone.

One more day with Jane all to himself might help him find his feet again. Right now Reid needed to be alone and come to grips with his mother's final moments. "I need some air."

She nodded. "I'll give you some space. I need it too."

THIRTEEN

The Divine Rights compound was just off Rock Ranch Road. The same opening they'd taken last time between two large oak trees was still there, and Jane held on as Reid maneuvered the four-wheeler.

They meandered through groves and thick brush heady with the scent of wildflowers, through heavy forest, and across small streams until they broke into the large clearing occupied by cabins, barns, and the meeting house. It appeared very much unchanged from what they'd seen several weeks earlier.

Several women peered at them as they approached, and Jane saw a young woman who could have been her twin, right down to the short stature. The fatigue and defeat in the woman's hazel eyes broke her heart.

If not for her dad's intervention, that could have been Jane.

From the shadows a man emerged who looked enough like her dad to be his twin, right down to his bushy white brows and muscular build. The four-wheeler rolled to a stop, but Jane couldn't make her muscles move to dismount. She was too gobsmacked by her uncle's appearance.

Edward Hardy might have been an inch or two shorter than her dad, but even the shape of his ears was the same. He wore a red plaid shirt under overalls that tucked into muddy boots. Gazing into his hazel eyes made her shiver. The hostility glaring back at her was terrifying.

She forced her limbs to move and stepped off the four-wheeler. "You must be Edward Hardy. I'm your niece, Jane." She smiled toward the young woman who had to be her cousin, Edward's daughter.

"Josie, get inside," Edward barked, and the young woman scurried away. "Where's your daddy?"

Even his voice sounded like her father's. Jane moved closer to Reid. "He doesn't know I'm here."

Watching his stony expression was like staring at a granite statue. No emotion, no life, and certainly no fondness for her. Maybe they shouldn't have come here. The last thing she wanted was to put Reid's life in danger.

"What do you want?" Edward slid his gaze over her. "Do you remember me?"

"No." She couldn't reveal what her mother had told her. This man might be searching for Kim as well as Gabriel. "Did you know Gabriel is in Pelican Harbor?"

The pipe in his pocket nearly fell out, and Edward shoved it back into place. "Who do you think let him go there? I run this place, not Gabriel."

Dislike for his arrogance was hard to hide. "What do you want from me, from my mom?"

"Nothing. That's Gabriel's bailiwick. I'll let him deal with you and your mother. You never answered my question. What are you doing here?"

"I'd heard you might be here, and I was curious to meet family I didn't know about."

"If your father didn't tell you about me, who did?" Edward challenged.

She should have thought about what to say before she spoke. "Is my grandfather still alive?"

"No. Your dad betraying us took a toll on him, and he had a stroke a few months later. You're lucky he's dead. He would have taken a horse whip to you for poking your nose into our business. And don't even mention your father and his desertion."

"Dad was in his twenties. He had a right to lead the life he wanted."

"Doesn't matter. Family is family, and your dad betrayed us. Someday he'll answer for it." Her uncle pointed a finger at her. "Get off my property and go back to Fairhope. You never should have come. You and your dad are dead to me and mine."

She wanted to argue, to ask more questions, but she saw the way several armed men drew closer. Without a word she swung around and walked back to the four-wheeler with Reid close behind. He started the vehicle and drove back the way they'd come. She didn't breathe easily until they were back on the road and a mile from the compound.

Reid pulled over and braked at a stop sign, then killed the engine. "You okay? A lot of hostility aimed at you back there."

"At least we know Edward's still alive. He's a wily one though and didn't reveal any reasons why he'd sent Gabriel to Pelican Harbor. He sure hates Dad."

"Maybe when you tell Charles you were here, he'll talk about it."

"And maybe pigs will fly."

"Good point." Reid nodded. "We can try."

She checked her phone. "Have you heard from Will? All this has made me worry. I kept thinking about what would happen to him if my uncle shot us both."

"A sunny thought." Reid smiled and pulled out his phone. "No texts. I'll give him a call and put it on speakerphone."

"Dad."

Reid's eyes widened. "What's wrong?"

Jane edged closer to hear.

Will drew in a shaky breath. "It's Lauren. She showed up here. I was fishing off the pier in our yard, and she grabbed the pole out of my hand. She was mad, madder than I'd ever seen her. She was yelling about how you owed her money and that she never wanted your illegitimate brat. She was scary."

"I'm sorry, Will. She might have gotten the divorce papers, and it sent her over the edge. I should have warned you not to be at the house at all."

"S-She slapped me. And she was waving some papers, so yeah, that was probably it. She tried to slap me a second time, and I caught her by the wrist. She fell backward into the water when she jerked away. I tried to help her out of the water, but she cursed at me and told me to leave her alone. I was so upset that I ran off so I didn't have to listen to her anymore. But maybe I should go out and make sure she's okay. Her car is still in the driveway."

Jane frowned, and a chill worked its way down her back. "Why didn't you call us right away?"

"I wanted to calm down first. And it's only been a few minutes."

Will's voice held a tremor, and their big, strapping son wouldn't want anyone to hear him crying. Lauren's words had to have hurt.

Reid glanced at Jane for her advice and mouthed, *What should we do?* before answering.

Jane leaned forward. "Call the station and tell the dispatcher what you told us. Say you're afraid to go out and look. Officer Brown will probably be the responding officer, and he'll take good care of you. If she's irrational, I don't want her assaulting you again. She might be out there waiting for you to show up. Is the door locked?"

"Y-Yes."

"We're going to hang up now so you can call. Call us back after you talk to the dispatcher."

"Thanks, Mom. I-I'm a little scared of her."

"It's going to be okay. Call right now."

"Okay, bye."

When the screen went blank, she pointed toward town. "We need to get home right away. I don't like the sound of this. And what was he doing at home anyway? He was supposed to be staying with Dad."

Reid nodded. "He likes fishing. Maybe Charles dropped him off for a bit."

"We'll figure that out later. You drive, and I'll see if we can get a flight out today."

While Reid accelerated away from the stop sign, she checked to see if there was an earlier flight. "Nothing tonight. We'll have to take our original morning flight."

At least it left at six, but the wait would be excruciating.

She could put the time to use. She placed a call to the district FBI office to inquire about Divine Rights. The agent she spoke to said the group knew the FBI was watching them and had kept out of trouble. For now.

"I don't think they'll be bothering us." She told Reid what she'd learned. "They aren't going to want to bring any attention to themselves."

Which was fine by her.

Jane paced the carpet of her hotel suite. Reid stood at the sliding glass door, looking out at the lights of town. From down below somewhere, the smell of pizza wafted up toward them. The little town bustled with summer visitors.

Reid turned back toward her. "I don't understand why Will hasn't called back."

"Dispatch would have kept him on the phone since he was afraid of being attacked again. And he might be with them down at the water, showing them where the confrontation took place."

"He's never without that phone. It's part of his arm."

"They wouldn't let him answer a call if they're interviewing him."

A dozen scenarios raced through her head. Will cuffed and taken to jail. Lauren's body forever lost and Will under suspicion for the rest of his life. Calculating stares around town.

"You're worried. I can hear it in your voice."

She gave a jerky nod. "Okay, fine. I'm worried something has happened to her. And that our son will immediately be implicated because of the argument."

"Like in maybe she's *dead*?" His voice rose and horror spiked in his eyes.

"The thought crossed my mind. I would have expected her to stomp off to her car and drive off. Why didn't she?"

The first people the police considered for guilt were those closest to the victim. In this case it would be Reid and Will. Maybe even Jane herself. She was the other woman. The thought was beyond distasteful. They all had something to gain from her death.

This long silence felt ominous and wrong.

Her phone's ring stopped her from admitting her worst fear. She quickly answered the call. "Jackson, what's going on there?"

"We found Lauren Dixon's car, but there's no sign of her, Chief. Your son told us she fell into the river, but other than a wet spot on the pier, there's no sign of the altercation."

"How's Will doing?"

"A little distraught. He keeps saying it's all his fault."

"It wasn't," she said sharply. "She assaulted him, and when he tried to stop her from hitting him, she jerked away and fell."

"So he said, Chief."

In spite of Jackson's affable tone, Jane inwardly cringed at the hint of doubt in his voice. This could go very badly if Lauren was found dead.

"When are you getting back?"

"Tomorrow by noon. We leave at six in the morning. We couldn't get a flight out tonight."

"What should I do with Will?"

"Take him to my dad's, please. Have you heard from my father?"

"No, ma'am. I tried to call him, but he didn't pick up. I left a message."

"He's bad about leaving his phone when he's in the bunker. I'll try to call him, but Will has a key. Just take him back and make sure he's okay."

"Will do. Safe travels."

"Thanks." Jane ended the call and told Reid what she'd learned.

"Lauren could be dead. Several gators inhabit the river by my house. What happens if her body is never found? Is Will in trouble?"

She wanted to reassure Reid, but she couldn't mislead him. "Maybe. A case could be made that he should have made sure she was out of the water before he left her. The blame for her fall could be placed on him."

"He's just a kid!"

She didn't want to mention all the kids she'd seen over the years who'd been tried as adults. Will didn't have a mean bone in his body, but the law could trap the unsuspecting. "I'll make sure his rights are protected."

"If she's never found . . ."

She nodded. "Lots of suspicion will fall on all of us. And she disappeared once before. What if she's doing it again? This might be more of her manipulation."

"What would she have to gain by this?"

"Money for her to turn up and prove she's alive. Or maybe she'll just sit back and laugh at the trouble Will's in. She could even plant false evidence. I don't trust her."

"Neither do I." He looked a little green. "You really think she'd do this on purpose?" He ran his hand over the stubble on his head. "What am I saying? Of course she would. It's her normal behavior. She wouldn't think twice about throwing us into quicksand. Even Will. He said she was acting crazy and saying she'd never wanted him."

"She's an evil woman."

"Should he lawyer up now?"

"It might be wise. You call Scott while I throw my things in the suitcase. Is your room all packed up?"

He pointed to his suitcase. "Yep. We'll get some sleep and head for the airport in plenty of time."

"Maybe we should just go to the airport."

He shook his head. "I want you to be able to stretch out for a few hours. We only have carry-on luggage so we can take the shuttle to the airport at four and be okay. Maybe you can at least close your eyes for a few hours."

She didn't think she would sleep a wink. This could ruin Will's life, even if he wasn't charged. A cloud of suspicion would hover over him once word of the altercation got out.

She should be in Pelican Harbor overseeing all this. Her lack of control was driving her crazy, but she forced herself to walk out onto the balcony and pray. This was out of her hands, but it wasn't out of God's.

FOURTEEN

The waves of worry radiating off Jane on the flight home and the drive out to her dad's compound kept Reid from thinking about the revelation of his mother's death. Their son was all that mattered now.

He followed her into her father's house where they found Will and Charles playing chess. Will was in denim shorts and a baseball T-shirt. His black hair stood on end from sleeping so he must have just gotten up, even though it was nearly noon. Charles gave a nod in their direction.

Parker gave a happy bark and left his position at Will's feet to rush to Jane. She stooped to pet him as Will stood with his hands in his pockets.

Reid eyed the circles under their son's eyes. "You okay, Will?"

Will shrugged. "I didn't sleep much. Are they going to arrest me, Mom?"

"We'll figure this out." Jane rose and went to hug him, but he stood stiffly in her arms and didn't return her embrace.

Reid went to them and put his arm around Will's shoulders. "You didn't do anything wrong, son."

Will turned tortured eyes in his direction. "I should have just let her hit me, Dad. It was wrong to fight with a girl."

"You didn't strike her back. You just tried to keep her from slapping you. She shouldn't have attacked you," Charles said.

"I could tell Officer Brown was upset with me."

Jane stepped back and dropped her arms to her side. "He was just investigating, Will. That's his job. I talked to Augusta at five thirty this morning, and they hadn't found Lauren yet. I tried to call her when we landed but had to leave a message. I'll head to the scene and see what we've got. You've heard nothing about anyone finding her?"

Will shook his head. "I talked to Mrs. Davis, and she said there's been no recovery of a body. And Lauren's car was still in our driveway when we left last night. Officer Brown hasn't been back so far today though."

"Olivia would know. So there's been no progress in the case."

It was Reid's property, and he felt a responsibility to walk the tree line along the water. He knew the property well, and if Lauren was there, he'd find something. "Let's take Parker to the pier and see if he can find her."

Jane buried the fingers of her left hand in the dog's red coat. "Good idea."

"Can I go too?" Will asked.

"Better not," Jane said. "If we find anything with you along, it could compromise the investigation."

Charles placed his hand on Will's shoulder. "She's right, Will. I can finish tromping you in this chess game. Let your mom do her job and try not to worry."

The grin Will sent his grandfather was his game face, the one Reid saw every time his son was scared but trying to be brave. His heart ached at what Will was feeling, but he sent his own encouraging smile toward the boy and turned to follow Jane back out to his SUV.

She loaded Parker into the back, then climbed into the passenger seat. "I have a bad feeling about this, Reid."

"So do I."

Her phone indicated an incoming call, and he fell silent.

"Jackson, I'm en route to the scene. Where are you?"

Reid strained to hear, but without the call being on speakerphone, he couldn't make out anything being said. He shot glances her way, but her expression stayed set. Nothing in her demeanor indicated Will was on the brink of being arrested.

"Okay, I'll see you there." She put her phone down and glanced at Reid. "He's got a forensic team going over things and is on his way there too."

"Do you need to recuse yourself from the investigation?"

"The mayor will probably demand I step away, but that doesn't mean my team will keep me in the dark about their findings. When do we talk with Scott?"

"He said to stop by when we got to town. He's concerned."

"There's plenty to be concerned about."

Reid pulled into his drive, where two other vehicles clogged the lane. A van and another SUV. The town's forensic tech, Nora Craft, nodded their way and pushed her humidity-fogged glasses up on her nose.

Jane was out the door before his SUV fully stopped. "Find anything, Nora?"

Reid got out and opened the back door for Parker.

"I've been through her car and collected hair and print samples. We've taken anything of interest from it. Nothing obvious from the pier, but I swabbed the fishing pole and anything I thought might hold trace materials. You just got back to town?"

Jane nodded. "Can we get a diving team down there?"

"Lot of gators, Chief. I don't think it's safe. And you can't go. Neither can Reid." Nora didn't have to say they were too close to the case. That much was obvious to all of them.

"Reid knows this property better than anyone else, and we'd like to see if Parker fixates on anything. Jackson is on his way here, and he can come with us."

So much unsaid. Reid could feel the tension and questions ping-ponging between Jane and Nora. They had to conduct this investigation correctly to make sure there were no accusations of a cover-up. Jane was walking a tightrope, but as long as she had other officers in attendance every second, there could be no questions of mishandling evidence.

Tires crunched on the blacktop, and he watched Officer Brown's car roll up the drive. Detective Richards was in the passenger seat. The entire small force was on scene, and for an instant Reid's face flushed as he clenched his fists.

Jane touched his arm and mouthed, *Calm down*. They had to do it this way. No one was pointing a finger at Will. Not yet. And they didn't want their behavior to cause anyone to think they were hiding something.

The two officers got out and came their way. Augusta glanced at Parker. "Ready to let your K-9 officer have a crack at this?"

"He's got some cadaver skills, but they're rusty," Jane said.

Cadaver skills. Though he'd known they were looking for Lauren, it still jolted him to think about the dog finding her body. Maybe she was lying in the cattails injured somewhere. That would be a much better outcome.

"Let's go," Jane said.

"This way." Reid led the way toward the water.

He hadn't let himself think about how much easier his life would be without Lauren in it. It wouldn't be worth the cloud hanging over Will's head.

Please don't be dead.

The thought and prayer played over and over in Jane's head as they tramped through high weeds along the water's edge. Mosquitoes buzzed around her head, and she kept her attention on Parker as he nosed through the fallen leaves and moss in the dense tree line. She heard a splash on occasion and jerked to look, but so far it had only been frogs or a gator's tail.

Reid kept close to her side as if he thought she needed his support. And she was more thankful than her sharp tone telling him to stay back indicated. She had grown to depend on him, and it made her feel weak.

She was the police chief, and she needed to shoulder that responsibility on her own.

They halted under a tall water oak tree dripping with hanging moss. She wiped the back of her hand over her damp forehead. The heat and humidity today were brutal, but her terror for their son was even more debilitating. The stench of rotting vegetation mingled with the sweet scent of wildflowers in the familiar smell of the marsh.

Parker stopped and raised his nose into the air. His ears and tail went up, and he whined low in his throat before bounding across a small stream toward a huge tree overhanging the main bay.

Jane leaped after him. "He's got something!"

She crashed through the underbrush to follow her dog, but he was a streak of red fur in his quest to follow whatever scent he'd detected. He aimed for a craggy, half-rotten water oak tree. Its gnarled tree limbs hung down into the water like fingers. Mats of moss hung low to the ground and obscured the tree even more.

Parker sat down and whimpered. He put his head on his paws and peered up at her with mournful eyes as she reached him. Her heart plummeted to her toes.

He'd found a dead body.

"Good boy." She petted his head and waited for Augusta and Jackson to reach the scene.

She had no doubt about what they'd find, and she couldn't be the one to discover Lauren.

Her team approached, and she rose. "It's his death signal. Something's here."

Reid touched Jane's arm, and she allowed herself the luxury of clinging to the comfort of his hand before she squared her shoulders and led them both away a few feet.

"Nora, would you take pictures as the body is brought up? I want to do this right, every step of the way."

"You got it." Nora moved closer.

Jackson waded into the water up to his thighs and shone his flashlight into the tree roots and branches. "Got a body, Chief. Looks to be a woman. Blonde."

Jane's lips trembled, and she swallowed. "Lauren."

"I think so." He stepped out of the water and pulled out a radio. He called Nora and the state forensic tech.

This all felt like it was spiraling out of her control. She couldn't let herself consider what it might mean for their son. Surely he wouldn't be implicated.

But even a charge of manslaughter could ruin the rest of his life. Her life felt as fragile as a spiderweb. There had to be some way to save Will from the train barreling down on them. She hadn't yet allowed herself to lock gazes with Reid. He would be as shattered as she felt.

Reid took her hand. "Look at me, Jane." His voice was a whisper so the bustling techs and officers didn't pay them any attention.

She dared a glance up into his sorrowful brown eyes. "This is going to be bad, Reid."

"I know. And we'll take it one step at a time. God isn't surprised by this. This is where our fear meets the bedrock of our faith. We can't let ourselves sink into a quagmire of doubt. We know Will is innocent of any wrongdoing. We know God is good. We can hold on to those two truths in this moment."

Something in her calmed as he held her gaze and squeezed her fingers. "You're right." She sank into the calm anguish of his eyes. He was afraid too, but he wasn't letting it take him under. And she couldn't either. She had to hold on to what she knew.

She glanced toward the team lifting Lauren's body from the water. "I've spent my whole life chasing justice for other people. I have to believe God won't let a miscarriage of justice happen now."

He squeezed her fingers tighter. "That's my girl. You've got good people on your team. They will unravel this mess."

Augusta rose from beside the body, and she beckoned Jane with a wave. "Chief."

Jane approached the body and let her gaze linger a long moment on Lauren's face. Dirty water pooled around her blonde hair, and her eyes were half open. There was no doubt she was dead. It took a moment for the reason for the summons to register. A large contusion dented the right side of her head.

Jane's vision wavered, and she took a deep breath. "She appears to have been bludgeoned."

Nora looked up from beside the body. "Maybe. It could have been postmortem."

"There's not a lot of current here," Jane said.

"True enough."

A look of understanding passed between them. Nora was asking with her eyes if Jane wanted her to help cover this up, but Jane couldn't do it. She was committed to truth no matter where it took her.

She gave a slight shake of her head. "You're the best tech I've ever seen, Nora. I have no doubt you'll get to the bottom of exactly what happened here. If Lauren's been murdered, we have to find out who did it. Let's call in help and see if we can find the murder weapon, just in case."

Sorrow vied with approval in Nora's eyes. She poked her glasses up on her nose and nodded. "If I were guessing from a cursory examination, I think we're looking for something heavy and square. Maybe a brick."

"The autopsy will tell us for sure. They should find trace materials of something in the wound."

Will had been fishing. Where was that old tackle box of her dad's he always used? She had no idea if it had been retrieved yet. She fought with the urge to find it and hide it.

She knew Will wouldn't hurt anyone. And God was good. That was all she could cling to right now.

FIFTEEN

"Y ou think I *murdered* her?"

Will's wounded eyes and hurt tone wrecked Reid's inner peace. They sat on their shady porch with the heat and humidity shimmering off the grass. Augusta had her notepad out and her first question was to ask about Will's tackle box.

Jane leaned over in her wicker chair and touched his arm. "Of course not, Will. I'm just telling you what we know so far. Augusta has to ask these questions. It's just part of the investigation."

Will didn't lean back in his chair, and his knee jiggled constantly. Reid willed him to stay calm. Agitation wasn't a good sign to the detective. The dog seemed to know too because Parker whined and pressed his head against the boy's leg.

"I didn't hurt her. I told you how it happened."

"Uh-huh," Augusta said. "Why didn't you get her out of the water then?"

"I told you I tried! She smacked at my hand and told me to leave her alone. I didn't know what else to do. She's an adult. Was I supposed to forcibly haul her up to the dock? She was too mad for me to handle."

The detective nodded. "I totally get it, Will. You've been taught well by your father, and you're a respectful kid. I like that about you. I'm just trying to fully understand what happened. Did you hate her for what she was doing to your mom and dad? No one could blame you."

Reid's leg wanted to jiggle too. Augusta was good, and if Will let down his guard, he might reveal something that would implicate him.

His phone vibrated, and he glanced down at a text message from Scott.

Don't let the police interrogate Will until I get there. Half an hour.

A little late. He cleared his throat. "Our attorney is on his way here now, Detective Richards. He has advised us to stop any questioning until he arrives."

Augusta's congenial smile faded. "If Will has nothing to hide, then there's no reason to cut it off. I'm merely trying to understand what happened."

"And we want to be open and honest. But Will is still shaken by what happened. I'm going to get him a sandwich while we wait on our attorney. Would you like something?"

"No, thank you. I'll wait in the car." She motioned to Jackson, and the two of them went to the patrol car parked in the drive.

Jane exhaled. "This is getting ridiculous. Will didn't do anything."

He rose and beckoned for Will to follow them inside to the kitchen. Reid found ham and cheese in the kitchen and fixed the three of them a sandwich while Jane made coffee before feeding her dog. All his assurances to Jane when things turned sideways came back to haunt him. It had felt easier to hold tight to his faith then, but now that they were faced with intense suspicion, his insides felt like a quivering mass of gelatin.

What would he do if Augusta arrested Will? And would she really arrest her boss's fifteen-year-old son? It seemed incomprehensible.

He slid a ham sandwich piled high with mayo over to Jane. His and Will's sandwiches were made with just a thin smear of mustard, and he watched a drip of mayo slide down the corner of Jane's mouth when she took a bite.

He reached over and wiped it away. "I may have gone a little overboard with your beloved mayo."

"Mom says you can never have too much mayo." Will devoured his sandwich in four bites. "Am I going to be arrested?"

"I don't think so, Will." Jane bit her lip. "Um, do you know where you put your tackle box?"

"I left it on the dock when I ran off to the house. I didn't even think about it until Augusta started asking me about it. Was Lauren really killed with it?"

"We won't know until we get the autopsy results back. Did you see anyone around last night except Lauren? Was anyone with her in the car?"

"I didn't see anyone else. I didn't even notice her car come up the drive since I was down the hill at the river. The first I knew she was there was when she started yelling. She asked where you were, Dad, and she got even madder when she found out you were out of state with Mom. She seemed jealous."

Jane looked stricken and put down her sandwich. "I feel responsible for what happened. If I wasn't in the picture, she might not have become so unhinged about this."

Reid put his sandwich plate down with a clatter. "It wouldn't have mattered. I still would've refused to pay her, and I still would have had to file for divorce. She was the one who started her little extortion game, Jane."

"If you say so." She took a sip of coffee. "I need to quit letting emotion cloud my thinking about this. If someone killed her, we know it wasn't Will. So who wanted her dead? And why?"

"And if that person used Will's tackle box to do the job, he might have *wanted* to implicate Will. Why?"

"To throw off suspicion?" Will suggested.

"Or something more sinister," Jane said. "Whoever it was followed her to your house. He may have intended all along to kill her and throw suspicion on one of you."

"If I hadn't been out of state, I'd be a suspect," Reid said.

She gave him a hard look. "You might still be. I can guarantee Augusta will look into whether you might have hired it done."

"I wouldn't implicate my own son!"

"You'd be surprised what people do to their own family members."

Reid gulped and went toward the chiming doorbell. Scott might be able to get them out of this mess.

The longest day on record was nearly over. Jane's head pounded in a sickening surge with every beat of her heart. Her adrenaline had spiked, and she was on a downward spin.

She dropped onto Reid's sofa and leaned her head back. "I thought Augusta was going to haul him off before it was all over. I wasn't sure we'd get Will to go to bed. He kept pacing and wouldn't even sit on the edge of the bed for a while." Pressing a finger against her temple helped her head only slightly.

"You have a headache?"

"The worst."

He tossed a soft throw onto the wood floor. "Sit down there and let me see what I can do with it."

She settled on the throw and nearly groaned when his fingers pressed a spot that relieved the pain for a few moments. "That's it right there."

He massaged her head for several minutes, and she lost herself in the firm assurance of his touch on her scalp. The radiating pain began to leave the spot behind her left eye, and she relaxed against him.

"Come up here and let me have your hand."

She scrambled up to the sofa with him, and he took her hand and clamped the webbing between her thumb and forefinger in a tight hold. The rest of the pain ceased in moments.

"That's magic. Where'd you learn to do that?"

"John's wife, Geena, used to get migraines, and I watched him get rid of them for her with this acupressure move."

"The truck driver who picked up you and Will when you escaped the cult?"

"Uh-huh." He released her hand. "Better?"

"All gone."

She didn't resist the pull he made to draw her back against him to settle in the crook of his arm. He smelled delicious after his shower. His hair still glistened from the water, and she ran her palm down the curve of his arm around her waist. All the resistance against him she'd been able to muster for the past few months seemed to have evaporated. All she wanted to do was turn her face up and kiss him until she didn't remember anything about today. A slow burn started in her belly.

She needed to get out of here before she made a fool of herself.

"I need a shower myself. I should go home." But she didn't want to leave his warm embrace.

"You could take one here. You have clean clothes in the suitcase out in my SUV."

"But I'd have to move, and I'm not sure I can." Her head turned of its own accord toward him, and she lifted her face to stare at him. "Has anyone ever told you that you're a beautiful human being?" She reached up to caress his freshly shaven face. "Your hair is really growing out." She ran her hand over the top of his head.

His eyes widened. "Did you find the wine the owners left behind in the cabinet or something?"

She smiled and shook her head. "Nary a drop. I think the trauma of the last few days has done something to me. I can't seem to summon any resistance to you tonight."

"You have to resist me?"

His mouth came closer, and she wound an arm around his neck. "Constantly. Even in my sleep."

A low chuckle rumbled in that big chest she'd admired before his head came down and his lips met hers. The jolt of pure desire shook her, but she met the passion of his kiss with her own. His warm, firm lips were more than she'd remembered, more than she'd dreamed.

He pulled her onto his lap and kissed her until she lost all sense of time and place. All that mattered right now was the scent and taste of him. She wanted to forget she'd helped bury his mother. She never wanted to remember the way her officers had looked at her boy. She never wanted to see another dead body or feel the weight of responsibility for justice on her shoulders.

All that mattered was this moment, this man.

She gradually realized his breathing had grown ragged and he'd pulled away a bit. Just enough to bring her back to the present. And to the problems that still hounded her.

She tore her lips from his. They felt somehow fuller and more tender than she'd ever remembered. "Sorry."

"For what? For being the only woman I've ever loved? For giving me the most perfect son a man could have?" He cupped her face in his hands and stared into her eyes. "I love you, Jane Hardy. I'm not going anywhere. Not ever. You're going to marry me and Will, and we'll live here for the rest of our lives, God willing. But you're hard to resist, and I was beginning to forget you don't have a ring on your finger yet."

Tears flooded her eyes. "I don't deserve you, Reid. I'd better get home before I lose all reason. Otherwise I might forget about that ring too."

His crooked smile made her heart melt. She pulled herself out of the warm security of his embrace and wobbled to her feet. She had maybe an ounce of resistance left, and she knew she'd better make use of it and get home.

Parker gave her a reproachful stare as he followed her to the door. This living in two separate houses would need to end soon.

SIXTEEN

There she was. Seated in the back corner of Pelican Brews, Reid lifted two cups of coffee in the air to show Jane he'd already gotten their breakfast. She looked fresh and alert in her crisp uniform. Ready to take on the problems facing them.

If anyone else was chief of police in town, he'd be even more worried.

She spoke to a few people on her way in and stopped to let a little girl pet Parker before she arrived at their table and slipped into the chair beside him. "Been here long?"

"About ten minutes."

"Where's Will?"

"Still asleep. Your dad's going to take him fishing after he gets up. It's been a grueling time for him, and he may sleep until noon."

She took the coffee he offered and sipped it. "I needed that."

"Receive the autopsy yet?"

"Not yet. I should get the report shortly." Her hazel eyes held a shadow. "Augusta requested a search warrant for your place to look for any possible weapon."

Reid winced. "Any fallout from the mayor yet?"

"Not yet, but it's coming." Recognition lit her face as she looked toward the door and lifted a hand in greeting.

Henry Williamson headed her way, winding his way through the tables to reach them. The confident way he walked told everyone he was bigger than his five-five stature.

"Good morning, Congressman," Jane said.

He nodded to her and Reid. "Chief, Mr. Dixon. I heard about the problem with your son, and I wanted to let you know my office stands ready to help in any way we can. He's just a boy, and I'm sure this misunderstanding will be cleared up soon."

"Thank you, sir. The investigation is in good hands with Detective Richards. The deceased attacked Will without provocation, and I'm sure the truth will come out."

Reid appreciated the way she was turning the fault back on Lauren. It was the truth, and he hadn't liked the way Augusta had made it seem like Will had been the aggressor. She'd just been doing her job, but Reid didn't have to agree with it.

"Is the autopsy back yet?"

"Not yet."

"I'll put in a call and see if they can expedite it. You're a good chief, and I don't like this cloud hanging over you and your family."

"Thank you."

The congressman nodded again and went to join his aide, who was in line for coffee.

"Nice of him to try to help," Jane said.

"You know how politicians can be."

She smiled. "You sound jaded, Mr. Dixon."

He grinned at her light tone. "Maybe so. Politicians get my back up."

"He's a nice guy."

"I was trying to say he's better than most." He saw the mayor's neatly coiffed dark hair enter the shop and she looked their way. "Uh-oh. Here comes Chapman. She looks ready to tackle an angry bear."

The fifty-something mayor held her head high, and her dark eyes blazed with determination.

"I need more coffee first." Jane took a gulp of her coffee. "Good morning, Lisa."

In high heels Lisa looked intimidating. "I wouldn't think you'd see anything good about it. I heard about Will, but I had to learn about it from my neighbor, of all people."

"Augusta is heading the investigation, of course. I'm not running it."

"You should have called me as soon as this went down. Your maverick attitude has to stop, Jane. You answer to me. After Victor Armstrong's arrest, the town can't afford more bad publicity."

Victor had been part of the city council, and he'd been behind the plot to blow up the oil platform. The news had shaken the community.

Reid saw the war battling behind Jane's eyes, and he logged the moment her anger won when her eyes narrowed.

"Look, Lisa, I've performed my job well ever since you hired me. There hasn't been a single time I've acted unprofessionally. If you want to replace me, then do it. Otherwise, get off my back and trust me to be impartial and fair. If you can't, then I'm not the right person for the job."

The mayor's mouth gaped, but she recovered her composure quickly. "I'm only asking you to keep me in the loop."

"My son was *attacked*. I had a few more things on my mind than making a call that wasn't pertinent to the investigation. I had a missing woman to find, and Parker did just that. I told you this morning via email. If you check your computer when you get to the office, you'll find a message from me running down everything we know so far."

Lisa's scowl eased. "Fine. When you keep me out of the loop, I feel hung out to dry when someone in my town knows more than I do about a crime. Any major crime. Surely you can understand that."

She didn't wait for Jane to answer but whirled on her heels and walked off to place an order at the counter.

Jane sagged back in her chair as her phone indicated a message. She glanced at it, then over to Reid. "Augusta got the search warrant for your place."

"We have nothing to hide."

She held his gaze. "I think we do, Reid. This feels like someone is deliberately framing Will. Can't you feel it? I sense walls closing in around us, hemming us in, trying to get us to make a mistake. This is too important not to take seriously."

"I am taking it seriously. I don't get why anyone would want to frame Will though. Me, sure. That would make sense. But Will is a kid."

"And he's *my* kid. My family has been attacked multiple times over the past few months, and I'm beginning to believe there's some purpose behind all of it."

He could see why she might think that. It had been intense. "What purpose?"

"I wish I knew." She picked up her coffee and rose. "I'd better get to the office. Keep an eye on Will. Maybe it would be better to keep him with you instead of letting him go with my dad. My family seems to be the center of this attack."

He wanted to remind her that he was part of this too, but he said nothing. Where had the closeness from last night gone?

Jane met Augusta in the hall. "In my office," she told her detective. She stalked to her office. "Shut the door and sit."

Augusta sank into the chair while Jane went around her desk, slung down her bag, and dropped into her chair. Parker went to his bed in the corner and plopped down on it. "A search warrant before we even get the autopsy report? Really?"

Augusta lifted a brow. "Chief, you haven't been walking the town like I have. We have to be aggressive in our investigation. People think it's going to be swept under the rug because of your connection to the case."

"I thought people knew me, trusted me." Jane's voice wobbled, and she cleared her throat.

"But they don't know Reid well yet. And someone has been spreading talk about Reid having hired a hit man. We have to be proactive and blatantly unbiased."

"Who would say such a thing?"

Augusta shrugged her slim shoulders. "It's like a wildfire spreading through town with no way to know who started it."

"How do we combat something so nebulous?"

"We find the real killer."

Jane's computer dinged with an incoming message. "Looks like the autopsy report is in. Come around and look at it with me. Henry must have made that call right away to get the autopsy prioritized." She adjusted her monitor so Augusta, standing to her left, could see it too.

She scrolled down the page to scan the highlights. "Metal slivers in the head wound indicate deceased was struck with a rectangular metal object. Just like Nora thought. And there are green paint flecks."

She tried not to show her dismay. That old tackle box Will used was green. "We need to find Will's tackle box."

"And what if there's blood or hair on it?"

They both knew the answer to that question. Will would need to be brought in for more questioning. And he would probably be arrested.

"But he already told us he left it on the dock."

Augusta held up a finger. "An admitted altercation with the deceased." She shot up a second finger. "The weapon belongs to him and is found with bodily evidence. That makes a pretty strong case, Chief."

"Circumstantial."

"But some pretty compelling reasons to look at Will."

"I can't deny that. So we have to find out who really did this."

"I'm working on Lauren's background. Where has she been? Why did she need money so badly? Was she involved in anything illegal? Lots of questions about Lauren Dixon."

If Jane had ever doubted her detective's abilities, she now recognized her stellar sleuthing skills. "How can I help?"

"Stay out of it. Mingle with people in town and tell them you're letting me handle it and that you believe in Will's innocence. And Reid's. Let that message permeate as Jackson and I figure out this case."

"What about Gail Briscoe's murder? Anything new there while I was out of town?"

"Not yet. You can take over that investigation and let me run with the Dixon case."

"All right, fair enough. You can't do it all."

Augusta gave a cheeky grin. "Well, I could, but I'd never see my family. The file is up to date and ready for you. Before the new murder, I'd planned to talk to some of Finn Presley's workmates at the fire station. And his ex-wife."

"You're focusing on Finn and not Gail?"

"First I wanted to discover if they knew each other."

"I'll start there too. You're a good detective, Augusta."

"Which is why you hired me." The detective went around the desk toward the door. "Was your trip to Maine successful?"

"Well, I met my mother. To say she wasn't thrilled to see me would be an understatement. When this other is over, I'd like to get your take on some evidence of an old murder."

"You got it." Augusta closed the door behind her.

Jane opened the Briscoe murder file and perused it again to refresh her memory. Gail's ex still looked good for a possible suspect, but Augusta's idea to eliminate any connection between the two victims was sound. When she talked to Drew, Jane wanted to find out if he'd had a sticker on the window. And he needed to be grilled about his abuse of Gail.

She rose and grabbed her bag before calling her dog. The firehouse was catty-corner from the police station, so it did not take long for her to reach the blast of air-conditioning in the firemen's break room. Four firemen were playing cards at a square table. Discarded Coke cans and littered popcorn around the chair legs showed they'd been at their poker game awhile.

The fire chief, Wayne Gardner, saw her first. "We got company, boys." He stood and came toward her. "I was expecting your detective today."

"I'm handling the investigation so she can focus on the new

murder. I want to leave it in her hands so there's no question about the evidence against my son."

The other firemen approached and clustered around Wayne. "Smart move, Chief." Wayne scratched at his bushy mustache. "How can we help you?"

"How well did you know Finn?"

"We're all as close as brothers. I knew when he washed his socks and what he took in his coffee."

Jane smiled. "What about his family?"

One of the younger firemen shook his head. "He'd been pretty broken up about his divorce. He didn't get to see his daughter as much as he wanted. He'd sued for joint custody, but his ex insisted he take a drug test, and he failed. Supposedly he was taking meth. Anyone who knew Finn realized that was an out-and-out lie. He hated drugs. I never saw him so much as take a couple of Tylenol. He was a health-food nut, too, and always talked about the fuel he put in his body."

Jane frowned. "Where is his ex now?"

"She lives over in Gulf Shores, out on Fort Morgan Road. I can give you her address. I went with Finn a couple of times to pick up his little girl."

"That would be helpful." Jane waited while he jotted down the address.

She desperately needed to be with Will and Reid. Maybe they'd take a drive out to the peninsula, and they could gather seashells by Fort Morgan.

SEVENTEEN

Were the police tearing his house apart? Had the killer planted any evidence?

Still carrying his coffee, Reid wandered down the street to the pier. The scent of the sea air normally soothed him, and he settled on a bench to watch boats moving out in the bay. Pete flew down to settle beside him. When Reid didn't offer to feed him, the pelican flapped giant wings and soared out over the water to scoop up a fish. Other pelicans dove and soared on the wind with squawking gulls and terns.

"You look as lost as a captain with no navigation equipment, son."

Reid gazed up at Alfie's drawl. "Morning." He pointed to the bench. "Have a seat. You just get back from shrimping?"

The old man reeked of seafood and still wore his once-white boots, stained red. A few shrimp scales clung to his pants. "Yep. Not tired yet though. You look lower than a snake's belly in a wagon rut. Need some cheerin' up?"

"Yeah. I guess you haven't heard what's happened." He told the old fisherman about Lauren's death and Will's involvement.

"That kid's good as they come. I'll bet Miss Jane is having a hissy fit with a tail on it."

"The worst one I've seen," Reid agreed.

Several young men in their twenties stopped a few feet away and stared at him. Reid didn't recognize any of them. They were too old to be friends with Will, and their expressions made him think they were punks looking for trouble. He glared at them as a warning to leave them alone.

"You throwin' shade at us?" one of them called. "Figures. Any dad who'd set up his own son for murder is a tool."

Reid rose and went toward them. "What'd you say?"

"Heard you hired someone to kill the ex, and your boy is taking the fall for it," the tallest boy said.

"That's absolutely not true. I'd never do that. Whoever told you that is spreading lies."

The guys stared at him, and one shook his head in disgust before they brushed past him, deliberately striking shoulders. Reid clenched his fists and glared after them. Was that really how people felt? He was new here, but how could anyone assume such a terrible thing? What father would do that?

He went back to the bench with Alfie, who'd heard the entire exchange. "That kind of attitude here surprises me. Whatever happened to innocent until proven guilty?"

Alfie pulled a toothpick from his shirt pocket and stuck it in his mouth. "Those fellas are as worthless as gum on a shoe. Pay them no mind, Reid. Anyone who knows you would never think such a thing."

"Thanks, Alfie. Hard to hear something like that. You heard anything more about the squatters out on the island? Gabriel might hate me enough to try to throw suspicion on Will."

"Saw smoke there yesterday. You saw yer little lady's mama, right? She didn't come back with you?"

Reid shook his head. "She couldn't wait to see the back of us. It was painful for Jane. Even though she knew her mom could have come to see her anytime, I think she'd hoped Kim would take one look at her and grab hold. Didn't happen. Kim was too afraid of anyone finding out who Jane really was."

"Poor little chief. Has to be hard."

"I don't know what Jane will do next. Probably let it be."

"Sounds like the woman is no real mother."

"She has two teenage girls with the guy she's with. Maybe when they're older, Jane can make contact. Her mom would refuse to allow it now, I'm sure."

Alfie took the toothpick out of his mouth. "Where's Will? With his granddad?"

"At the moment. I'm going to go do something with him, try to distract him. There's a search going on at my house right now."

The worry about what they were finding wouldn't leave him alone. It wouldn't be good.

"And you're feared someone planted something?"

"Yeah. If someone wants to implicate Will—and it looks that way—the police will find something else. I keep hoping and praying the killer wasn't purposely trying to frame Will, but I think it was deliberate. And Will's tackle box is missing."

"That dog won't hunt for anyone who knows your boy."

"The problem is most don't know him. We're new here."

"Folks who think that way just got one oar in the water. But be patient. Truth always comes out."

"I guess it usually does, but I don't want Will to have to wait in jail for it to show up."

Alfie gave a slow nod. "Something about this smells bad enough to gag a maggot."

Reid rose and stretched out his back. "I'd better go get my boy. Waiting to hear what they find at the house is like waiting for paint to dry. But I might wish I didn't know what they discover."

He walked back across the street to his SUV and glanced at the police station parking lot. Jane's SUV was still there. He was tempted to stop in, but in the end, he got in his vehicle and left town.

Let her do her job. Maybe she could stop this runaway train.

"There's the house." Reid pulled into the drive of the cute coastal home painted a light turquoise.

Palm trees swayed in the breeze, and flowers bloomed beside the walk. A large water oak shaded the front lawn, and two cattle egrets followed behind a neighbor's mower, eating bugs.

Jane opened her door. "I wish you'd stayed with Will on the beach."

She'd argued about it in the five-minute drive from Fort Morgan to the house, but Reid hadn't budged about accompanying her. Someone was after her family, and she might be a target. She needed backup.

He reached over to put his hand on hers. "Parker will take care of him. There are plenty of other people around, including some of his baseball friends. He's playing volleyball. Nothing harmful in that. He's fine."

Music, something tropical with steel guitars, floated through the screen door and open windows. The occupants either didn't have air-conditioning or didn't like it. The heat and humidity shimmered off the drive, and his forehead beaded with perspiration the minute he got out of the SUV.

He fell behind Jane and let her go to the door first. She pressed the doorbell, and the distant sound of a vacuum cut off before light steps came to the door.

An attractive brunette in her twenties appeared in shorts and a tee. She opened the screen door, and her gaze flickered when she took in Jane's uniform. "Is this about Finn?"

"I'm Jane Hardy, Pelican Harbor chief of police. You're Amy Presley? I have a few questions."

"I am." The woman glanced behind her. "I'd rather make sure my daughter doesn't overhear." She stepped out onto the porch and pulled the door shut behind her. "What do you need to know?"

"Do you know of any enemies your ex-husband had?"

Her brown eyes widened. "Whoa, he wasn't *murdered*. He died in a fire."

"We aren't sure yet what went on. Did he know Ms. Briscoe?"

"Not socially. She owned the lab where he got his drug test. He hated her, you know. I'm surprised he was willing to try to rescue her when the fire broke out. They had words on several occasions."

Reid saw no sign of deception in her expression. How did Jane do this every day? Ask questions, prod deep into people's personal lives. It was enough to make you lose faith in humanity. This young woman seemed to have no regret about what happened to her ex. And from what he'd heard about it all, demanding a drug test had been an act of meanness.

"Words?" Jane asked. "What was their disagreement?"

"He claimed she'd falsified the drug test and that he'd lost custody over it." Amy shrugged her slim shoulders. "That was Finn though, always passing the buck."

"Why did you request a drug test? Was he a known drug user?"

The other woman's eyes flickered, and she glanced away from

Jane's face. "Well, sure. He'd been addicted to meth when he was a teenager. I suspected he'd gone back to it."

"His coworkers claimed he hated drugs, that he was a health nut."

The Presley woman bit her lip. "That kind of thing can get a hold of you."

"Was your relationship amicable?" Jane's voice was deceptively soft.

"He was . . . difficult. Always wanting more and more time with Bexley, our daughter. He'd fly into a rage when it wasn't convenient."

"You say you're surprised he tried to help. Anything that might let us know why he went in there when he was told not to?"

Amy lifted her chin. "I thought maybe he tried to kill her."

"I see. Did he threaten Ms. Briscoe?"

"He said someone should end her reign of terror. He was planning on suing her. I tried to talk him out of it, but he could be bullheaded."

"Were you surprised when the test results came back?"

"Not really."

"You wanted to find something to use against him."

Relief lit Mrs. Presley's eyes at the sound of a child calling for Mommy. "I'd better go. That's all I know anyway."

When she vanished inside the house, Reid took Jane's arm and they walked back toward the SUV.

"What did you make of her story?" Jane asked.

Reid loved the way she trusted his opinion. "I dislike women like her—ones who use power over their children to hurt their exes. And she was lying about believing he was doing drugs. She was probably more surprised than anyone when it came back positive. Something is fishy about the whole thing."

"I think so too. But her point about the test being falsified needs investigation. Maybe something's there. The team is checking out disgruntled customers. I'd call Finn one of those."

"Me too," he agreed. "It sounds like a setup. It makes me wonder if maybe Mrs. Presley knew Gail and asked her to falsify the results. I didn't believe her to be credible at all."

Jane smiled. "You're picking up police terminology."

They got in the SUV, and she started the engine. "That didn't take long. Will won't be ready to go."

"We can hang out and watch him play for a while. It's a hot day. He'll be ready to get ice cream soon."

Reid buckled his seat belt. "Have you heard if they've searched my house yet?"

She glanced at her watch. "They should be there now. You want to grab Will and head back to watch?"

"Scott is there and told me to stay away. He's probably right. I don't think I could stop from interfering."

She squeezed his hand. "Augusta has it under control. She'll figure out who really did this."

Reid wished he could believe her, but he was getting more and more worried about their son. If it looked like Will would be arrested, he planned to confess himself. He couldn't let their son's life be ruined.

EIGHTEEN

Watching the seabirds swoop and catch fish should have calmed her. Jane sat on a rock overlooking the water and watched Will throw a ball for Parker. The whitecaps deposited more seashells on the sand before rolling back out in a soothing motion, and she tasted salt on her lips. The wind lifted her hair, and she knotted her hands together and tried to breathe through her anxiety.

Was this one of her boy's last free days?

She couldn't bear the thought of what seemed to be barreling down on them. And to be shut out of the investigation added more stress. They could be finding something at Reid's house right this minute that would further implicate Will.

Beside her on the rock, Reid plucked her hand off her knee and held it. "Rough day today for all of us. Will seems calm though."

The boy shouted and dropped to the sand before he threw his arms around Parker's neck. The volleyball game was still going on with teenagers down the beach, and Will had been invited to continue to play, but he didn't seem to want to be too far from his parents. It was the only sign of stress Jane detected in him.

She let sand trickle through the fingers of her free hand. "I should have gone to the house. It's hard to wait here not knowing what's happening."

"Augusta would have kicked you out anyway. And a reporter might have snapped a picture of you there. It wouldn't have ended well."

He was right, but it didn't make the wait any easier. His hand enveloping hers calmed her racing fears and slowed her pulse. She brushed the sand from her hands and exhaled as she lifted her face to the salt-laden breeze. Out in the distance she could see a big boat cruising by a couple of the oil platforms.

"What did you make of Amy Presley's information?"

She turned her head to Reid and smiled. "I know what you're trying to do. And I love you for it. I need to talk to some of Gail's coworkers and see if they know whether Finn threatened her. What if he started the fire himself and it moved faster than expected? He might have been caught inside."

"All neatly tied up with a bow and then you can move on to figuring out Will's problem."

"Maybe. It's hard to know. There's still a lot of investigation to go. Gail's ex still looks good for it too, and Finn could have been caught up in that war."

Will got up and brushed the sand from his legs before sauntering toward them. He dropped to the beach in front of them. "Anything from the search warrant?"

"Not yet. Try not to worry though. Things like this take a while. And be prepared to have to clean up a mess when we get back. They'll be taking fingerprints and pulling belongings out of dressers and closets. I'll help tidy up. And I thought I'd make some gumbo for dinner. Maybe Olivia and Megan can join us."

At the sound of Megan's name, his lips curved. "I haven't seen her for a few days. She's been at cheer camp. I think it ended yesterday though."

"She's probably ready to see you too."

The budding romance between the two was cute to watch. She glanced at Reid. Did other people see the love sizzling between them? Probably. Neither she nor Reid had made much effort to hide it.

Reid shaded his eyes with his hand. "Speak of the devil. There's Megan and Olivia heading this way. The beach must have been calling them too."

Jane winced to see Olivia using a walker. Was ALS supposed to move this fast? She'd thought Olivia's decline would be much more gradual. Megan walked beside her with two beach chairs.

The other two hadn't seen them yet, so she lifted her hand and waved. "Olivia, Megan, over here."

Olivia's smile was lopsided, and she was winded when she reached them. Megan unfolded a chair for her mother and dropped the other to the sand to help her mom sit. Once her mom was settled, Megan spared a quick smile Will's way.

"Hey," he said.

"I talked Mom into coming as soon as I got your text."

He colored and shot an apologetic look at Jane. "Uh, sure. Mom was just saying she was going to invite you to dinner once we clean up the mess at the house."

"I'll help."

Megan seemed to know all about what was going on, so Olivia would too. Jane removed a bottle of water from the cooler and handed it to her friend. When Olivia struggled to uncap it, Jane took it and untwisted the cap, then handed it back.

"Thanks." Her hand trembled, and water splashed out as she managed to get the bottle to her lips.

Jane saw the worry in the girl's big blue eyes.

Megan unfolded the other beach chair. "I want to swim."

"I'll come with you," Will said.

Megan's ponytail bounced as she and Will ran toward the water with Parker on their heels. Olivia's smile was wistful. "Young love." Her words were slurred.

Jane chose her words carefully. "You don't seem to be having a good day. Didn't you have a doctor's appointment on Tuesday?"

"I had blood drawn. He called this morning to give me some test results." She paused and studied Jane's face. "Surprising news, Jane. I was going to call you but decided to tell you in person. He doesn't think I have ALS. He says it's moving too fast."

Not ALS? That had to be good news, though Jane didn't like the sound of *moving too fast*. "So what is it then?"

"He thinks it might be Guillain-Barré. That's good and bad news."

The term was vaguely familiar, but Jane didn't know much about it. "It sounds like all good news to me. Let's hear it. I need some good news."

"I might be perfectly fine in about six months. Seventy percent fully recover." Her smile made an appearance then.

Seventy percent! Jane wanted to clap and cheer. "Olivia, that's wonderful!"

Olivia held up her hand. "The bad news is that I'm going to need care. I'll likely be this bad or a little worse for months. If they'd caught it sooner, treatment might have shortened it, but it's a little late now."

Jane exchanged a long look with Reid. "We've already talked about this. Reid has plenty of room, and we want to help."

Olivia nodded, and her throat worked. A tear slipped from one eye, and she fumbled in her purse.

Jane found a tissue for her. "I'm here for you and Megan. Reid and I both are."

"You've done so much already. I hate to be a burden. I could go to a nursing home if you can take Megan."

"You're not going to a nursing home. We'll figure this out."

But how? She had a job to do, and she couldn't ask Reid to play nursemaid. Could they hire someone to help out?

Reid took her hand. "I'm here too. We can take shifts caring for you, Olivia. I've got plenty of room at my house. I'll get a room ready for you and one for Megan."

Jane had never loved him more than in that moment. How many men would be willing to do something like this? Not many. But even as she thanked him with her eyes, she didn't see a way through the maze of problems that faced them.

Reid parked behind the detective's car. They'd come this way the minute Scott had called. He wanted to tell them in person what the police had found, and Reid hadn't liked his attorney's somber tone.

His stomach was doing calisthenics, and he knew Jane was just as rocked by what was going on. He glanced at her before he got out with Parker. Her outer calmness was a mask her eyes couldn't hide behind.

"Will, you can go inside and start cleaning your room. We need to get ready for Olivia and Megan to move in with us."

That bombshell left the boy speechless for a moment. His eyes gleamed. "Really? When is this happening?"

"In the next couple of days. Olivia needs help."

That sobered Will in an instant. "She's dying? Oh, man."

"Actually, no. They've found out it's something that is likely temporary. But she'll need too much help to stay at home. She might be here for three months or maybe six. But we don't want her to go to a nursing home."

"I'll do whatever you need to help. Olivia's awesome." He went to the porch, and the dog went with him.

"That'll keep Will occupied," Reid whispered to Jane as she came around the front of the SUV.

Scott rose from the chair on the porch. The front door stood open, and even from here Reid registered the mess inside. The officers had been thorough. He might have to order pizza instead of cooking something.

Will bolted past them to reach Scott first. "Is everything okay?"

Reid and Jane hurried after him, and Scott waited until they were all on the porch. "It's not good, guys. They found a tackle box in Will's closet. Looked like it had blonde hair and blood on it. The officers were quite excited, as I'm sure you can imagine."

Reid tried to speak and couldn't find the words. This was horrible beyond his worst fears.

Jane gasped. "It had to have been planted."

"You and I know it, but the police are heading back to seek an arrest warrant. I'll push for Will's release into your custody, but you can probably expect at least a night in juvie, Will. I didn't see any way to sugarcoat this news. Sorry. You'll want to pack a bag, son. Try to be calm. I'll get you out as quickly as I can."

Reid's words welled up from some place deep inside. "I did it."

"You did not. You were with me," Jane said in a wobbly voice. "Don't go there, Reid. It will make it look like you think Will did it. And we know he's innocent. We have to trust God like you said.

And Augusta. Trust justice. Someone is trying to hurt my family, and I'm going to find out who is behind this."

He opened his mouth to list all the ways he could have had Lauren killed, then closed his mouth. She was right. Any detective would see straight through his confession. And it would make it worse for Will, not better. He hadn't thought his plan out well enough. There was no trail leading to him at all. It would be a confession with no substance.

"What do we do next?" he asked.

Even though she had tears in her eyes, Jane tipped up her chin. "We follow the law. Will is innocent, and we'll prove it."

How did they go about proving Will's innocence? While the evidence was circumstantial, it was compelling. Blood and tissue.

Will bolted for the house, but not before Reid saw the tears in his son's eyes. He wanted to go after him, to tell him he wouldn't have to go to juvie, but it would be a lie. They all had to face this tsunami heading their way.

"We have no witnesses, no proof. But someone evil is moving us around like chess pieces."

"We'll find something." Jane blotted her eyes. "The person behind this can't stay hidden for long. Augusta told me everything she's looking into. She's a good detective. She'll find some path to the truth. And so will we."

"Like what?"

She held his gaze. "Elliot is good with online stuff, right?"

"He's great at it. So am I."

"Now that Lauren's been found, we might be able to track down who she left with eight years ago. We still know so little about Lauren's whereabouts. And what about talking to the neighbors? Someone might have seen the altercation between Will and Lauren."

Hope bubbled in his chest. "I'll call Elliot. He's been going stir-crazy while he's recovering. Computer work will be right up his alley."

Scott nodded toward the end of the drive where another police car rolled toward them. "Get Will. I'm sure they have an arrest warrant."

"I'll get him. You talk to Augusta," Reid said.

He wasn't sure he'd be able to hold his temper with the detective. Jane trusted her, but Reid found it hard to believe anyone would work as hard as he wanted to clear their son's name. It was going to be up to them.

NINETEEN

D on't do this, Augusta." Jane barred her detective's path up the porch steps of Reid's large brick home.

Reid stood with Will by the front door, and she wished with all her heart she could prevent seeing her boy handcuffed and loaded into the patrol car's backseat. Parker knew something was wrong, too, and he whined low in his throat at Will's feet.

Augusta's brown eyes were shadowed, and her uniform held creases from her long day. "Chief, you know I have no choice. If this were a neighbor, you'd be right there making the arrest. We have to follow the evidence." She looked toward the door. "Where's Jackson?"

"Searching around the outbuilding. Did you find anything else besides the tackle box?"

"The deceased's fingerprints were inside the house, so we're going to have the house and building checked with Luminol when it's fully dark. She might have been killed inside." She peered around Jane's shoulder. "Reid, was Lauren ever inside your home?"

"Not to my knowledge. I always intercepted her on the porch or in the yard." He glanced over at Will. "Did you ever let her in?"

"Like I'd let her in."

Jane inwardly winced at his dismissive tone. That wouldn't help. "So maybe she broke in."

Augusta lifted a brow. "I'll take a look at the locks."

Jane stepped out of the way so the detective could check the front door. She turned on her flashlight to closely examine the brass tumbler. "Scratches on it. It's possible someone broke in."

"She might have wanted to wander around and see if she could find money to steal," Reid said.

He stood shoulder to shoulder with Will, who had a backpack slung over his shoulder. If Jane didn't know him so well, she would have guessed he was calm by his expression, but he was clenching and unclenching his fists. They were both helpless to prevent what was about to happen. Maybe they should have loaded Will in the SUV and taken off to hide out, but she was an officer of the law. She couldn't abandon her duty.

She believed in justice like she believed that water was wet. It had been her life, and it wouldn't fail her now. Would it?

Jackson, his dark skin beaded with perspiration, came around the side of the house with something in an evidence bag. Her heart seized, and she took an involuntary step toward him before she caught herself. Asking what he'd found was Augusta's duty. Jane could only watch from the sidelines.

Augusta spotted Jackson and moved to talk with him out of earshot. He opened the bag and showed her the contents, but Jane couldn't hear what they said between them. Augusta's face looked grave when she turned around.

Jane blocked her path. "What is it?"

"A woman's bloody sweater."

"Someone planted it," Reid said.

Jane's throat constricted, and she shook her head. "Surely you can see this is all a setup."

"I think so too," Jackson said. "But the evidence is adding up."

What else had they found?

Augusta put her hand on Jane's arm. "You have to let this play out, Jane. We don't believe Will did this, but we have to follow the evidence. If this is a setup, we'll find out who is behind it."

No matter how much she wanted to look professional, Jane couldn't stop the tears from leaking from her eyes. "I want to believe that, but it's hard to let you walk out of here with my boy."

"I know. We'll take good care of Will, but we need to take him into custody. I've already called ahead to the judge and let him know I'll be arresting him as a juvenile. If Jackson hadn't found blood, I could have booked him for involuntary manslaughter, but this changes the charges. That's about the best I can do in the situation."

Jane had instantly understood how damaging finding blood meant to the case. Her son was facing an uphill battle to prove his innocence.

"I appreciate it." At least Will wouldn't be locked up in the regular jail but sent to juvie until they could get him out. She released a heavy exhale. "I'll get Will."

Her knees barely held her as she walked back to the porch and looked up at her son, whose dark eyes were wide. His lips trembled, and her heart failed at his pleading expression. "You'll have to go with them, Will. They will ask more questions, but Scott will be with you, and it looks like they will book you as a juvenile. They won't object to your release into our custody, but you'll have to go to juvie until a judge rules."

Will swallowed hard and went pale. "Okay." His voice wobbled and he swayed.

Reid grabbed his arm. "Steady, son. We'll get through this."

Will took several deep breaths. "Can you guys come with me?"

"We'll be right by your side. Scott will meet us at the station. This will all take several hours so we have to be prepared for a grueling time."

They went down the wide steps arm in arm. Jane gave Will a final squeeze, then loosened her grip and moved away. "He's ready." She stepped back and loaded Parker into the backseat of Reid's SUV.

Hearing Augusta read Will his rights brought tears surging to Jane's eyes. This was some kind of nightmare. If only she could wake up. But this was all too real.

Jackson cuffed him and gently guided him into the squad car's backseat. He squatted by the door and spoke to Will too softly for Jane to hear, but Jackson patted his knee before he stood up and sat in front. The squad car turned around in Reid's circle driveway and pulled out to head for town.

Jane's jumbled thoughts were hard to pin down as she rode in the passenger seat of Reid's SUV. She couldn't have driven if her life depended on it. Her hands kept shaking, and her mouth was dry. Reid was holding it together, but then she knew what faced their son and he had never seen this play out.

When it was over, it wouldn't be something they'd ever want to remember.

Augusta blocked the interrogation room door. "I'm sorry, but only one of you can go in with him. There's no room for more since his attorney is also in there."

Jane curled her fingers into her palms and glanced at Reid. Everything in her wanted to be with Will, but maybe Reid would be the better choice. The two had always been close, whereas she had only been in her son's life a few months.

Reid's anguished gaze locked with hers. "I want to be there, but you know more about the law."

Augusta cleared her throat. "If I might offer my advice. I'd like to be able to say the chief exerted no influence on her son's answers during this questioning. It might be safer for Will's acquittal if you're not in the room, Jane. You can listen in so you know what's happening."

Her detective made good sense, but Jane didn't want to agree. She wanted to be able to touch her boy or shake her head to warn him off of answering something. But Scott would be there. He was a good attorney and would protect Will's rights.

She took a step back. "You're right. Go ahead, Reid."

He paused long enough to squeeze her hand. "I'll tell him you're watching so he knows you're with him."

She gave a jerky nod and touched the top of Parker's head for courage. "I'll be right here." The words *when he's taken away* refused to leave her lips. Had it really come to that? Arrest? Her boy behind bars for murder?

Reid and Augusta entered the interrogation room, and she ran with Parker around to the viewing room. She slipped into the booth and directed Parker to lie down in the corner.

She drank in the sight of her son and Reid. Both so alike in appearance, temperament, and their care for other people. While she couldn't claim a hand in Will's upbringing, she couldn't imagine a son she could be prouder of. There was no way he was guilty of harming Lauren.

Augusta smiled at him and turned on the recorder. "So let's go over the events officially. I'm going to read you your rights first before I ask you to answer any questions."

Jane checked out mentally as Augusta went over the familiar rights list. Her gaze wandered to Scott on Will's right at the table. Reid was scooted up close to Will on his left.

"Do you understand?" Augusta asked.

"Yes," Will said in a nearly inaudible voice.

"How did you come to be fishing at the dock?"

"I was staying with Grandpa while my parents were out of town, but I was getting bored with playing video games so I asked him to drop me off for some fishing."

"What time was this?"

"About one. I was hoping to catch some frogs. Grandpa was going to show me how to fry up frog legs. He was supposed to pick me up at six unless I called him sooner."

"So you were at your house alone?"

"Yes, until Lauren showed up."

"What time was this?"

"I'm not really sure. I wasn't watching the time."

Augusta looked at Reid. "According to your father, he spoke to you about four."

"Then it was just a few minutes before that. Maybe three forty-five. I'd just gotten back to the house when Dad called."

She glanced down at her notebook. "What happened when Lauren showed up?"

Jane had heard this part multiple times, and Will recounted the same details. Lauren had been yelling and waving some papers. She wanted to talk to Reid, then flew into a rage and attacked Will. Jane could only pray a judge would take that attack into account.

"So she started to strike you again, and you grabbed her arm?"

"Yes. She jerked her arm out of my hand and lost her balance. When she fell into the water, she came up mad and sputtering. I reached down and tried to help her up. The water was only to her waist or so. She wasn't drowning or anything like that, but I wanted to help her. She started yelling at me again and told me to leave her alone. She smacked at my hand. So I ran away from the pier and went to the house." His voice trailed off to a softer volume. "I shouldn't have left, but she was yelling and screaming at me. Cursing too. It scared me."

Her son was a strapping six-footer, but he was only fifteen. When a kid was that big, it was easy to forget his real age. Of course it scared him to have an adult berating him. Jane watched to see her detective's reaction, but Augusta's expression was neutral and interested. Scott frowned though and shook his head.

"Then what?" Augusta asked.

"I didn't know what to do. I-I tried to call Grandpa, but he didn't answer. He often doesn't have his phone on him." Will tipped up his chin. "You can check with him. His phone would show I called. I was rattled. Then Dad called. I told him what had happened, and that her car was still in the driveway. He instructed me to call 911, so I did. I waited until Officer Jackson arrived, and we went back out but couldn't find her. You know the rest."

"So you were watching the driveway?"

Will nodded. "I didn't want to go back out until she was gone. She was yelling so much, and I wanted to be away from her." His voice trembled. "I didn't bring my tackle box back in. I ran off and left it on the dock with the fishing pole."

The fishing pole! Jane saw the same thought register on Reid's face.

He held up his hand. "Did Officer Jackson find the fishing pole on the dock?"

"He did. We took it into evidence."

"Why would he have taken his tackle box and left the fishing pole? It's clear he left everything."

"Please, Mr. Dixon, I'll ask the questions." Augusta rose. "That's all for now. We're booking you for manslaughter, Will. That may be upgraded to murder as we investigate. The DA may weigh in also. I'm sorry. You'll be detained in the juvenile center jail, and your attorney can ask for you to be released into your parents' custody when we see the judge tomorrow. Good luck." She had Will stand so she could cuff him again before she took him out to be transported.

Manslaughter.

Jane ran from the room to see Will one last time before he was taken away. He was pale and tears pooled in his eyes when he exited the room with Augusta.

"I didn't do anything, Mom."

She hugged him tightly. "I know, Will. I know. Stay strong. It's just one night."

At least she prayed it was only one night. Reid joined Jane and she threw herself against his chest and wept as Augusta led their son away.

TWENTY

His son was in juvie for manslaughter.

The very thought was surreal, and Reid's insides felt made of glass as he parked outside Elliot's houseboat. Lamplight glimmered on the water and pushed back the shadows as he and Jane got out. If only light could drive away the shadows of fear in his heart.

"Elliot knows we're coming," he told her.

The door opened as they walked along the dock to the boat, and Elliot waved at them. "I'm ready for something to do. What's going on? I heard a rumor at the coffee shop that Will was arrested for manslaughter. That can't be right."

"It's all too true, I'm afraid," Reid said. "That's why we need your help."

Elliot stepped aside to motion them in. "Man, that's just wrong."

His curly blond hair was patchy where the doctors had shaved his head for brain surgery after his injury. Though he was only twenty-five, he was one of the smartest people Reid knew.

The living room was decorated in a beach theme with coral and turquoise colors. The scent of hand sanitizer hung in the air like usual, and a large, industrial-sized bottle of the stuff sat beside the computer. There were neat stacks of computer magazines next to various computers.

Reid explained what had happened. "Someone is trying to frame him."

"You sure you're up to working? How are the headaches?"

"Getting better, ma'am. I have some special glasses that are helping me with computer work. I'll spend every waking minute on it. I love that kid. What do you need from me?"

"Find out everything about where Lauren has been these past years. Who has she been with? What has she been doing? Has she made any enemies? She had a fake ID, and we have that name and the social security number she's been using so that should make things easier."

"Piece of cake, boss." Elliot glanced at Jane. "You doing okay, Chief?"

"No, neither of us are." Her voice was thick with tears, and she wandered over to stare at the bank of computers along the wall. "These last months have been nearly unbearable with the constant attacks, but this is the worst. The cloud of suspicion over him will never go away, even if he's acquitted. Not unless we find out who is doing this to us and why."

"I'm on it." Elliot's blue eyes were bright with determination. "I'll see if I can hack into her emails."

Reid handed him a paper with all the information they'd been able to glean about Lauren's past movements. "She's been going by Lauren Haskell. You have a picture of her fake driver's license, which was issued by Vegas, so that must be where she's been living."

Elliot took the paper and scanned it. "I should have some information for you by tomorrow."

"Don't stay up all night," Jane said. "You need to rest."

"I'm wide-awake. I had a nap this afternoon because there was nothing else to do. Walking around still makes my head ache, but

I can rest when I need to. I'll be able to sit right here and work. I'll call you as soon as I have something."

"You don't know how much we appreciate it, Elliot," Jane said. "We're hoping he'll be released tomorrow, but it will be up to the judge."

At the anguish in her voice, Reid clasped her hand, and they moved toward the door. "Thanks, Elliot." They exited into the humid night air. As he closed the door behind them, he heard the clack of computer keys.

He slipped his arm around Jane's slim waist. "Want to get something to eat before I take you home?"

"I'm not hungry. But I don't want to be alone. Want to come home with me for a while? I have leftover pizza if you're hungry."

"I'm not hungry either. I've got my laptop, and the two of us could see what we can dig up."

She paused, then stepped into his embrace and rested her head on his chest. "This can't be real, Reid. It's not right. Justice is failing me."

"Everything in this life can fail. I have to keep reminding myself that only God is faithful and never fails us. Things are bleak, life is unfair, but this isn't over yet. We will see God work."

She leaned her head back to stare up into his face. "I'm trying to believe that, but it's so hard. Do you really think it's true?"

"Yes, even though I have doubts as big as tidal waves. Every time they try to take me under, I grab hold of God's promises. It's hard right now. Harder than I ever dreamed it could be. We have to keep reminding ourselves that he has the power to fix this."

She dropped her arms back to her sides and turned to go to the SUV. "I pray you're right. I vacillate between total trust and total doubt."

"He's not afraid of our doubts. I'm scared too." And he was. Fear was a suffocating companion that constantly tried to smother his faith. "These past few hours have taken every bit of my strength to hold on, to refuse to let terror make me forget who really rules the universe." He opened the SUV door for her.

She smiled up at him. "So you're not the Superman of faith?"

"Hardly. Faith takes more work than I ever dreamed. But when we get through this, we'll look back and realize this trial will make the next one easier because we'll have seen how God worked it out."

She slid into the seat. "I'm ready for it to be over—for Will to be home with us. And it's not just Will's situation, but it's Olivia too. And my mother. It's like trying to touch faith through fog."

She was so right. He went around to sit behind the wheel and drive the few blocks to her apartment. If only he could go to sleep and wake up with Will safe at home. But trials had to be walked through. They had no choice.

The microwave beeped in the kitchen where Reid was warming up pizza. Jane sat on her sofa and fingered the brass key. It was worn smooth from being handled over the years, and the name of the manufacturer had been rubbed off. She wished she had the safe-deposit box. Seeing the evidence of what had happened so long ago might distract her from her fear for Will, even for a few minutes.

But there were so many other important things to do. She could make a list of who to question about Gail's death. And talk to more of Finn's coworkers or family. That investigation was still her job.

But Will was the most important thing in her life.

Parker yawned and jumped onto the floor before looking at her quizzically, as if to ask if she was ready to go to bed.

The grueling last two days had left her body exhausted, but her mind still buzzed. She felt wired and alert, though she also wanted to crawl into bed and pull the covers over her head. She reached for her laptop and called up the bank website.

Reid came into the room carrying two plates of pizza. "Dinner is served."

The aroma of garlic and tomato sauce made her stomach turn. The thought of eating was nauseating, but she accepted the plate he offered anyway. She set it on the coffee table in front of her. Maybe her appetite would return later.

He settled beside her on the sofa. "Find anything?"

"I decided to look up hours for getting into the safe-deposit box at the bank."

He'd reached for a piece of pizza, but he drew his hand back at her words. "I'm not sure I want to see the pictures she mentioned. I don't think I can handle what happened to my mom right now."

She closed the webpage. "You're right. This can wait. I was looking for a distraction, but I obviously wasn't thinking it through."

He picked up his laptop on the sofa and opened it. "You have access to more information than I do. Have you done a search for Lauren?"

"Not yet." She went to the NCIC site to log in. The National Crime Information Center had data of virtually all possible crimes. "Augusta will have already done this, but I might see something she missed. Or something that leads me in a different direction."

His shoulder brushed hers, and his breath brushed her face. "Will this tell us where she was?"

"I hope so. Let's try the stolen identity first. She had to get that identity somehow because she used a social security number." Jane started the search and waited a few seconds before the results appeared. "That social is for a Penelope Haskell, which is probably how she came up with the last name she was using. Penelope died ten years ago. Let me see if there are any outstanding warrants for her arrest." She executed another search. "Nothing there, so she was keeping her nose clean. What's the address on her driver's license?"

Reid pulled out the paper and read off the address to her. "Let's search Google Earth. We could see what houses are nearby, maybe call neighbors and see what they can tell us."

"Good idea." She pulled up the program and typed in the address.

A neighborhood popped onto the screen, and she navigated to a street view to study the houses. "She came here dressed to the nines and reeking of money, but this place is very middle class."

The modest green ranch house in Baxter, Kentucky, couldn't have been more than a thousand square feet. Scraggly crabgrass poked through the dirt in places, and the shrubs seemed half dead from lack of care. The paint on the door and window trim was peeling.

She called up a real estate website and scanned for house prices. "She probably didn't pay more than eighty thousand for that place."

Reid touched a finger to the screen. "That's her car, so it's definitely her house. This must be an old picture."

"Most of the photos on Google Earth aren't current time." Jane peered at the computer. "Looks like it was taken three years ago, so she'd been there awhile." She zoomed out to check out another view from the other side. "Someone's in the backyard. A man. It's too blurry to make out his face though."

"Could Nora do anything to enhance it?"

"I can have her try." Jane saved the picture and shot it off in an email to Nora with her request. "I'll have to pay her overtime. She's got to be torn in a million directions with all that's going on."

"Can you read the street addresses on either side?" Reid asked.

"Sure." She navigated until the numbers on the house to the right were visible, jotted them down, then moved to the house on the other side.

"And on the opposite side?"

She positioned the screen until she got the information about the three closest houses across the street. "It's too late to make any calls tonight, but we can look up the phone numbers and be ready to talk to them tomorrow."

She spent ten more minutes searching for the addresses and phone records of the neighbors while Reid ate his pizza. "The one directly across the street seems a good one to call first thing. According to the owner information, an older woman lives there, and she might be the type who pays attention to what's going on in her neighborhood. We can divide up the names and call."

He wiped his fingers on a napkin before he accepted the paper she handed him. "Any other ideas?"

She rubbed the back of her neck. "I'm too tired to think."

"I'll go home and let you try to get some rest." He drew her close for a good-night kiss that gave her more comfort than he knew. He was such a steady rock in her life. "C-Could we pray for Will before you go?"

He stilled and nodded. "I was thinking the same thing."

His deep voice rumbled through her like an electrical current as he asked God to protect and comfort Will when they couldn't. Tears burned her eyes and leaked out from under her closed lids.

She had been trying not to imagine how alone and scared Will must feel right now, but it had been impossible not to picture him in that cell.

God would be in that cell with Will even though they couldn't. It would have to be enough for tonight.

TWENTY-ONE

He shouldn't have shut Jane down about the key.

Coffee in hand, Reid sat on the back deck as dawn pinked the eastern sky over the trees. Frogs croaked in the marsh, and he heard the splash of something in the river. The hearing was set for nine, three hours from now, and it couldn't come soon enough. Every minute ticked by like a year.

He just wanted Will safe and sound at home.

Headlights came up the drive, and he recognized Jane's SUV. He got up to greet her as she got out with Parker and came up the back steps.

"You're up early." He pulled her into his arms and held her close.

She was trembling, and he could see how fragile her emotions were. His own were just as bad, but he as a guy, he felt he wasn't supposed to show them.

"I didn't get a wink of sleep," she said in a husky voice.

"Me neither." Not with their boy locked up. He kissed her, then pressed his cheek against hers. "We'll get him out this morning. The judge knows you. He'll let us take him. It's going to be okay."

She pulled away and shook her head. "Getting him out of juvie solves nothing, Reid. We've got Everest to climb ahead of us."

"I know, but at least he'll be where we can protect him."

She bit her lip and stepped back. "Got coffee?"

"A whole pot." He gestured to the hot pot on the table. "I'll get another cup." When he returned from the kitchen, he found her in a chair, looking at her phone. "Any news?"

"A text from Scott. He's already talked to the DA and she won't argue against Will's release. So it should be routine to get him out."

"Thank the Lord." He poured her a cup of coffee and handed it to her.

She wrapped her hands around the mug. "It's probably too early to make any calls to Lauren's neighbors."

"Unless we want to make them too mad to talk to us."

They sat sipping their coffee in companionable silence for several minutes.

"Have you talked to your dad this morning?" Reid asked.

"He called at five. He'd been up all night and offered money if we needed it for bail." Jane took a sip of her coffee. "Nice of him, but juvie doesn't take bail. They either release him into our custody or they retain him."

"He feels responsible since he didn't stay with Will. He was putting in some equipment in the bunker and thought he'd be okay for a few hours."

Jane's eyes widened. "I hope he isn't thinking they will charge him in adult court."

"Could they?"

"Oh yes. Alabama is hard-core with crime, no matter how young the offender. Many kids have been handed over to adult court for serious crimes like this." She shook her head. "They can't do that. I don't think Augusta would go for it."

"What if the DA is insistent?"

"It could happen then. I have to admit I keep wishing Dad had stayed with him the whole time. If he had been there, we wouldn't be in this mess. There would have been a corroborative witness. Now we have nothing but Will's word, and a whole lot of evidence that contradicts his story."

Reid snapped his fingers. "Witnesses. Has either of your officers put out a request for anyone driving past at that time? Spoken to any of my neighbors?"

"Augusta said no one has come forward. Olivia called this morning too. She said she was going to look for a nursing home instead of staying at your house, but she needs us to take Megan. I told Olivia we still wanted them. That's okay, isn't it?"

"Of course it is." Though he had no idea how they would work out care. "The kids can probably help out too."

"She has insurance that will help pay for an aide. We can look for someone. I didn't want her to go to a nursing home." Jane raked her fingers through her light-brown hair. "Everything is a mess, Reid. How did we get here in only a few days?"

"I don't know, honey. All we need is one break to lead us to Lauren's murderer and get Will out of trouble."

"And Olivia. I vacillate between feeling overwhelmed and wanting to help all I can. There's so much going on I can't even evaluate the situation properly. I can't think or reason. Everything is resting on the outcome today."

He nodded. "I'm sorry about last night. I didn't mean to bite your head off about the key."

She reached over and took his hand. "I understood. I'm not sure I'm ready to go there either. A murder that old isn't high on our list to solve. It was more for distraction than anything. I don't even know if Gabriel is still in town."

"He's still in town. Alfie saw smoke from campfires out there. I've wondered if Gabriel is behind this. He hates me and your mother."

"But this?" She shook her head. "Seems extreme, even for him. He's been waiting to hear if I spoke to my mom."

"But maybe he wanted to give us extra incentive to deliver what he wants."

Her heart twisted in her chest. "What our boy is facing . . . . It's awful, Reid."

He held out his arms. "Come here, honey."

She moved over to his lap and put her head against his chest. He wanted to reassure her, to comfort her. He was a strong guy, but even his strength couldn't hold back the forces marshaling against their son.

***

Jane had been in the courtroom in Bay Minette many times before, but never with so much at stake. It was the first time she'd noticed its true odor—one of fear and despair. She held Reid's hand at the back of the room and scanned the front tables for their son.

"There he is," Reid said as Will twisted around at the defendant's table to stare at them. Reid gave a little wave, and Will nodded in their direction.

He seemed smaller today, younger. The poor kid, dressed in an orange jumpsuit, looked scared and near tears. She knew his night hadn't been pleasant, but they'd bring him home today, and she'd bake chocolate chip cookies for him. He'd forget all about the past eighteen hours.

They slid into the front row right behind Will. Jane gave him an encouraging smile and leaned forward to whisper to him. "This will be over soon, Will. Stay strong."

"Sure, Mom." His wobbly voice was soft, and he swallowed hard before he turned back around.

A movement to her left caught her attention. Megan helped Olivia slide into the seat beside Reid. Jane's father was with them. Their support here was like a balm to her hurting heart. Her dad hadn't said much when she dropped Parker off to run in the woods while she was busy today.

Thank you, she mouthed. Jane glanced over at the prosecutor's table and bit back a gasp. The district attorney was here. Why would Wendy Chan bother with a juvenile case like this?

Jane clutched Reid's hand and leaned over to whisper in his ear. "I don't like that the DA is here. They usually send an assistant." She glanced around for Augusta, but the detective wasn't present.

If only Jane had her phone . . . but none were allowed in the courtroom. Maybe Wendy was there because of the high-profile nature of the case, with the accused being the teenage son of the Pelican Harbor chief of police. Media would be hungry for the salacious story.

"All rise," the bailiff announced. "Judge Glen Cole presiding."

They rose as the tall, lanky judge entered the courtroom. He'd always reminded Jane of Morgan Freeman, right down to his kindly manner. He was a true gentleman, and she was glad he was adjudicating. Fair and impartial, he always seemed to see directly into the heart of every case. There'd been rumors he planned to retire this year, but she didn't see him ever leaving the bench.

He settled behind the bench and addressed the DA. "What do you have for me this morning, Ms. Chan? I'm a bit surprised to see you here."

Wendy rose and came around the end of the table. "This case is complex, Your Honor. And new information emerged this morning. The state is charging Will Dixon with murder as an adult based on this new evidence."

Jane gasped and half rose, but Reid grabbed her forearm and kept her in her seat. She reached out and grasped the rail in front of her. What was going on?

"Will Dixon wantonly and with malice aforethought took the life of his mother, Lauren Dixon."

"She's not my mother!" Will started to rise, but Scott grabbed him and kept him in his seat.

Jane closed her eyes and gulped. Will's anger would testify against him.

The judge glared at the defendant's table. "Control your client, Mr. Foster."

"Yes, Your Honor."

"Proceed, Ms. Chan."

"The police discovered clothing covered with Mrs. Dixon's blood at the accused's property. There's also blood spatter and a pool of blood inside the outbuilding, which identifies it as the murder location and not the water as the defendant claimed. This elevates the crime beyond manslaughter to first-degree murder, which is what the state charges this morning. May I approach the bench?"

The judge motioned to her, and she brought documents to the bench, then handed a copy of the same papers to Scott. Jane felt faint. This couldn't be happening. The judge wouldn't release Will with a first-degree murder charge. Will would stay incarcerated until trial. Even worse, he'd be remanded to the adult jail unless Scott was able to get a stay on that because of his age.

The judge perused the documents and looked at Scott. "What do you have to say, Mr. Foster?"

He cleared his throat. "This is a gross miscarriage of justice, Your Honor. My client was attacked by the deceased, and in defending himself, Mrs. Dixon fell into the water. When he tried to help her, she ordered him away. He's just a kid, only fifteen, so he did as she directed. He didn't strike her with anything. There's no evidence he hit her. He left his tackle box and fishing pole at the river, where anyone could have taken it and attacked her. Further investigation will prove someone is trying to implicate an innocent child. We are asking for his release into the custody of his parents."

"A hidden tackle box was found in his closet with her hair and blood on it. And his fingerprints," the judge pointed out. He stared for a long moment at Will before he sighed and turned to his bailiff. "Request granted, Ms. Chan. Bailiff, please transfer Mr. Dixon accordingly."

Jane gasped and leaped to her feet. "Your Honor, please! This is not right."

Judge Cole's expression was kind. "I understand your dismay, Chief Hardy, so I won't sanction you for your outburst. You must let justice play out in this case, and I have to protect the community."

Scott splayed his hands at his sides. "Your Honor, I beg the court to allow the lad to stay at juvenile hall in light of his very young years. He just turned fifteen. An adult jail would be beyond harmful to him. You know this, sir."

The judge pressed his lips together and glanced from Will to Scott, then back to Will. He finally nodded. "I'll grant that request. Juvenile court can retain custody." He exited the bench and vanished through the back door.

Will turned toward Jane. "Mom, what's happening?" His eyes were filled with horror and fear.

Ignoring protocol, Jane went past the railing and embraced him. He quivered like a frightened puppy, and she had to use all of her strength to keep from sobbing against him.

She patted his back. "We're going to get you out, Will. Your dad and I will spend every minute finding out who did this. Stay strong."

"Yes, we will," Reid vowed at her side.

He had his arm around both of them, and Jane hadn't realized he'd followed her.

The bailiff took her arm. "I must take him now."

At least his voice was kind and understanding. It could have been worse. Jane released Will and stepped into the circle of Reid's strong right arm. Her legs were wobbly, and she wasn't sure they would hold her much longer. Nausea roiled in her stomach, and she had to swallow the bile at the back of her throat.

She sent an appealing glance at Scott, who shook his head.

He put his hand on her shoulder. "There's nothing we can do today. I'll talk to Wendy and see if we can reach some kind of agreement."

"No plea deal! Will is innocent, and he's not pleading guilty to anything."

"Of course."

"And we need a bail hearing since he's being charged as an adult."

"I'll get that done." Scott's flat tone told her he didn't hold out much hope.

She watched the bailiff lead Will off before she let the tears flow against Reid's chest.

TWENTY-TWO

"Everything about this is wrong." Jane sank on the hard seat she'd vacated and looked up at Reid, Olivia, her father, and Megan. The courtroom had emptied, and only the five of them remained.

She eyed the judge's door. Maybe he'd listen if she talked to him in his chambers.

Olivia leaned across her walker and took her hand. "It won't do any good, Jane."

In spite of her trouble speaking, Jane had no problem understanding her. "I know. But it's so wrong, Olivia! I've spent my whole adult life upholding the law and justice. It has failed me at the most crucial time in my life. I feel like I've wasted all these years for something that's false."

Olivia maneuvered around until she could sit beside Jane. She took her hand again. "Honey, what you're looking for right now is mercy. The judge can only evaluate based on the evidence, and that's piling up against poor Will. We know the truth though. God knows the truth too. He's the ultimate judge right now."

Her words didn't ease the ache in Jane's chest. "Justice, mercy, what difference does it make? I've been wrong about everything. I feel like I'm at sea without a rudder. What do we even *do* now when the law has failed us?"

"It hasn't failed us yet. Augusta is still out there searching for answers. This is just the preliminary skirmish."

"But Will's being charged with murder. First-degree murder! They believe he planned to kill Lauren." She bit back a moan and fought against the panic rising in her chest.

Reid's expression betrayed that he felt as stricken as she did. "Our son is being railroaded. I've heard about it before, of course, but I never thought it would happen to my own son. I don't know what to do with the knowledge that the law could be so unfair."

Olivia's grip on her hand tightened. "You've always been an excellent officer, Jane. You can move forward making sure you don't let injustice happen under your watch."

"This is under my watch, and I can't do anything about it."

"Who says? You've got your team." Olivia gestured to herself and around to Megan and Reid. "You've got us. And most importantly, you have God. Evil can't win."

"How can you say that? You of all people? If evil can't win, why are you sick? Evil wins all the time!"

"Death isn't evil, Jane. It's only death of the body, and it comes to everyone. And if injustice happens in this world, God will bring about ultimate justice in eternity."

"So you're telling me it's okay if Will goes to jail for the rest of his life because eternity will be different? How is that supposed to be comforting? It's monstrous!" She leaped to her feet and ran for the door.

Solitude was what she needed right now. A place where she could think and figure out how to deal with today's events. Reid called after her, but she ran faster. Down the elevator and outside where she stood blinking in the harsh sunlight and oppressive humidity. Where could she go to lick her wounds?

Blackburn Park.

It was two blocks away. She ran as fast as she could, but though the wind rushed through her hair, she couldn't leave behind the injustice, the fear. A warm breeze caressed her face as she reached the park, and she nearly collapsed onto the bench by the gazebo.

Thankfully, the park was deserted. She buried her face in her hands and leaned forward. Nausea still churned in her belly, and she felt faint, both from the heat and from the trauma of being unable to help her son. A train rumbled past across the street, and she grounded herself with the sound and vibration.

What good was her job if she couldn't help her own child? This was wrong, so wrong. Where was God right now? She couldn't feel him.

Forsaken. That was the feeling rising in her chest.

The word brought up something she'd read in *The Screwtape Letters.* "Be not deceived, Wormwood, our cause is never more in jeopardy than when a human, no longer desiring but still intending to do our Enemy's will, looks round upon a universe in which every trace of Him seems to have vanished, and asks why he has been forsaken, and still obeys."

Obey? What did God want of her right now? Faith. And that was hard. She didn't think she was capable of having that kind of trust in this moment.

"There you are."

She looked up at Reid's deep voice and saw him standing by the gazebo. "You followed me."

"I always will." He moved to join her on the bench.

His bulk beside her should have been comforting, but she felt so alone, so lost. Nothing made sense in her world. Nothing.

He took her hand. "You're cold."

She realized she was shivering in spite of the heat and humidity. "Shock, I guess. I wanted this over today."

"It will be soon. We have to hold on."

"And when is it over? When Will goes to prison?"

"We have to trust God, even when it's hard."

"How? I don't even know how to do that. What's he want from us?"

"The book of Micah says God requires us to do justly, to love mercy, and to walk humbly with him."

"What does that even mean? I've pursued justice. It's how I got to be chief of police."

"So we pursue it even more. We trust God to lead us in the right direction. To guide us on where to look and what to do." Reid's voice trembled.

This whole trust thing was as hard for him as it was for her. "You're saying that to help yourself as much as me, aren't you?" she whispered.

He nodded, and she felt the shudder that skittered down his body. This was so hard. How would they bear it?

She gripped his hand and took several deep breaths. Faith was about walking where you couldn't see the path. That's about all she could do right now because what stretched in front of them was a gaping chasm with no bottom.

But she knew God loved her. And Will and Reid. God was the only Rock she could cling to at the moment.

———

Jane seemed to have recovered a little color in her cheeks during the drive back to Pelican Harbor. Reid parked, and they got out to walk to the waterfront. The sun broiled their skin, and when they reached the pier, they sat with their legs dangling over the water. Parker settled beside them, pausing to stare at squirrels mocking him from nearby trees.

Pete had immediately flown down to land on the pier the minute he saw Jane. She opened the small cooler she carried and tossed small fish into Pete's gular pouch. His throat bulged as he swallowed down his food. When the cooler was empty, his large wings lifted him back into the air, and he continued to hunt on his own.

Jane bent over and rinsed her hands in the seawater. "They're probably bringing Will lunch about now."

Reid nodded. The pain of knowing what Will was going through was almost too much to bear. Reid was hanging on to his composure by his fingertips. All his words to Jane haunted him too. It was one thing to proclaim that he trusted God and another to actually feel it past all the doubts clamoring to be heard.

God was all they had right now. And he was enough. He had to be.

"I talked to Augusta. She tried to call to warn me of the blood spatter evidence that had turned up, but I'd already gone inside the courthouse without my phone. She was going to call Lauren's neighbors this morning, so I gave her the names and numbers we collected. She hadn't gotten that far yet."

"I thought you wanted to call them."

She stared out over the water. "I did, but Augusta insisted she and Jackson should do it. She's right. I've got to trust them."

"We love him more than they do."

Jane brought her anguished gaze back to him. "But if we interfere, that evidence might be inadmissible. We could be accused of tampering with things or leading the witness. It would be awful to have the evidence that would release Will and then see it thrown out because of something we did. I have to back off. I *have* to."

He didn't want to agree, but there was no choice. "So what's next?"

"I've got Gail's case to investigate, but we can also be thinking of anything we can throw Augusta's way to check out. I told her about the Google Earth picture I sent to Nora, and she's going to follow up on it."

He shifted and frowned. It felt wrong to leave this in someone else's hands. It had been one thing to do it when they thought they'd get Will out, but the stakes were higher with him accused of murder.

"I know, I know," she said, reading his expression in a glance. "It doesn't mean we aren't looking into things too. But she needs to be the one interrogating possible witnesses."

He leaned back on his hands propped behind him. "I don't know what to do."

He'd been trying so hard to be strong—for her, for Will. Faced with inactivity, his confidence wavered. How many days would their son have to spend behind bars? And would he even be the same kid when he was released?

"I'll be constantly thinking of other places to dig, and Augusta promised she'd look under every rock I find. I'm barely holding on to doing the right thing here, Reid. You have to be with me."

"I'm with you." He took her hand. "Of course I'm with you. I need to keep reminding myself that doing the other investigation will free up Augusta and Jackson to find out the truth. We're doing our part."

"Exactly." She consulted her notepad. "Have you heard anything from Elliot?"

"Not yet. He thought he'd have something by today, so I'm trying to be patient."

Gulls gathered at their side, and Reid stood and shooed one away when it tried to peck at his shoestrings. Parker growled and lunged at it, and it flew away. Reid wished he could drive off his fear as easily.

Jane got to her feet as well and consulted her pad again. "I need to take a look at Gail's lab. If Finn believed his test was falsified, maybe other complaints exist. I'm going to call the Department of Public Health and see what I can uncover."

He nodded. "I'll give Elliot a call and see if he's got anything too." Anything was better than twiddling his thumbs out here by the water, as beautiful as it was.

While Jane walked farther out on the pier toward the sailboats bobbing in the waves, he pulled out his phone and dialed Elliot.

"I was just about to call you, boss." Elliot's voice held a thread of excitement. "You won't believe what I found. Lauren knew that other victim, Gail Briscoe."

"What? How do you know?"

"I found Lauren's email account and hacked in. They met when Lauren first came to town, and they became drinking buddies. Gail was helping her gather information about you."

"Wow. Are you suspicious Lauren killed Gail or am I grasping at straws?"

"You nailed it, boss. Gail was asking for money or she was going to tell you what she knew about Lauren. They had an argument by email. I've compiled their conversations in one document, and I'm emailing it to you now."

This made Jane's investigation into Gail's murder all the more pertinent. Or did it? Even if Lauren killed Gail, who killed Lauren?

Unless there was an accomplice behind both of them.

"Any idea who the man in Lauren's life was?"

"I haven't been able to get into her other email account. It's encrypted, but I'm working on it."

For the first time since the nightmare began, Reid started to think they might solve this, that they'd find the faceless figure behind this mess.

TWENTY-THREE

J ane stood at the end of the pier and stared out over the white-caps. The breeze lifted her hair, and she inhaled the aroma of seaweed and saltwater. Pete had followed her out here and perched on the end of the pier by her feet. He eyeballed Parker when the dog plopped beside him, but after several years of contact with the dog, he wasn't frightened off.

"Ms. Briscoe was about to be arrested?" Had Jane heard that right? This would turn the entire investigation on its head.

"That's correct, Chief Hardy. A complaint was filed against her, and we have proof she forged a doctor's signature about drug test results. We were about to execute the warrant when we learned of her tragic death," the board of health employee said.

"Any chance the author of that complaint was Finn Presley?"

"Mr. Presley brought that charge, yes."

"And he died in the fire too."

"Our investigation ended when Ms. Briscoe died, so I was un-aware of that detail. I'd heard a firefighter died, but I hadn't heard the name. An interesting development. I wonder if Mr. Presley would have known her address when he went into the house."

"I spoke with his ex-wife, and I believe he knew where she lived and had tried to talk to her."

"Interesting. Let me know what you find out."

"Could you send over details of your investigation?"

"Of course."

Jane gave the woman her email and ended the call. She turned to find Reid striding toward her on the pier. His excited expression made her heart leap. Could Will be about to be released?

He reached her and held up his phone. "Elliot found out that Lauren *knew* Gail!"

Jane absorbed the news. "That's definitely odd, but Gail died before Lauren, so their friendship doesn't seem to have anything to do with Lauren's death."

"Maybe it does. We still don't know who her lover was. What if he's the one behind all of this? Maybe he killed both women."

Adrenaline shot through her. "That's true. This might lead to something important."

"Gail was blackmailing Lauren. Elliot found emails about it. She was so desperate for money she was trying to extort her own friend. She threatened to tell me what she knew about Lauren. I wish she had. Things might be different now."

"Could that be why Lauren was pressing so hard for money?"

"It's possible. What did you find out?"

She took his arm, and they began to walk back to shore. Parker padded beside her. "Gail was falsifying drug tests. Finn placed a complaint, and the investigation showed that the doctor verifying her work never signed off on them. She forged his signature."

"Wow. That's huge news."

"Finn's complaint started an investigation, so there was definitely bad blood between them."

"And he knew where she lived. With his anger against her, would he have risked his life for her? It seems fishy."

"What if he killed her, then set the fire and was caught in the blaze himself?"

Reid nodded. "That wouldn't have anything to do with Lauren's death."

"I'll have to investigate and see what we can find out. There might be a connection, or it might not mean anything about Lauren's death. I'm going to tell Augusta about it." She pulled out her phone and called the detective, then put on the speakerphone so Reid could hear too.

"Chief, I was just about to call you," Augusta said. "I spoke to Lauren's next-door neighbor, and she saw the man in her life a few times. He was older than Lauren and obviously wealthy."

"We figured he had money. Maybe he dumped her, and that's why she was desperate for Reid's money."

"The neighbor never heard them argue. And listen to this. Over the back fence a few days before she left, the neighbor heard the man tell her if she managed to pull 'this' off, whatever 'this' means, he'd make sure she never had to worry about money again."

"Whoa. So the two had some sort of plan that involved her coming to Pelican Harbor. On Google Earth, we found an image of a man in her backyard. I sent it to Nora to see if she could enhance it. I haven't heard from her yet, but she might have been able to do something with it."

"I'll check on it."

"Anything from other neighbors?"

"Just that the man drove a black Lexus."

"Anyone provide a description more than he's older? Some way to identify him?"

"He had white hair, but no one got a good look at him."

White hair could be anyone over forty or fifty. "So that's a dead end. And there are a lot of Lexuses in the country."

"But I found it interesting that she wasn't here to get money because she broke up with her sugar daddy. Quite the opposite. One other thing—the neighbor said she was home for a few hours last week, and the man met her there."

"I don't suppose anyone got a license plate number?"

Augusta huffed out a sardonic laugh. "We should be so lucky."

"I have some interesting news for you too. Lauren knew Gail Briscoe. And Gail was trying to blackmail her."

"Wow. I wasn't expecting that. You're thinking maybe this unseen guy killed Lauren? As well as Gail?"

"Maybe. There's more though. Finn Presley hated Gail. She had falsified his drug test, which caused him to lose custody of his daughter. The health department was checking into the allegations. Yet he died in a fire at her house. Did he set the fire and get caught? Or is there more than we're seeing?"

"Good work, Chief. Let me know what else you find out. I tracked down Drew's attorney. That information is in the main file."

"I'll give him a call." Jane ended the connection and turned to Reid. "At least Augusta isn't saying I shouldn't be involved now that Gail's case might tie to Lauren's death. Since they are two separate investigations, we can plow ahead. I'm going to arrange a meeting with Drew and his attorney."

"You think he'll agree?"

"If he refuses, I'll bring him in to the station for interrogation. I think he'll go for it." She logged into the file and found the attorney's name and number. Ms. Jenkins had a meeting with Drew in an hour and agreed to let Jane come by with questions.

She put her phone away. "She's in Foley, and Drew is on his way there now."

"Fast work."

"She didn't want Drew to be hauled into the station."

It was a start. All Jane could do was pray something led to their son's release in the next few days.

―――――――

"Thanks for allowing me to interview your client so quickly." Jane shook Chloe Jenkins's hand and stepped into the massive, expensively appointed office.

Ms. Jenkins had red hair that brushed her shoulders and a sprinkling of freckles that gave her a girl-next-door look. She was around forty with a professional, pleasant manner. She'd play well to women jurors.

Jane glanced around and spotted Drew Briscoe on the sofa in a seating area to the left. "Mr. Briscoe."

His glower didn't lighten. "This is ridiculous. I already told you all I know."

"Have a seat." Ms. Jenkins settled beside Drew on the sofa.

Jane and Reid settled on opposite chairs, and she took out her notepad. "One small thing I wanted to ask you about—did you put a sticker in the window of the home you shared with Gail that read 'Save My Pet'?"

He blinked and shook his head. "I've never seen a sticker there. Gail hated animals. She didn't want a dog or a cat. Not even a gerbil."

Jane underlined his answer. She'd have to puzzle that out.

"Let's circle back to your relationship with the deceased. You broke her jaw and sent her to the hospital several other times."

"Don't answer that," Ms. Jenkins said.

"I'll answer it. I have nothing to hide." Drew's fists clenched, and his face reddened. "I'm not proud of that, but you don't know what Gail was like. She knew just how to push my buttons and tip me over the edge. She'd smile." He shuddered.

Abusers were always alike—the spouse had it coming. Jane kept her expression and tone neutral. "I'm going to need your whereabouts on the morning of May 30."

"I didn't kill her!"

"Just answer the question," his attorney said quietly. "Let's get this over with."

"Where were you that morning?"

"Home. It was a Saturday, right?"

"It was."

"I got up at seven, fixed breakfast. Probably eggs and bacon, but I don't really remember. Went for a jog, showered about nine. That detailed enough?"

"Anyone see you?"

"The neighbors probably saw me jogging. I didn't pay any attention, but I think I heard mowers going down the street."

Jane made a note to follow up with neighbors. "She was killed early. Any proof you were home in bed? Phone calls, someone else in the house?"

He shook his head and frowned. "I live alone. My vehicle was in the garage."

"I'm sure you can find neighbors who saw him go home," his attorney said. "Do your job, Chief Hardy."

So no real alibi for the time when Gail was murdered. He would stay at the top of her list for now.

"Were you aware Gail was about to be arrested? She had been forging a doctor's signature on lab results."

He lifted a brow. "I hadn't heard that. Why would she do that?"

"I assume money. She would have had to pay the doctor for his time, and this way she could run through more results. There is some question she might not have been running the tests at all—just filling out forms and sending them back. She would save the costs of testing materials as well. Do you know why she might have been in such dire financial straits? According to bank records, she earned nearly 150,000 dollars a year."

He relaxed. "She liked to spend money. It was one of our biggest sources of arguments. Jewelry, nice cars, new furniture every few years."

"I see. Do you have any idea why she was so desperate right now? Was there something she wanted to buy? Some debt she owed?"

"I already told you she was taking me back to court for more money, but she didn't say why she needed it so badly. Just that she couldn't live with the agreed property division."

"Do you have a girlfriend, Mr. Briscoe?"

He straightened again. "What's that have to do with anything? It's not a crime. We were divorced."

"So you do have a girlfriend?"

"That has no bearing on this," Ms. Jenkins said. "You don't need to answer that, Drew."

He shrugged. "I've been seeing a woman for about a year. So what?"

"Did you complain about Gail to her?"

"Well, sure. When you're in a relationship, you share your thoughts and problems."

"Gail was definitely a problem."

"I didn't say that!" He ran his fingers through his brown hair. "You seem determined to pin this on me."

"I'm sorry you feel that way. That's not my intention. I want to get to the truth. What's your friend's name?"

He pressed his lips together and glanced at his attorney who nodded. "Fiona Hamilton. You probably know her. She owns the bridal shop Tropical Weddings."

Jane darted her gaze down to hide her shock. "I know her. I'll have a chat with her."

"She was shocked to hear of Gail's death. Fiona liked her."

"Have you thought of anyone who might have hated Gail enough to kill her?"

"No one in particular. Have you spoken with her employees? She has two that I know of."

"Not yet." Jane had added their names to her list of people to interview.

"Is that all, Chief?" Ms. Jenkins asked.

Jane rose. "For now. I'll need to try to verify your alibi, Mr. Briscoe."

"Sure you do," he said in a weary voice. "I hope you figure out who did it so people stop staring at me."

Jane had firsthand experience of what that was like now. She thanked them and exited the office with Reid.

He took her hand as they went toward the SUV. "What do you think?"

"I'll need to check with the neighbors, but he might be telling the truth. I find it hard to believe Fiona would ever drug someone and leave them to die in a fire. We might need to look elsewhere."

Which brought the lab back under suspicion again. "We're not far from her lab. Let's stop by there."

TWENTY-FOUR

ail's lab was in a small block building in a strip mall in Foley. It looked open, which surprised Reid. He'd thought with the owner's death it might have been closed. He navigated through the tourists parking at the ice cream shop next door and found a spot as someone else was backing out.

He held open the door for Jane, and they stepped into a small reception area with a digital check-in kiosk.

A harried-looking young man in a white lab coat shot them a glance, then stopped in his tracks at the sight of Jane's uniform. "Is this about Gail?"

Jane flashed her badge. "It is. You have a few minutes?"

"I guess." He glanced through the plate-glass window into the lot. "A couple of people will be coming in soon."

"This shouldn't take long."

Reid glanced around while Jane was asking questions. He looked at some awards on the wall for the lab. At one time the lab was humming along legitimately. What had changed for Gail? His eyes fell on a desk with paperwork covering the top. Lab orders and results.

He turned back to sidle beside Jane.

"Did you ever have any disgruntled customers show up here?" Jane asked.

The man shifted from foot to foot. "There was one guy who came in madder than a hatter. It was that fireman. He was waving his results, and I thought he was going to hit her. Gail was scared, and she finally locked herself in the office there." He pointed to a door off the reception area. "I had to get him to leave. There was a bulge in his pocket, and I thought he might have had a gun."

So Finn had been mad enough to kill her?

"Were there any other disgruntled customers?" Jane asked.

"Not like that. I mean, when you work with drug addicts, you're going to get a few people who aren't happy that the test comes back positive. She had her tires slashed about a week before her death, but we never found who did it. The security camera showed a man all in black sticking a knife in them, but we couldn't see his face."

Jane stopped writing. "Was this reported?"

"Yeah, to the Foley police."

What else did the Foley police know?

Jane scribbled in her notebook. "Did Gail ever mention her financial difficulties?"

He nodded. "She had to lay off a couple of people. We lost some government contracts to another lab. She was worried about paying her mortgage and keeping this place open."

"Do you know why she lost the contracts?"

"Just business. Another lab had better prices and faster service. It upset her though."

The door opened and a man stepped in. Reid assumed it was one of the clients the employee had mentioned.

Jane put her pad away. "Thank you for your time. If you think of anything else, please call me." She slipped her card into the employee's hand, and he put it in his lab coat.

Reid held open the door, and they went out to his vehicle. "So at least you know the reason for her financial difficulties."

"I wish we'd found out more. Let's go back to Pelican Harbor and talk to Drew's neighbors."

"You sound discouraged."

"I am. I wanted to find a solid clue so we could get Will out of juvie." She got in the passenger side and shut the door.

When he got behind the wheel, he found her with her forehead pressed to the dashboard. He put his hand on her back and felt her sobs. "We'll get there, Jane. What investigation reveals the answer right away?"

"None," she said in a muffled voice. "But this is so important. What's happening to our boy?"

"I'm trying not to dwell on it. We can't think about it or we won't have the focus we need to figure it out."

She lifted her head. "I know, I know. I'm not sure where to go next, what to do. All these piddly questions don't seem to be getting us anywhere."

"I don't think it's Drew, do you?"

Her hazel eyes were wet, and she shook her head. "Not really. He's a bully, but I think he was telling the truth about the day Gail died."

"So go with your gut, Jane. If your gut says this is the wrong direction, let's focus elsewhere. We can talk to Finn's associates and see how else he might be connected to this. We can check with the doctor whose signature she forged. Maybe she did something else to him and he did it. But you know who I keep circling back to?"

"Who?"

"Gabriel. Who else would want to cause us pain? Who has a motive to frame Will in order to make us hurt?"

She chewed her lip. "We could go out to the island and talk to him again."

"I think we should."

She swiped at her face. "Thanks for keeping me on track. I'm about to go out of my mind with worry. I'm a professional. I should be able to think more clearly. I don't know what's the matter with me."

"You've been under a crazy amount of stress."

"I know, but I shouldn't let it affect me like this. I have to get it together. I feel like I'm about to shatter into a million pieces."

He leaned over and cupped her cheek. "I wouldn't let that happen. I have faith in you, Jane. I know how good you are at your job. It might take longer than you want, but you'll find the killer. We're going to get Will released. Have faith in yourself. And faith that God will lead you in the right direction."

"I'll try." She pressed the back of his hand where it rested on her cheek. "You're the best, Reid. Let's talk to that doctor today. I have his name, and he's here in Foley too."

The doctor's office was packed, but Jane wasn't about to let something like that deter her. She marched to the reception desk and flashed her badge at the woman behind the glass. "I need to see Dr. Bix for a few minutes."

The receptionist gave an exasperated sigh. "He's got a packed schedule. We should be closing in five minutes, and it's going to be seven by the time he sees everyone."

"I understand, but this is important. It shouldn't take more than fifteen minutes."

The receptionist rolled her eyes but got up and went out. Her jaw was tight when she returned. "The doctor is down the hall to your right. His nurse will take you to him. Please be considerate of our patients and make this as quick as possible."

The door opened, and a nurse beckoned to them. She didn't look as annoyed as the receptionist. Instead, her blue eyes held an avid curiosity. She escorted them to a small inner office.

A bald man was at a desk, and his dark eyes glanced Jane's way as he rolled out from his desk a bit. "You're here about Gail Briscoe."

"I am. I appreciate your taking a few minutes. I know you're busy."

"Crazy busy. Allergy season." Dr. Bix stretched out his legs. "I have to admit, I was shocked she was forging my name. I'd wondered why she wasn't sending labs over to be reviewed, but I thought maybe she'd found someone else to analyze them."

"Were you upset?"

He gestured toward his waiting room. "You saw it out there. You think I need more work? I was disconcerted that she put my name on something false and ruined people's lives, but I didn't do it. I did receive a few threats though."

Jane's ears perked. "Threats? Did you report them?"

"Nah, I didn't take them seriously. Phone calls, a note or two from a man claiming I ruined his life and would pay for it. Some graffiti on the office windows. I knew they'd stop once the news media got a hold of the arrest."

"You knew there was a warrant out for her arrest?"

"I assumed so when I was interviewed. It was a serious accusation. You can't have people impersonating doctors."

Jane nodded. "Was anyone in your office upset?"

"No. We have plenty of work."

She put her pen and pad away. "Well, thank you for your time, Dr. Bix. I'll let you get back to your patients."

She and Reid went back through the packed waiting room and out into the heat. "You were right. I think this line of questioning is wasting our time."

Reid glanced at the sky. "We should wait until tomorrow to confront Gabriel. By the time we return to Pelican Harbor and rent a boat, it'll be getting dark. You don't have enough manpower to crash in on him in the dark."

While that was the prudent thing to do, she wanted to find out something now. She glanced at her watch. "We have a little time for some kind of investigation. Any ideas?"

"We have a ton of emails Elliot found on Lauren's computer. Let's grab some dinner and take it back to your place to review them. Once that's done, we have more cleaning to do at my house. Olivia and Megan move in tomorrow morning."

Jane felt such a sense of urgency, but she knew he was right. So much was pressing down on them right now. They had to take this step by step.

TWENTY-FIVE

I got the document from Elliot pulled up." Reid looked up from his laptop screen. He didn't want to read it without her. They were both stressed and might miss something, but together they made a formidable team.

The remains of takeout shrimp étouffée permeated the air in her apartment, and the sounds of laughter and jazz music floated through the open balcony door to where they sat making notes and planning a strategy.

He patted the space beside him on the sofa, and she scooted over to read the emails with him. The vanilla scent of her hair made him want to nuzzle in closer, but there was no time for romance, much as he wanted to kiss her. Their son's freedom hung on everything they did for the next few days.

He enlarged the screen and propped the laptop so they could both easily see it. Elliot had arranged the conversation from first to most recent at the end. The lengthy document was a list of emails and responses between Gail Briscoe and Lauren.

The first email was from Gail to Lauren, thanking her for a fun night at the bar. The first few messages were about mundane things like cooking, work, and friends.

Jane tensed beside him and he knew she'd just read what he

spotted—Lauren telling Gail she'd deserted a husband and his "little brat" eight years ago and that she'd tracked them to Pelican Harbor.

Jane leaned back against the sofa. "Lauren's love for Will was always fake. That breaks my heart. I wish I'd been there to see him take his first steps, to hear his first words." Her voice was thick with heartache.

He hugged her to his side. "I know. Me too. One of these days we'll look at videos I took of him when he was little."

"I'd like that. I'm so glad he won't ever read this."

"I think Will always sensed it. That was why he hung on to her so much. He wanted her to love him and knew it was all pretense."

Jane slipped her hand around his bicep and leaned in close enough for his chin to brush the top of her hair. Her close contact gave him comfort.

He scrolled slowly enough that they could both read the next email. "Lauren quickly asks for Gail's help with any information she can get about you and me. She was clearly using her."

He scrolled down a few more pages. "Let's see if she mentions the mystery man she's involved with."

Jane nodded. Outside the sliding screen door, a Harley roared by and the sound of a Weed Eater droned on. He blocked out the noise and concentrated on the words on his screen.

He kissed the top of her head before he started to read again. "He bought her a house. We should check the deed to her place. Maybe it's in his name."

"He's been very circumspect. I'll bet it's in either her name or a shell company." She reached for her phone and tapped out a text. "I told Augusta to check."

He didn't hold any hope for information there either. "What

would make someone so paranoid about keeping their relationship secret?"

"He's married. That's for sure."

"But it has to be more than that. He must've cared about her because they've been together for several years."

"Or else she's been useful to him," Jane said.

"He bought her a house. I think it's more than that."

"Maybe his wife is the one with the money, and he'll be tossed out on his ear without anything if she finds out."

He nodded. "That works. What else?"

"He's in some kind of government work. That kind of thing would destroy a political career. Maybe he's a spy and doesn't want his cover blown."

He grinned. "James Bond with white hair."

She tipped her head to the side and smiled. "You'd make a good Bond. Tall, dark, and handsome." She reached up to touch his hair. "I can't wait to see how it looks in another few weeks."

He rubbed it too. "Hey, it's a whole half-inch long now. I'm going to need a haircut soon."

"You and Will look so much alike. I always saw it, but it's even more obvious now." Her message alert came, and she picked up her phone. "It's Augusta. The deed is in Lauren's fake name."

"Figures."

She went back to the screen. "Back to the drawing board."

They read through more pages of Lauren talking about her wonderful mystery man and her perfect life by a lake in Kentucky. "She's lying to Gail," he said. "Her house wasn't on the water, and it was very modest."

"Gail says a few things that indicate she's jealous. Lauren doesn't seem to see it. She just keeps going on about how much money she has. And it's all a lie. This might be why Gail thought she could blackmail her."

They reached the part where Gail began to hit Lauren up for money. She threatened to tell Reid about Lauren's lover.

Which meant the stakes were very high for the guy. High enough to kill?

Saturday morning Jane wanted to get out to the island as quickly as possible and confront Gabriel, but first they had to get Olivia and Megan settled. Jane had loaded up on some supplements she wanted Olivia to try too. Once Will was out of jeopardy, she'd research more about Olivia's condition.

Olivia was on the sofa and looked exhausted. Parker lay at her feet as if to guard her.

"This is all you have?" Jane glanced over the assortment of boxes and suitcases in Reid's living room.

She'd expected more things, but then again, this wasn't forever. There was a good chance Olivia would recover. She had to consider the long term and the next few months.

The men Olivia had hired had deposited her meager things, and Jane had tipped them. They departed while Reid was driving Olivia's car over with the hanging clothes that didn't fit well in a suitcase.

Olivia nodded. "I have no need for furniture and other things. This is mostly our clothes and the important items from Megan's room. I found a renter for my place. Our new temp at the office."

"That's convenient."

Megan had already hauled two boxes to the room assigned to

her and her mother. After talking it through, they'd all decided it would be best if Olivia had someone with her at night, and Megan wanted to be that person. The room was the master on the first floor so Olivia wouldn't have to climb any stairs. Reid had offered to bring in two double beds instead of the king, but Megan wanted to sleep beside her mom so she could be closer to her.

Jane didn't blame her. She'd take that spot in a heartbeat. When she got Will home, she wanted him close.

She'd had Augusta check on him, and she assured Jane he was in a private cell in a wing that held few juveniles. Jane had asked the guards to take special care of him, and they'd even brought him some books to read. He was as comfortable as possible.

Not that there was much comfort in that.

Guards could get distracted. Bad things could happen. Jane had seen most of them. It should be better in juvie though.

Olivia touched her hand. "What were you thinking about? It's very dark."

"I'm worried about Will."

"I've been praying for him, and God told me he'll be all right. This will turn out for his good in some way. Have faith, Jane."

"I'm trying, but it's hard."

"Just keep walking in the dark. God will show up."

She believed that deep in her heart, but practicing it was hard. "You want to lie down and rest? I can put things away while you do."

Olivia smiled and shook her head. "It's a pretty day, and if you'll help me to the back deck, I'll soak up some vitamin D."

"You bet." Jane helped her out the back door and got her settled in the chaise lounge with a book, though she suspected Olivia would fall asleep.

She went back inside and rolled the turquoise suitcase down the hall to the master where she found Megan hanging up jeans and tees in the large walk-in closet.

The room still held the faint aroma of Reid's spicy cologne, and it made Jane ache to have him beside her. Without him here, fears crowded in on her.

Megan was pale, and her blue eyes held pain and confusion as she turned to face Jane. "Lots of room here. I feel guilty that Mr. Dixon gave up his room for us."

"Your mom couldn't climb the steps, and he was glad to do it. The rooms upstairs are all large, and Will won't mind sharing the bathroom with his dad."

"You think he's coming home?"

"I know he is, honey."

"This is all so hard." Megan sat on the bed's edge and stretched out her long and tanned legs. "Do you think Mom will really get better, or is she trying to make me not worry?" She dipped her head, and her ponytail swung across her cheek.

Jane sat beside her. "I haven't had time to do a lot of research yet, but she has. She said 70 percent improve."

"It doesn't seem right. Where is God right now? Mom loves him, but I hate him right now."

"I know how you feel. I've spent my whole adult life pursuing justice only to find out it's failed me when I need it most. Reid reminded me that's what faith is all about though. We keep walking the right direction in spite of not being able to see the path. So that's what I'm trying to do. I remind myself that God loves your mom, and he loves Will even more than we do. Just like Reid said—this isn't over yet."

Megan lifted her face, exposing eyes glimmering with tears.

"What if it's over for Mom? What if she's one of those 30 percent who don't recover?"

Jane didn't want to give her any easy answers. "You think it's over when we die?"

Megan bit her lip. "No. Not really."

"Me neither. No matter what happens, we'll see your mom again. And she loves Jesus. Have you seen that picture on social media? The one where the woman is hugging Jesus with everything in her?" When Megan nodded and began to cry in earnest, Jane slipped her arm around her. "That will be the expression on your mom's face when she sees him too."

Megan buried her face in Jane's shoulder. "I know you're right, but it's so hard. I know it's hard on her too. She's always been so active. It's going to be excruciating the next few months. I want to be home."

Jane answered for herself too. "One day at a time. And we'll be here with you. We're your family, Megan. I love you."

Parker whined and put his head on her knee as if he felt their pain.

She held the sobbing girl and cried with her. For Olivia who was facing such a rough time, for Megan who would be lost without her mother, for Will waiting in a cell not knowing if he'd ever be free. And for herself when she didn't know how to find her way out of this morass.

TWENTY-SIX

Tourists and residents thronged the brick sidewalks of Pelican Harbor for the jazz festival starting today. Music played on the street speakers, and vendors were setting up to sell Cajun dishes and seafood. The party vibe was already in full swing.

Reid tried to ignore the judgmental stares of a few people on the street as he and Jane headed from the SUV toward Scott's office. Why did people always assume the worst? Did it make them feel superior that their child had never been accused of anything? Did that make them better parents?

He wanted to shout out Will's innocence, but Jane took his hand and pulled him inside the office where the cool blast of the air-conditioning tamped down his anger. "Can you believe the gall of people like that?"

"I've gotten messages of support, you know. A few accusatory comments, too, but by and large most people have been great."

With her job visibility she had to have heard from a lot of people. The stares outside were probably mild compared to what she'd been experiencing.

They'd planned to go to the island in spite of the huge swells out there today, but Scott had called with an urgent meeting request.

Reid stopped inside the lobby under the chandelier. "Did you see those pointed looks though? What makes them so superior?"

She tucked her light-brown hair behind her ears. "I used to think something like this couldn't happen, not on my watch. I was so wrong."

They went down the hall to Scott's office. He met them in the doorway. "Have a seat."

Reid didn't care for his somber expression. "You said you had news?" He and Jane sank onto the chairs.

Scott went around the other side of his desk. It was Saturday, and he wore khaki slacks and a green golf shirt, so he clearly hadn't expected to come into the office today. His dulling red hair looked freshly cut, and Reid spotted a set of golf clubs in the corner.

"Yes. I've been in contact with Ms. Chan. She's willing to drop the charge to manslaughter if Will chooses to plead guilty."

Jane leaned forward in her chair. "Absolutely not! He is totally innocent, Scott."

"I know, but she agreed to ask only for a two-year sentence. And he could serve it in juvie."

Reid clenched his hands into fists. "It's still wrong. Will isn't guilty. We're finding information that will lead to the actual killer. I know we are." He glanced at Jane, who nodded.

"Reid is right. Gail Briscoe knew Lauren and was blackmailing her. We're pursuing that avenue with the thought that Lauren had an accomplice who might have murdered both Gail and Lauren."

"And in the meantime, your son could face the death penalty."

What if they didn't solve this? Jane was like a terrier with a captured rat—she'd shake the truth out of someone, wouldn't she? But people went to jail all the time for crimes they didn't commit.

But Jane was shaking her head before Scott finished talking. "Have you requested a bail hearing?"

"I did. It's set for Wednesday, but I'm not optimistic the judge will agree to release him even when we give our evidence. And if he gives him bail, it won't be cheap. Count on five hundred thousand dollars for a first-degree murder charge."

Jane gasped, and Reid's gut clenched. He'd transferred every penny he had from savings to checking in preparation for paying Will's bail, but that kind of money was out of his reach. Maybe he could get a loan on the house he owned in New Orleans, but that would take time too.

Scott sighed. "Do you want to talk to Will about the deal before I turn it down? He might want a say."

"He's a minor," Reid said. "He doesn't understand the ramifications of pleading guilty."

Jane glanced over and held his gaze. "I think we should at least tell Will and explain the right decision. He's old enough to have some input on this."

Did they have the right to make that decision for Will? If he was being prosecuted as an adult, maybe he ought to have the opportunity to weigh in before they rejected it outright. But Reid couldn't agree to any kind of guilty plea. He just couldn't. "Can you get us in before visiting hours tomorrow?"

"I don't think so. I'm sure Chan knows we can't talk to him until tomorrow," Scott said. "But I really think you ought to consider it without rejecting the idea out of hand. I know Will is innocent, but the evidence is bad. He's admitted to fighting with her. He could be convicted."

Reid glared at the attorney. "We're fighting for his life, Scott! This isn't some kind of game. Even if he was incarcerated for two years, Will's life would never be the same. We can't sit by and let him be railroaded by some unseen enemy."

Scott sighed. "Very well. I'll let Chan know you'll have an answer on Monday morning."

"The answer is no," Reid said. "No matter what Will says, the answer is no."

Jane put her hand on his arm. "Let's talk to Will. I agree with you, but he has to have a say in this." She leaned toward Scott. "What can we do to better our chances for release?"

"An idea of who might be behind this would be helpful. And have your dad attend as well."

"I'm sure he will."

Even waiting until Wednesday felt like an eternity. He wanted to hear his son's booming laughter and heavy footsteps. The sight of his goofy grin always brought Reid joy. The two of them hadn't been apart more than a day or two ever since the kid was born. It was agony, pure and simple. Not being able to fix things for Will and make sure he had enough to eat felt wrong.

Everything about this was wrong.

He thanked Scott for the information, then he and Jane exited into a drizzling rain that expressed the despondency they both felt. He took her hand, and they ran through the puddles to the SUV.

At some point they would need to talk about the elephant in the room—the murder of his mother. Every time the thought came up, he'd managed to suppress it, but he wouldn't be able to do that much longer. It was starting to affect his sleep with nightmares.

An old murder wasn't high on the list right now, but maybe it should be. He'd had a dream last night that it held the answer to what was happening to Will. When he awakened, he dismissed it as the usual weirdness of dreams, but Gabriel wanted the pictures badly. Was there more in them than his mother's murder?

He needed to gather his courage and take a look.

"I know you hate asking Dad for money, but you're not. I am." Jane pushed open her door and stepped into the deluge of rain, which soaked her in an instant. She ran through the mud puddles to her dad's front porch.

It had taken a lot of persuasion to get Reid to come out here. It was only when he understood she was doing it with or without him that he agreed to come along. It had to be a blow to his pride, but they could never manage a $500,000 bail on their own. And it might be more than that. Even a percentage charged by a bondsman would be tough. And there was no guarantee a bondsman would take them. The judge would be reluctant to agree to bail because of Reid's contacts and constant jetting around the globe.

She waited for Reid to join her before going inside. The television blared the sound of a baseball game, and she found her dad in his recliner with lemonade and a half-eaten pizza on the table beside him.

He put his feet down. "Jane. I wasn't expecting you." His gaze cut back to the game before he picked up the remote and paused it. "Have a seat." He gestured to the sofa.

Jane and Reid sat shoulder to shoulder. The sudden silence shriveled her courage a bit, but she had to do this. "There's a chance Will could be given bail at the hearing on Wednesday. Scott says it's likely to be at least five hundred thousand dollars though. Even with pooling all of our money, we can't come up with that kind of cash. Do you know a bailsman who might be willing to cover us?"

"We don't need a bailsman. I have the money, and I've made sure I can get to it. Will is my grandson."

"Thank you, Charles," Reid said in a low voice. "I didn't want to ask you, but we didn't know what else to do."

"You didn't even need to ask. I love Will and I miss him."

"Thank you, Dad. We have some interesting evidence too."

She told him about the connection between Gail and Lauren as well as the charges that would've been brought against Gail.

His bushy white brows drew together. "I'm not surprised. Finn believed his case wasn't the only one she'd botched."

"You knew Finn?"

"I mentored him. He was interested in building a bunker, and we'd spent a lot of time together."

"This is the first you've mentioned it."

"You haven't been out much since his death."

Her dad was always so hard to talk to. He wore his secrets like a second skin, and the shield was as impenetrable as steel. With all that had happened with Will the moment they'd come home from Maine, she hadn't even told him about her visit with her mother or that she'd met his brother.

Did her dad even love her? He never said it, but at least he freely admitted he loved Will. That was enough, more than enough.

She gathered her thoughts back to the case. "Did you get the sense Finn might harm Gail?"

"He was enraged, but who wouldn't have been? He hated drugs of any kind. That test was totally bogus, but I don't think he would have tried to hurt her. I talked to Wayne, and he said they were all out at Gail's house until Finn saw the 'Save My Pet' sticker on the window. He went back inside to try to find the dog."

"But she didn't have a dog. And Drew never put a sticker on the window. That's an odd piece of evidence, and we haven't figured out how it fits."

"I know. It seems suspicious to me. Finn loved dogs. He volunteered at an animal shelter and worked on finding homes for dogs every day. He had three of his own."

"I wonder what happened to his pets?"

"Wayne found homes for two of them. Finn's ex-wife took the puppy for their daughter."

Jane hadn't given much consideration to the sticker. "Could someone have put that sticker there as an enticement for Finn to go in and end up dying? That seems a stretch. I mean, there would be no certainty he'd even notice the sticker. And why would he go in and not one of the other firemen?"

"Was the sticker on the outside of the window or the inside?"

She thought about it. "I don't know."

"Someone who puts a sticker in their window wants it to last, so they put it on the inside facing out."

"I'll check that out."

"Wayne dislikes dogs, and Finn was the only rabid animal lover in the fire department. He was young and impetuous." Her dad reached over for his lemonade. "But you're right—it would be a stretch to assume he would act that way."

Jane frowned as she thought about it. "They'd gotten Gail out by the time Finn saw the sticker and went back inside. It's odd for sure."

But she didn't see any way the sticker could play a role in some kind of plot to kill Finn. "What if Finn killed her and set the fire?"

"Autopsy?"

"Drugged with a roofie and left to die. So definitely murder."

He gave a slow nod. "You can't completely know another human being, but Finn was a gentle soul. He loved his little girl, and he thrived in his job of helping people. It would be out of character for the man I knew."

She wanted to point out that he hadn't done a good job of even picking a girlfriend, but she kept her mouth shut. Charles didn't have a good track record when it came to understanding human nature.

"I talked to Mom."

His hazel eyes flickered. "I assumed you did, but I figured you'd tell me about it when you were ready."

"I found out about my three missing days fifteen years ago. She drugged me so I wouldn't remember a murder." Jane launched into what her mother had told her.

Charles ran his fingers across his lips. "She gave you a safe-deposit key? What are you going to do with it?"

"We haven't examined it yet. Will's situation is more important than an old murder right now."

"Is Gabriel still in town?"

"We were going out there this morning until the storm rolled in. We'll go out as soon as it's safe. I'll let you know."

"He's always been an angry young man."

She nodded. "Would you come to the bail hearing with us? You're friends with the judge."

"I was planning on it. In the meantime you should check on Gabriel. His presence here is probably not a coincidence with the murders that have occurred. And have you thought about the fact that he might be behind Will's predicament? He warned you that he'd make those you love pay."

She wet her lips. She had to tell him about his brother's threat and see what he had to say.

TWENTY-SEVEN

This wouldn't be easy. Her dad never gave up information easily. "Mom told me some other information, Dad. I didn't remember that we'd been in another compound before going to Mount Sinai."

He straightened, and a lock of shaggy white hair fell onto his forehead. His brows came together. "You were young."

"I decided to go to Cumberland, Dad. On our way back from Maine."

Red ran up his neck and his eyes bulged. He rose and stalked to the window. "You had no right."

"Your dad is dead, but Edward is still there. He's joined up with Gabriel."

Her dad whirled to face her. "That's impossible. Divine Rights and Liberty's Children have very different philosophies."

"Edward is running things. He's very arrogant and unlikeable."

"Just like Dad." Her father's eyes narrowed, and he pressed his lips together. "Lawless, full of self-importance."

"Why does Edward hate you so much? I mean, he *hates* you. He ordered us off the property and told us never to come back."

"Water under the bridge," her dad said. "It's not important any longer."

"But what if it is?" Reid said. "We already know Gabriel is here because of something Kim did. What if there's more to it? I know talking about the past is hard for you, Charles, but Will's life might depend on it. We need to know what's going on. If you love Will as much as you say you do, you'll tell us."

Heat radiated from her dad's face in waves. He was holding his rage in check, and she knew pushing him was dangerous. But she had to for Will's sake.

"Dad, what happened when you left Kentucky?"

"It has nothing to do with Will."

"And what if it does? You're a lawman. You just told me we need to talk to Gabriel, that he might be involved in this. What if Edward is too?"

The fire ebbed in her dad's eyes, and he went back to his chair and nearly fell back into it. He dropped his face in his hands and sighed before looking up again with such an air of defeat that pity squeezed Jane's throat. If it weren't so important, she would tell him it was okay, that he didn't have to talk about it. But she had to know.

"I couldn't stand the lawlessness. My dad and brother loved power, and they took anything they wanted from the towns around us. I'd thought we were doing God's work and found out we were doing my father's. We had an argument, and I left with you and your mother. I wanted to find a different way of life, one that didn't feed on the weaknesses of others."

"From the frying pan into the fire," she said softly.

"I know that now, but Mount Sinai seemed different at first. It wasn't, of course, but I was young and full of zeal."

"I can understand why your father was upset, but why is your brother still so angry?"

Her dad rose and went to the door. "I don't want to talk about it anymore."

The door slammed behind him, and rain began to strike the windows as the storm picked up.

Jane exhaled. "Let's go talk to Gabriel. Maybe there's more here than we realize."

If she could only get him to talk.

Reid and Jane huddled under the canopy as the police motorboat battled the wind and waves. The covering did little to protect them from the rain that poured down in sheets. Water sluiced down Reid's face and drenched his clothing. Jane was soaked through as well. The warm temperature kept them from any real chill from the inclement weather.

"Maybe we should have waited." Jane lifted her voice over the sound of the wind. "The waves are ferocious."

Reid shook his head. "If there's any chance at all Gabriel orchestrated framing Will, we need to figure it out. If we can find proof he's behind this, Will could be free today."

He'd felt so helpless and useless the past few days. At least now he was doing *something*.

The island grew closer, and he peered through the windshield to search for signs of movement, but all he saw was the wind whipping the bushes and tree limbs. The weather had erased any marks in the sand, and the rain obscured any boats that might be hiding in the vegetation.

"I don't see the inflatables that were here before," Jane said.

"Maybe they pulled them farther into the trees so they wouldn't blow away."

If Gabriel and his men were gone, what would they do next?

They needed to talk to him and see what he knew about Lauren's death, if anything. It could be a wild-goose chase, but they had to find out for sure.

"I texted Augusta about our plans." Jane handed him her phone, then went to the starboard side. "We'll need to drop anchor out here and wade in. It won't be easy in these waves."

He nodded and let the engine putter slowly as close as he dared to the land. When Jane made a cutting motion with her arm, he killed the motor. She tossed the anchor over the side, then sat and pulled off her boots.

He took off his shoes and stowed Jane's and his phones, then went back to attach the ladder. The waves slammed the hull and the boat rocked hard. He grabbed the railing to avoid falling.

"I'm not sure you can withstand the waves, Jane. Let me go in by myself. I know him better anyway."

With her hair slicked flat to her head, she looked even smaller and more fragile, but she lifted her chin. "I don't trust him, Reid. You're not going there alone. I'm a strong swimmer."

"It's the current I'm worried about. There's a bad riptide. Look." He pointed out a main rip along a rocky outcropping and a feeder current running parallel to the shore. "So if we're going in, stay away from that area. I'll hang on to your hand. Let me get in the water first."

She nodded, and he climbed down the ladder. His toes touched bottom, and he braced his knees against the surge. The water was chest high, and salty waves pulsed into his mouth and nose. He choked and sputtered before swallowing it.

Jane peered down at him. "You okay?"

"Yeah. It's going to be over your head, and you won't be able to take your gun. I'm going in alone."

He'd barely gotten the words out when he saw the splash and her head bobbed just above the surface. "Stubborn woman," he muttered. He reached out and grabbed her hand as the current started to drag her away.

Hanging on to her, he fought the waves and current a few inches at a time. His thighs burned, and his knees ached with the effort of keeping his feet planted and the two of them upright until the water was shallow enough for Jane to stand. She staggered through the water, chest deep to her and waist deep to him, as the land drew closer. They reached the beach, and she sank to her knees in the wet sand. He was winded himself, and they both paused long enough to gulp in lungfuls of air.

The rain was still coming down hard enough to make it difficult to see. He rose and tried to get his bearings. He thought the pathway through the underbrush to the settlement was to their right.

Jane took his hand to get up, and she shielded her eyes from the rain with her hand. "That way, I think." She pointed in the same direction he'd been considering.

"Let's get into the trees. Maybe there will be enough shelter from the rain to be able to see."

She clung to his arm as they rushed along the vegetation. The path had to be close. He spotted it and veered into it. In a few feet they were under a large canopy of trees that broke the deluge assaulting them.

He stopped and wiped the water from his face as Jane did the same. "The path looks well worn. They're probably still here."

She nodded. "Got any idea what to say?"

"How about we tell him we spoke to your mother, and she gave us what he wants? We'll give it to him, sight unseen, if he helps us prove Will's innocence."

"I'm not sure I can. That time in my life was awful, Jane. Losing my mom, then losing you. The camp totally destroyed by fire and my dad dead. It's all a nightmarish jumble I'm not sure I want to relive."

She hugged him around the waist and stared up into his face. "I understand. I don't like to think about it either, but there might be some leverage in the pictures we can use if he refuses to help us."

"Okay." He embraced her and rested his chin on the top of her head. Her hair smelled of the sea and rain. "We'll cross that bridge when we come to it." He lifted his head and dropped his arms from around her. "I'm ready to do this."

The mishmash of lean-tos and tents looked even more dismal in the rain. Reid wiped his dripping face and studied the clearing. The scent of mud and wet leaves swirled around them in a suffocating stench. He didn't want to leave the trees' shelter until he was sure of the lay of the land. It was too risky to Jane. While she might think Gabriel would be amenable to their request, Reid knew him too well to assume anything.

He leaned over to whisper in her ear. "I saw movement in that big tent on the right."

He narrowed his gaze on the entry to the large tent and saw a figure lift the flap and step out into the rain. Before he could say it was Gabriel, something rustled behind them, and he turned to see a man with a rifle trained on them.

Reid lifted his hands. "We're here to see Gabriel. He's expecting us."

The man gestured with the rifle's barrel. "I'm sure Gabriel will be glad to see you. Move."

Reid and Jane tramped through the mud to the big tent, and Reid wished there had been some way to bring their guns with them. Or even their phones. But the immersion in seawater would have been problematic. Maybe they should have risked it. Jane had texted Augusta, but by the time she realized there was a problem, it might be too late.

Gabriel gestured for them to step inside out of the rain. The scent of cooking meat filled the tent, and he glanced around. A small propane cookstove occupied the center of the space, and several cots topped by sleeping bags hugged the canvas walls. Camp chairs circled the stove, and Gabriel, who stood staring at them, was the only occupant.

He handed them each a towel, and Reid mopped at his hair and face. Gabriel still hadn't said anything, and Reid took the time to gather his thoughts. He'd feel easier about the tough conversation if Jane hadn't insisted on coming along. He had to protect her as well as get to the bottom of this mess.

Gabriel gestured to the camp chairs. "Have a seat."

Reid guided Jane to the seat farthest from the one Gabriel dropped into. Reid eased into the chair beside the other man and tossed the towel on the floor.

Jane continued to dry her hair, and Reid didn't like the predatory gleam in Gabriel's eyes as he watched her.

"So, pretty lady," Gabriel said. "Did you see your mother?"

Jane dropped the towel to the tent floor. "We did. She was . . . surprised to see me."

He grinned. "I'm sure she was. What did she have to say about my demand?"

"Kim gave us a safe-deposit key. She said the box contained pictures of you and my dad killing my mother."

Gabriel's expression remained impassive. "She said? You didn't look at the pictures?"

"We haven't had time to go to the bank," Jane said. "But you're not getting the key either unless you help us clear Will."

Gabriel glanced away for an instant before he gave a quick shake of his head.

Reid felt a sickening rush of intuition. "You didn't frame Will. You're using his predicament to try to gain possession of the pictures." Reid rose and held out his hand to Jane. "We're done here."

"What about the key? I'll take it, and you'll never see me again."

Reid started to tell him he couldn't have it, then remembered they still had to get out of here in one piece. What was to stop Gabriel from killing them and sinking their bodies into the sea?

"It's back on the boat. We'll go grab it."

"You go fetch it, Dixon. The little chief of police stays here."

Reid crossed his arms across his chest. "Then you don't get the key."

"Sure I do. My men can find it."

"Let them try if you like. It's little and you have no idea where it is. We both go or you get nothing."

Gabriel's lazy smile flattened, and his eyes went cold. "No funny business. Walter here will have his gun on you the whole time. One hint that you're double-crossing me, and you're both dead."

If they played it Gabriel's way, they'd both be dead anyway. Reid nodded, and they filed back outside. The rain had changed to a sprinkle, and the hint of more light told him the storm was past. The one above them, at least.

TWENTY-EIGHT

If Gabriel didn't frame Will, then who did?

The question burned through Jane as they trudged back through the drizzle to the beach. The shrubs and trees dripped with moisture, and she was drenched again before they'd gone ten feet. The mud sucked at her bare feet, and her legs felt heavy from the effort of pulling herself free with every footstep.

Sunset was coming, and the sun that had begun poking through the clouds began to sink in the west. And she was tired, so tired.

The gun pointed at them made her back itch. Walter could trip and shoot one of them in the fall. At the first opportunity she planned to get that rifle away from him. Most men underestimated her because of her small stature. This big guy would do the same, and he wouldn't see her coming until she disarmed him.

In spite of her tired muscles, she had to summon the strength somehow.

They broke through the line of vegetation bordering the beach and stepped onto soggy sand and slick rocks. The boat still bobbed in the water. She hadn't been sure the anchor would hold. The swells were ferocious, bigger than they'd been when they came ashore. The tide was coming in, amplifying the surging waves.

Fighting that surf felt impossible right now with her legs aching, but she had to do it. Safety was on the boat, and every minute they stayed on the island increased the risk of never getting off of it.

Reid took her hand. "Hang on to me."

"Hold up," Walter said from behind him. "I don't think Gabriel wants it done this way. The water is too rough."

Too rough to keep his rifle dry for sure. Which was very good.

"Back to camp," the big guy said. "We can wait awhile."

Now or never. She caught Reid's gaze and saw the same determination in his face. She gave a slight nod and turned.

Walter gestured with the rifle. "March."

She looked past him and frowned. "What's he doing here?"

When Walter turned, she kicked out with her right foot and struck him in the knee. He went down, and Reid snatched up the rifle and tossed it into the churning water. The two of them raced into the waves to get to the boat before the guy could summon help.

The waves snatched Jane up and tossed her to the sandy bottom. Salty water filled her nose and mouth. Which way was up? Her hands grasped sand. Wrong way. A strong wave rolled her over again, and she began to panic. She needed to breathe.

A strong hand grabbed her arm and hauled her to the air. "Hang on to me!"

She nodded and gulped in blessed air. As she clung to his hand, he plowed through the rollers to reach the boat. The faint sound of shouts rose above the thundering surf. Saltwater churned over her head several times and forced itself into her mouth.

She was breathless and sputtering when Reid pushed her hands onto the ladder's rungs.

"Climb!"

Boosted by his strong arms, she staggered up the ladder and fell gasping onto the boat's deck. He was right behind her.

He thrust her gun into her hand. "I'll get us out of here while you cover us." He paused long enough to haul up the anchor, then rushed to start the engine.

She got onto her knees, wiped her dripping hair out of her eyes, then took aim at the shore where men were beginning to stagger into the water after them. Her finger pressed the trigger, and she shot twice over their pursuers' heads. They all lunged for the ground, then crawled into the bushes. Several rifle barrels poked through the vegetation.

The report from a few rifles came in quick succession, and their thunder rang out over the sound of the surf. They had plenty of manpower.

She ducked as a bullet whistled past her ear. "Get us out of here!"

A roar from the engine starting answered her, and the boat slewed in the water, then took off away from the island. A bullet banged the hull's side, and she peered up over the side to watch the beach fade into the dim twilight. Angry shouts followed them, but she didn't see anyone hauling out an inflatable or any other kind of boat to pursue them.

The rain lessened to a drizzle, and the men rose and disappeared into the woods.

Once they were out of range, she stood and went to sit beside Reid as he aimed the boat to Pelican Harbor as fast as it could go. "That was close. You weren't shot?"

"Not a graze. You weren't injured, right?"

"I'm fine. Shook up, but fine."

Reid laughed. "You're a dynamo. When you took Walter down with one kick, I was ready to cheer."

"You really think he was lying about framing Will?"

"Positive. I know the guy."

Not what she wanted to hear. Jane had wanted to find evidence and take it straight to Augusta to give to the DA. "Then who is behind this?"

"I wish I knew." He reached over and took her hand. "I think we need to find the evidence the key unlocks."

"Why now?"

"I don't want to leave any stone unturned. Especially not out of fear of facing the past. I think he was lying, but what if I'm wrong and the pictures hold a clue? While I'm not eager to look at the photos, I have to. Just in case."

"It's Saturday, but the bank manager will let me in, I think. I just have to make a call. We can grab the key and meet her at the bank. We can scoop the contents into a box and take them back to my apartment to go through."

"Let's get dinner and eat it while we go through the stuff."

"I'm not hungry."

"You're losing weight, Jane. Your cheeks are hollowed out, and your pants hang on you. I'm not hungry either, but we have to stay healthy. For Will. For each other."

"Okay, I get it. What do you feel like eating? I'm sick of pizza."

"Shepherd's pie from Mac's Irish Pub? We haven't had that in a while."

Her mouth watered a bit at the thought. "Okay, you found my weak spot."

Darkness was beginning to fall fast. Reid switched on the boat's lights, and the glimmer from downtown Pelican Harbor began to twinkle on the horizon.

Every muscle in her body ached from battling the surf, and the stress from the past few days was beginning to take its toll. Her brain felt sluggish, and she struggled to focus on what needed to be done next.

Would this nightmare never end?

———

Reid and Jane sat on the sofa of her living room with their food on the coffee table. In addition to shepherd's pie, they'd also picked up a box of beignets on the way home as well as coffee for the long evening ahead. After getting the contents of the safe-deposit box, they'd both showered, and he'd squeezed into a set of Will's sweats he'd found in the closet. Jane's hair was still damp and gleamed in the lamplight. Cleaning up had done a lot for his mental attitude, and she seemed brighter and more alert as well.

Reid didn't want to do this, but he had to.

The contents from the safe-deposit box sat on the coffee table in front of him like a Pandora's box he didn't dare open. He'd need to eat before reviewing the contents. The pictures it contained were likely to kill any hunger he had.

They'd haunt him for the rest of his life.

Jane handed him his shepherd's pie. "Our visit with Gabriel wasn't what I'd expected."

He nodded and took the hot bowl. He ladled in a bite, and the rich taste of ground beef, garlic, and spices rejuvenated him. "I'd hoped for more answers. Instead, we have more questions."

The dish was thick and tasty, and his appetite kicked up at the flavor. His spoon scraped the bottom before he realized it, and he put the bowl on the table, then reached for a beignet. He demolished it in three bites and had two more.

Jane set her empty bowl on the table and helped herself to a beignet that left powdered sugar on her lap. She brushed it off before Parker could get to it. "I'm ready when you are."

His belly contracted, and he exhaled before he nodded. "I'm ready." But was he really? No part of him wanted to see his mother's murdered body or a bloody knife in his father's hand.

She pulled the box onto her legs and opened the lid of the old shoebox they'd taken from the bank. Inside was a jumble of pictures.

His soul cringed at the thought of fully facing his father's evil. Was there any part of that madness in him? He didn't think so, but the doubts would rise once he saw the proof in this box.

Jane removed the pictures and placed them faceup. A sheaf of pictures all designed to give him nightmares.

She lifted the first picture into the light. A twilight setting in the woods with the trees providing shadows interspersed with shafts of fading sunlight. A woman lying on the ground with two men looming over her. He recognized his father and Gabriel at a glance. His mother was still alive in this picture, and her right hand was reaching up in a beseeching gesture.

The picture gutted Reid, absolutely gutted him. His eyes flooded, and he smelled his mother's scent—homemade lye soap and Secret deodorant. He remembered her smile and the fierce hugs she always gave. The sound of her voice. A thousand small things overwhelmed him.

A keening sound came, and he realized it was coming from his own throat.

Jane squeezed his hand. "Are you okay?"

He took several deep breaths. "Give me a minute."

She put the box aside and crawled into his lap. With her arms around his neck and her fresh scent in his nose, the horror began to fade. "I'm okay." He nuzzled her neck and inhaled. "Let's continue."

She moved her hands to his cheeks and stared into his eyes. "You're sure?"

"We have to do this."

"Okay." She slid off his lap and reached for the pictures again.

His mother's raised hand was a plea the two men above her showed no sign of answering. His father's right hand was raised with a knife in it, and blood stained the blade. At the sight of the blood, his gaze went back to his mother, and he saw blood on the arm she'd lifted. A defense wound.

He closed his eyes and breathed in and out a few times.

"You don't have to look at more, Reid. I can do it."

He opened his eyes and stared into her face. A face full of concern and love. He drank in the expression in her eyes and the curves of her cheeks. This wasn't something she should do alone. It would take both of them to make sure they gleaned every clue from every picture.

"Just give me a minute." He pulled her into another embrace.

She was his port in the storm, his anchor when waves battered him. She grounded him, completed him. And he didn't think she had any idea of how much he loved her. He wasn't an eloquent guy. He preferred to show his feelings, not spout flowery words. Hopefully she could sense his love in everything he did.

She nestled against his chest and nuzzled her nose against him. "You smell clean and yummy." Lifting her face, she pulled his head down for a kiss.

He kissed her with every bit of the love filling his heart. She tasted of sunshine and vanilla. Of forever and family.

He pulled away and rested his chin on her head. "I see what you're doing. Distraction can only go so far. This job is still in front of us."

She gave a throaty laugh. "But you don't have to do it, Reid. I really don't mind. These kinds of pictures are the terrible things I have to see all the time."

The touch and smell of her rejuvenated his determination to do what had to be done. To face this horror.

He kissed the top of her head. "This isn't any easier for you. It might bring back memories of that night. Got any glimmers yet?"

She shook her head. "Just that same initial feeling of holding a shovel and a sense of panic. Maybe that's all I'll remember."

"I hope so. I know it had to be terrible. Go ahead. Let's see the next picture."

She sighed and lifted it into view. This one showed Gabriel with his knife buried in Reid's mother's chest. He tried deep breathing for a few seconds. Maybe his father hadn't been the one who killed her. But the next picture shattered that hope. His dad's knife was in her throat. He'd executed the final cut.

"What an evil man," Jane murmured. "I'm sorry, Reid, so sorry."

His throat was too tight to answer, so he pulled her close and buried his face in her hair until he calmed again.

"How many more pictures?" he muttered against her cheek.

"A bunch. Want me to look at them first?"

He lifted his head. "No, let's just do it. One after another quickly, then we can go back and examine them for details. That way I'll know what I'm facing."

"Okay."

They saw several pictures of his mother's dead body followed by several pictures of her in a shallow grave. Jane inhaled at the final photo of herself shoveling dirt onto his mother's prone body in the hole. She was easy to identify because of her very pregnant belly.

Tears tracked down her face.

"It's okay, honey. There wasn't anything you could have done to stop it."

"Why can't I remember this? I need to remember." She shoved the pictures off her lap and clutched him.

She couldn't look at anything more. Not tonight. She had to remember.

TWENTY-NINE

Even with the air-conditioning going, Jane was hot, so hot. She threw off the covers and sat up in bed.

The clock on the nightstand blinked 2:00 a.m., and she and Reid had gone back to his house at eleven. The past three hours had been filled with tossing and turning. Maybe it was the unfamiliar space. This large bedroom decorated in an impersonal style wasn't home.

Memories of that forgotten night floated like fog through her brain. Too diaphanous and faint to catch hold of an outline. But there was something important she needed to remember, if she could just snatch it out of her brain.

Parker lifted his head and stared at her from the foot of the bed. "Sorry to wake you, buddy."

She slid her legs off the mattress and padded downstairs to the living room. She gazed outside into the blackness, then grabbed her sketch pad and went out to sit on the back deck. The mosquito zapper emitted a constant crackle, and the night air was thick and hot, dripping with humidity after the storm.

She settled on a chair and threaded the pencil through her fingers for several moments before she opened her sketch pad to a fresh page. She stared out into the dark yard into the space under a tall tree. Her fingers began to move of their own volition, and she closed her eyes and tried to think back to that night.

An owl hooted from a nearby tree, and she heard the squeak of a mouse. Hunter and prey. The way of the world. But humans shouldn't act that way. Moses Bechtol had killed his own wife— the mother of his only child—and that kind of atrocity happened every day.

The whole thing was an affront to her sense of justice.

She continued to scratch the pencil across the page, the sound a soothing litany in the back of her mind. She barely heard it as she tried so hard to remember. Sights, sounds flooded her consciousness. It had been cold that night with a skiff of snow, hadn't it? And windy. Her ears had been cold.

The screen door behind her squeaked, and she opened her eyes. Reid exited with rumpled hair and a sleepy expression. He dropped into the chair beside her. "You're going to get eaten by mosquitoes."

"The zapper is getting them. I haven't gotten a single bite. You look good enough to eat though." She reached over and mussed his hair up even more. "I wasn't sure I liked you with hair, but it's growing on me."

He rubbed the dark thatch. "I need a haircut. What are you doing out here?"

"I feel like I'm forgetting something really important. If I could just remember, it might be the key." It had felt like she was on to something for a while, but it had vanished like a dream upon waking.

"Or it might make you feel worse." He leaned over. "What are you drawing there?"

It was too dark to see, so she shrugged. "Just doodling. Sometimes it helps me think. It didn't work this time."

A mosquito buzzed by her ear. "Let's go back inside. Maybe some decaf would help me sleep. Did I wake you?"

He rose and held out his hand. "I heard a door squeak, and I'm kind of on guard right now. I keep thinking Gabriel or one of his minions will try to forcibly take the key and the pictures we found."

"It could happen." She walked with him to the back door and went through the kitchen.

She laid her sketch pad on the island and went to make some decaf. "Want a cup too?"

"Sure." He picked up her sketch pad and held it up. "May I?"

"Sure."

He flipped through the pages, and she tried to remember all she'd done in the book. A few pictures of him, but he'd seen those. Some of Will. A couple of Olivia. And tonight's sketch. "Did you look at what you were drawing?"

"No, it was dark. Like I said, it was nothing."

"Check this out, Jane." He came to her side and showed her the sketch from this morning. A pile of guns were heaped in a wooden box under a twisted tree. There were several AK-47s on top of the pile. Several smaller crates held boxes of ammo.

"Any idea what that's all about?"

She stared down at the sketch, and a crawling sensation made its way up her spine. The memory was close, so close. The tree seemed familiar, and in an instant she recognized it as the tree in the pictures. Those twisted branches had been the last thing Reid's mother had seen before Moses snuffed out her life.

With a shaking hand Jane traced the largest branch. "Recognize that, Reid?" When he inhaled sharply, she knew he'd seen the same thing she did.

He took the pad back and stared at it for a long moment. "Was this before or after she died?"

"Before." When he looked at her, she bit her lip. "I don't know how I know that, but I do." Then a torrent of memories hit her. "Guns. Your dad sold guns. I heard a guy buy these. I can almost see his face." She covered her eyes with her hands. "Oh, why can't I remember?"

He grasped her wrists and pulled her hands down from her face. "It's okay, honey. Really. It will come when it's ready. Don't try to force it. Gun running. That's interesting. I never knew that was going on, but I shouldn't be surprised. Guns were everywhere in camp."

"I think it was more than guns. I think there was a really dangerous bomb of some kind." She covered her mouth with her hand. Where was this coming from? Was she right or was this something her subconscious was making up?

"A bomb?"

She nodded. Measuring with her hands, she showed him what she remembered of it. "It was a lead cylinder, I think, and it had a funny symbol on it. I remember now! It had that black-and-yellow radiation symbol on it. The trefoil."

His gaze was troubled. "This might be more important than Mom's death."

But did it hold any significance for Will's situation?

"Let's look at those photos again." Reid stuck the breakfast dishes in the dishwasher, then fed the last piece of bacon to Parker before he washed the odor from his hands.

He'd been mulling over the picture Jane had sketched of the guns. How had that activity been hidden from him? He'd thought he'd been an integral part of his dad's leadership of the camp. What else had his father hidden from him?

Megan hopped up from the island bar. "I'll wipe down the counter and wash the skillet."

Olivia sat at the island counter in her wheelchair. Shadows smudged the thin skin under her eyes, and her mouth was drawn. But her dark-blue eyes were alert and clear. "I'd like to see the pictures too. If you don't mind."

"I'd love your input." Jane rolled Olivia's wheelchair to the dining room table. "I'll get the photos." She stepped into the living room and quickly returned with the shoebox in her hands. She slid into a seat beside Olivia's chair, and Parker settled by them on the floor.

Reid dried his hands and sat on Jane's other side. "The pictures aren't pretty, Olivia. Steel yourself."

"I've seen many awful things people have done to other people, Reid. I'm sorry for your loss though. And for the shock this all must be. Thank you again for taking us in."

"I wouldn't have it any other way. I'm honored to have both of you here."

Jane slipped her hand over to his lap and squeezed his fingers. While he cared about Olivia, he'd done this for Jane. He returned the pressure.

She picked up the photos in the box. "Wait. Some of these are stuck together." She gently peeled them away from each other to reveal three other pictures. "Look here. That's the cylinder I remember."

The picture showed a close-up of a lead cylinder with a trefoil on the lid. The next picture showed a box of guns lying in the bottom of a hole, and in the last one, he recognized the bricks of plastic explosives instantly. "That looks like C-4." Reid's gut clenched and he exhaled. "Jane, I think those are the ingredients for a dirty bomb."

"Seriously?"

"I did a documentary about terrorism and was at the ATF headquarters. I saw something similar to this. It's terrifying to think about whose hands it might have fallen into."

"Could it still be buried somewhere in the woods?" Olivia asked. "Do you know for sure someone dug it up?" She flipped the picture over and gasped. "Did you see this sketch of a map on the back?"

"No!" Jane took it and stared at it, then looked up at Reid. "What if this is what Gabriel is after?"

Reid studied the map before leaning over to scoop up the rest of the pictures to leaf through. He stopped at the third picture and pointed out the cabin. "I think that's the cabin where you stayed with your mother." He traced the road on the map with his finger. "This leads back to camp. And look, there are directions for finding it. We need to see if it's still there."

"That's clear up in Michigan. We can't go there right now, not with Will's situation."

"Of course not. But you could ask the Michigan state police to check it out."

She nodded. "True enough. I can send them this picture along with any other instructions I can find. The officer who headed up the raid that day was Captain Nick Andreakos. Let me see if he's still working for the department. I could contact him directly since I'm sure he remembers it."

Had Reid seen the captain? He vaguely remembered a big guy shouting orders and firing. And hadn't Andreakos been the one who found the woman his dad had kidnapped?

She snapped pictures of the map and the cabin, then ran a search for Nick and found him. "He's with District 3. There's a phone number." She placed the call, then turned on the speakerphone.

"Captain Andreakos," a deep voice answered.

"Captain, this is Chief of Police Hardy in Pelican Harbor, Alabama. I'm in the Gulf Shores area. Do you have a moment?"

"What can I do for you, Chief Hardy?"

"Do you remember a raid on a cult called Mount Sinai? This would have been back about fifteen years."

"Clearly." His lazy tone sharpened. "That day was not something easily forgotten."

"I was there that day too." Jane launched into the circumstances of the days with her mother she'd forgotten. "In my possession I have a map of that area. I have reason to suspect the group had the makings of a dirty bomb they buried in the woods nearby. If I send you the information I have, would you be willing to go out and search for it?"

"Let me give you my email. Send it over, and I'll go out there right now. This could be very big. If something like that is out there, we need to find it." The captain cleared his throat. "Looks like you might be right. And you think that stuff is still there?"

"One of the splinter groups is after these pictures. I assumed it had something to do with an old murder, but now I suspect he's searching for the map to the radioactive material and the C-4. We need to reach it before he does."

"I'll call you after I check this out. Thanks for the tip."

Jane put down her phone. "That's the best we can do right now. But this definitely ups the stakes on why Gabriel wants these pictures. And it would provide a powerful motive for framing Will in order to force us to hand them over."

A trickle of unease slithered down Reid's back. "I'm still not convinced Gabriel framed Will. Something still smells off to me."

"Maybe, but it's the best direction we've got right now."

"Let's not give up on the investigation connecting Lauren to Gail. Just in case, we have to cover all the bases. I still think Gabriel was lying about being behind this."

She placed the pictures back in the shoebox. "Let's go talk to her brother, Ned Berry, again. Maybe he knows something about that friendship. Or about her trying to blackmail Lauren. At least it will give us something to do while we wait to see Will at four fifteen."

The hours would drag until Reid got to see his son again.

THIRTY

The glowering clouds flickered with lightning, and the radio blared the warning of possible tornados. Jane drove her SUV through the darkening air to Ned's house again. Reid rode shotgun and was staring out the window with a morose expression. She knew how he felt.

It had been a couple of hours since she talked to Captain Andreakos, as they had waited to leave until Rebecca, the nurse's aide, came to watch over Olivia. How long would it take for him to find the buried weapons—if they were even still there?

She pulled into the driveway of Ned's place. Had it only been just over a week since she'd first spoken with him? So many things had happened in so short a time.

When she got out, she spied the Harley-Davidson through the open garage door. Wet tire tracks showed it had recently been out for a ride, and she caught the stench of engine exhaust. She and Reid went to the door, and she pressed the doorbell of the modest ranch home with a sense of déjà vu. He might not be able to tell her much more than he had last week.

Ned opened the door and stared at her. "I figured you'd be back at some point." He stepped out of the way and gestured for them to come in.

She walked past his bike boots sitting under a hook that held a black leather jacket. His hair was windblown.

"Looks like you just got back from a ride," Reid said.

Ned gestured for them to follow him. "I've got burgers on the grill out back. You can talk to me there."

They followed him through the small living room to a dining room that had a sliding door opening onto what seemed like a new deck. The wonderful scent of grilling meat wafted on the breeze.

Thunder rumbled overhead, and Reid glanced up. "Better hurry. We've got a storm brewing."

"Yeah, lunch is almost done. So what do you need, Chief?"

Jane positioned herself out of the ribbon of smoke from the grill. "I wanted to personally let you know about your sister's autopsy."

He flinched. "Murder for sure?"

"I'm afraid so. She was drugged and died of smoke inhalation. I think it's some comfort she was already dead before the fire got to her."

"At least she didn't suffer burns or anything." He cleared his hoarse voice. "Thanks for letting me know."

"Did you ever meet Gail's friend Lauren? Lauren Haskell?"

"Lauren Haskell?" He flipped over four burgers, then shut the grill's lid again. "Met Gail and Lauren for drinks one night. Man, she was quite the looker. Had all the guys salivating over her in the bar, and she knew it." His eyes widened. "Say, is that the woman who was killed along the Bon Secour? They arrested the kid? Your kid, right? I didn't notice the victim's name. That's too bad. She was hot."

"Yes, Lauren was the victim." Jane should have known he'd have heard the news.

"Gail talked about her a few days before the fire. Said she was loaded and that she hoped Lauren would help her out with a loan until she could get back on her feet from her scumbag husband."

A loan. Jane didn't want to reveal what they'd been told about the so-called loan. "And did Lauren help her out?"

"I don't think so. Gail was mad about it. Said Lauren's rich boyfriend should have been more understanding."

"Did she and Lauren have an argument?"

"She was yelling at Lauren on the phone the day before the fire. I heard her saying something about 'you'll be sorry' and 'wait until your ex hears about the plans.'" Ned glanced at Reid. "That would be you, I assume?"

The guy had heard more than he'd let on at first. "Did she ever mention people in her lab being angry about the results?"

"Oh yeah." He lifted the grill's lid again and scooped up the burgers, then transferred them to a plate. "Some guy came by her place once when I was there. He banged on the door and was yelling that he was going to turn her in for fraud. But she said he was just mad his drug use got found out."

"Did she go to the door?"

He shook his head. "She hushed me when I wanted to go talk to him."

"Did you see him or did she say a name? Was it the man who was suing her that you mentioned?"

"I think it might have been the same guy. I peered through the window when he got in his truck. He had a fire sticker on his window and a bubble on top. I think he might have been a fireman."

Finn. She exchanged a long look with Reid. "Well, thanks for your time, Mr. Berry. We'll let you eat your lunch. If you think of anything else, let me know." She passed a card to him. "We'll go around the side of the house."

The first drops of rain fell from the dark sky as they hustled to the SUV. Jane hurried the last few feet and slung herself under the wheel. "Those clouds are scary."

Huge black clouds hung low, lit by occasional slashes of lightning. It was early afternoon, but it was dark enough to be dusk.

Reid dashed around to get in as the deluge started. Jane started the engine and drove toward her office.

Her phone rang, and she glanced at the screen. "It's Olivia. I'll call her back in a little while. The roads are too flooded to make it safe to talk."

And she didn't like the greenish cast of the sky at all.

———

The tornado siren blared from several light poles in a deafening shriek. "Come on, we need to seek shelter!"

Reid leaped from the vehicle and grabbed Jane's hand as she came around the front of the SUV. Thunder rolled over them, and the sky seemed eerily blackish green. Lightning crashed nearby, and he caught the scent of ozone as the wind picked up.

The storm was on top of them.

He spotted the twister's tail as it roared toward town. Dozens of plate-glass windows would be shedding their frames any minute, and he glanced around for a place to shelter. The closest building was the bridal shop, and he pulled Jane to the door. They practically fell inside with the force of the wind propelling them.

Reid spared a glance over his shoulder at the tornado, now on the ground, bearing toward them. It was big. Scary big.

"This way," the blonde owner shouted. "I've got a storm closet back here."

Half carrying Jane so she could keep up, he ran after the blonde, forgetting her name in the chaos. She opened a heavy door and flipped on the light, and the three of them plunged into the small space built of concrete blocks.

The sound of breaking glass came as he shut them in and locked the door. His heart pounded, and he held Jane upright. Her hazel eyes were unfocused, and a trickle of blood trailed down her forehead.

"Are you okay? Jane!" If he hadn't had her gripped by the shoulders, she would have fallen over.

She swayed and put her hand to her head. "I think I'm going to be sick."

He got her seated on a bench along the back wall and put her head down. "Take deep breaths."

He wasn't sure what had hit her, but she'd taken enough of a blow to knock her silly. Crashing and banging blared from outside, and something struck the door where they sheltered. It shuddered but stayed locked.

Jane took several breaths before she raised her head. Her eyes were clear this time, and she dabbed at the blood with her fingers. "I'm bleeding."

"Yeah. I didn't see what hit you."

"I think it was a piece of glass." She gazed around the space and saw the woman. "Fiona, I'm so thankful you're okay. We're in your storm shelter?"

The woman's bun had come half undone and lay in blonde swaths on her shoulders. "I think my shop is coming apart."

The racket outside was ear shattering, and vibrations rumbled through the floor. Stuff hit the door again, and Reid sat between Jane and the door, blocking anything from getting to her if the thing didn't hold.

She buried her face in his chest as the sound reached a crescendo. He could feel her heart beating through the shirt on her back, and he held her in a comforting grip.

Fiona sat in a corner with her knees pulled to her chest and her head down. Her face was white, and she was praying aloud, though Reid caught only an occasional word.

Then the chaos was over. The wind lessened and the clatter ceased. Reid wanted to make sure it wasn't coming back, so he hung on to Jane. "Let's wait a few minutes before we open the door."

Jane raised her head. "Fiona, I heard you're dating Drew Briscoe. True?"

Reid hid a smile. Ever the cop. Plus, he suspected she was trying to distract her friend.

Fiona lifted her face, and her lips eased into a tremulous smile. "True. He went through a lot with Gail, and he's been so good to me."

Jane bit her lip. Reid knew she wanted to warn her friend against the man. She shouldn't waste her breath. When a person, man or woman, wore that kind of besotted expression, they didn't listen to reason. "Okay."

"You're listening to the rumors about him. I know he wasn't necessarily kind to Gail, but he's changed. He'd never hit me. I'd clock him with a frying pan if he tried."

"You remember that," Jane said. "Did you ever talk to Gail?"

"Never, other than once when she came in here searching for a gift. She was nice enough."

"Did she know you were dating Drew?"

"Oh yes. I could tell by the way she glared at me. But I never gave her the opportunity to warn me off." Fiona's light laugh held a trace of unease.

Reid rose and went to the door where he waited for total silence. When it finally came, he cracked open the door and peered out into a scene of utter destruction.

Wedding dresses were off their hangers, soaked and covered in mud and debris. Shelves lay upended, and the front counter with its cash register was missing. The windows had all blown out. Glass and debris crunched under his shoes as he walked out. Sunlight touched the destruction, and he looked up to see the roof mostly missing.

"Wow," Jane whispered behind him. "It's all gone."

Fiona followed her out too and stood openmouthed at the loss of her shop. She stared at the missing ceiling, then back to the front door. It was the only glass in the place that was still there.

She drew in a shuddering breath. "At least we're still alive. I've got insurance, too, praise God. Everyone okay?"

"Yes." Jane squared her shoulders and headed for the door. "I need to see what's happened to my town."

Reid followed her out into a scene of unbelievable destruction. This store had been hit, and two other places were missed. Down the other direction, the other side of the road was hit harder.

Ambulances wailed in the distance, and Jane ran to begin checking businesses for casualties. He glanced at his watch. They still had a few hours before they could see Will. Hopefully Bay Minette had been spared, and Will wouldn't hear enough to worry about them.

THIRTY-ONE

Jane's head ached, and she was bone weary after checking on residents and picking up debris in the affected shops for the past two hours. It could have been worse. She spotted Reid working too. He had mud on his face and arms from tossing out splintered boards and mud-covered merchandise. Mayor Lisa Chapman too.

She glanced at her watch. She had fifteen minutes before they needed to leave for Bay Minette. It would take nearly fifty minutes to get there without heavy traffic, but if she needed to, she could flip on her lights and siren to get there in time to see Will.

She turned when Reid called her name. He cradled a little redhead in his arms who looked to be about five. The little guy had a gash on his head, and he was staring up at Reid with something akin to hero worship.

"Parents?"

"Can't find them. I think his cut might need stitches."

The boy reached for her, and she took him. "Let's get him to a nurse."

His sturdy frame in her arms made her remember again all she'd missed of Will's childhood. She'd shied away from too much contact with children over the years. Being around them was such a painful reminder of what she'd lost. She kept all that walled in, along with her desire to never hurt that much again.

She glanced at Reid walking beside her. She'd kept herself from him too. Too much even now. She needed to talk to him about it. Explain herself.

She handed over the little boy to one of the nurses running triage, and a frantic redhead came running up. "My son!"

"He's going to be okay. Might need stitches, but that's all."

"The wind snatched him right out of my arms." The mother put her hands to her face and sobbed. "I thought he was dead."

Reid put a comforting hand on her back and guided her forward. "In there."

"We need to go," Jane said.

"I know. I've been watching the clock. Want me to drive?"

"I can do it. It's my vehicle. I don't want residents to see me looking weak and ineffective. They'll need reassurance that we're going to get things fixed."

His indulgent smile reached his eyes and turned her insides to mush. She wasn't always the easiest person to love. She took her duties very seriously, and she was always a little prickly about people judging her because she was small. People had accused her of being a porcupine, and maybe she wielded a few quills for protection.

They reached her SUV, and it took several minutes to drive carefully around the debris and people. It would be a miracle if she didn't have nails in her tires. On the outskirts of town, she was able to increase the speed.

"Other than a few downed limbs, it doesn't look like a tornado hit anything out here," Reid said.

"I got a text from Dad. His house is okay, but I saw Olivia's and it wasn't as lucky. I hate to have to tell her the roof is off."

He winced. "I hadn't seen that."

"I thought I'd tell her in person. At least we have no fatalities that I'm aware of."

"If not for Fiona's storm closet, we might have died."

"God was looking out for us."

Reid smiled. "He always is." He glanced down at his grimy hands. "We're kind of a mess. I hope we have time to wash up before we see Will."

She checked the clock on the dash. "We should have about ten minutes."

He stared at her. "You're smiling funny. What are you thinking?"

"About carrying that little boy. I haven't held a kid that age. When his arms went around my neck, I imagined it was Will at that age." She shot a glance over at Reid in time to see his expression of pain. "I'm getting past that though, Reid. That's what I wanted to tell you. Holding that cute little guy, I realized I'd missed out on so much because I was too afraid to risk being hurt."

"I knew that."

"I am officially taking down the wall. If I get hurt, it's part of life, right? Pain and joy—they're part and parcel of a full life. You'd never know real joy without the sorrow to compare it to. God told me it was time almost audibly as I was holding that little guy. I have to do it."

His smile warmed his brown eyes. "I've never heard it quite put like that but you're right. I'm glad you're going to try, but it's not always easy to lay down the quills."

She laughed. "I was thinking earlier about how much like a porcupine I can be. You sure you weren't reading my mind?"

"I often wish I could. You're so smart and quick-witted. I can see a thousand thoughts darting through your head and wish I could catch hold of just one of them."

She wasn't sure she could make him see how she felt the minute she stepped out into the damage left by the storm.

"Hiding in that storm closet made me realize every day is a gift. I didn't have you and Will for fifteen years, but I have you both now. And that's good enough. God willing, I'll have a lifetime of years ahead with you. I'm going to savor every one of them. We'll get Will out. I know we will. And one day we'll look back and see how this made us stronger, just like you said."

He reached over and squeezed her right hand lying on her leg. "Preach it, girl."

Now to try to lift Will's spirits as much as they could without losing sight of what she'd just learned.

After relinquishing all personal belongings, Reid followed Jane's lead as the guard directed them to the visitation area where Will waited. Reid's heart pounded at the thought of seeing Will, and he knew Jane felt the same way. It would be so hard to leave him behind after this fifteen-minute visit.

Fifteen minutes wasn't nearly long enough.

Jane's epiphany still warmed his heart, and he saw a new determination and hope in her eyes. They had to convey that hope to their boy today too. They'd get through this.

They were led to a private room where Will waited. When he spotted them, a relieved grin replaced the fear on his face. He rose to greet them with a hug.

Reid kept his right arm around him in a tight embrace and pulled Jane in with his left.

"Hey, son." He squeezed as much reassurance as he could before he finally released them.

Every part of him wanted to grab his boy and get out of there, away from this place reeking of sadness and pain. Will didn't belong there—he didn't. Reid had to force himself to stay seated and smile when he heard kids crying all around the room.

Jane brushed Will's cheek with her lips. "It's so good to see you, Will. Have you had any problems?" She sat on his other side and grabbed his hand.

"I'm okay. I'm in a cell by myself, and the guards have been nice. Some of them know you, Mom. One of them told me I'm getting a bail hearing on Wednesday. Am I getting out?"

Reid looked away from his son's hopeful gaze in time to see Jane wince. "We hope so, Will," he said. "We're working on it. There's a lot going on with the case, and we're hoping to do more than get you out on bail—we're working to get you exonerated."

Will exhaled. "By Wednesday?" He ducked his head. "It's not likely, is it?"

A hard question to answer. "We're doing the best we can, but there are no guarantees. Stay strong, son. We're going to get through this. And your grandpa is helping us with the bail money—we'll be all ready to pay up and get you home in your own bed."

"I don't get it, Dad." Will twisted his hands together. "Why would anyone try to make it look like I killed Lauren? And in cold blood. It's crazy."

"We don't know yet, but we think it might be coming from someone who hates me or your mom."

Will shook his head. "Like revenge. That's messed up."

"It is. You're just a kid, but what hurts you hurts us more than you can know."

Jane cleared her throat. "Um, Will, the DA has offered a plea bargain."

"Plea bargain. What's that?"

"She's offering a reduced charge of manslaughter if you plead guilty. Two years in jail."

Will's mouth gaped. "You want me to say I did it?"

Jane grabbed his hand again. "No! We know you didn't do it. But you're being treated as an adult, and you should have some say in this. If you're found guilty, you could get the death penalty."

Reid winced and wished she'd sugarcoated that one. "I don't think that would happen."

"I don't either, but it could. So you need to tell us what you want. Your dad and I initially said no, but we are duty bound to at least mention it."

His eyes went wide. "No! I didn't do it, and I'm not going to say I did. You'll figure this out, Mom. I know you will. I'll be patient. Don't make me say I did it."

Tears glistened in Jane's eyes. "We'd never make you say that. I'll find the truth."

Will sniffled and nodded. "For a minute, I thought . . ."

"No, never," Reid said in a low, fierce voice. "I know your heart, Will. You could never do this."

"Thanks, Dad." He swiped his eyes. "How's Megan? I thought maybe she'd come too."

Jane inhaled and visibly pulled herself together. Her eyes twinkled. "Oh, so we're chopped liver? You'd rather see her?"

Red flared in Will's cheeks. "What? No, I didn't mean that. I-I just thought . . ."

"Relax, she isn't dumping you," Reid said. "She wanted to come, but only parents are allowed. She and her mom have moved into our house though."

Will smiled. "Wow, when did that happen?"

"Yesterday."

Will's grin went to nuclear wattage. "I'll help out whenever I get out of here."

The guard stepped to their room. "Time's up, Chief. Sorry."

Already? Reid wanted to protest, but he rose as Will got to his feet. He embraced their son, then Jane hugged him too, her nose red and her eyes moist.

"We'll see you Wednesday, honey," she said. "Love you."

He clung to her, then turned to Reid again. "Love you guys. Can you leave me some money at the front? If we want any snacks and stuff like that, we have to have money in our account."

"I'm on it." Reid clapped Will on the shoulder and tried to keep a smile on his face, but his insides were shredded like shattered glass.

How could his boy be going through this? It wasn't right.

His eyes burned as he and Jane made their way back to the front where Reid used his debit card to load Will's account with as much money as was allowed.

Back out in the late-afternoon heat, he and Jane were silent as they went to her SUV. Nothing they could say would change what they'd just seen—their young son, scared and alone. Their helplessness to alter the situation right now was a hard pill to swallow.

Even Jane's optimistic words from earlier seemed hollow, though he knew he'd cling to them when this shock had passed.

Jane flung herself under the steering wheel and leaned her head forward as she sobbed. "He's counting on me, Reid. And I feel like I'm failing."

From his seat on the passenger side, Reid leaned over and embraced her across the console. Though he wanted to weep himself, he had to be strong for her. "You're not failing. It's early days, Jane. We're going to find the killer. I know we will."

She lifted streaming eyes. "We've got to get him out, Reid. We just have to. I don't care what it takes. I'll break him out and flee to another country. I'm not letting him stay in there. How can the law perpetrate such a miscarriage of justice?"

"I know, honey. We'll get to the bottom of it."

"We keep saying that, but it's not happening. There's nothing I can produce in that courtroom in three days that will convince the judge to release him. I have to find it!" She banged her head on the steering wheel. "If I could only remember those three missing days."

"Maybe it will come to you. Let's get home and check on Olivia. The aide will be leaving in a while."

As they pulled away, Reid stared back at the correctional facility. If only he could break in and rescue his boy. Instead, they had to drive off and accept this despair.

THIRTY-TWO

Odd. The back door of Reid's house stood open.

He entered through the front door with Jane on his heels. "Hello?"

"Olivia?" Jane called.

They went through to the living room, and he stopped dead in his tracks. Cushions were scattered on the floor. Drawers from the end tables had been upended, their contents strewn on the floor.

Jane pulled out her gun. "Olivia! Rebecca!" She held out her arm for him to stay back. "Call 911 while I clear the house."

Reid pulled out his phone and put in a call for help, then stayed on the line as he followed Jane down the hall to the master bedroom. His gaze took in the scene in an instant. The bed was empty, and the door to the closet hung open. Piles of clothing and boxes lay heaped on the floor.

He stepped to the bathroom and gasped at a figure lying on the tile floor.

"Rebecca!"

He knelt by the prone woman and touched her neck. A pulse beat steadily under his fingertips. "She's alive." A brass lamp was on the floor a few feet away.

"Don't touch anything," Jane warned. "Where's Olivia?" Her voice was a thin strain, and her eyes were full of fear.

"I don't see her wheelchair."

"Let's check the upstairs."

He backed out of the bedroom and followed her upstairs to see if Olivia was there, though she couldn't get up the steps unless someone carried her. The other three upstairs bedrooms seemed intact. No drawers dumped. The beds were still made, and the closet doors remained closed. They'd found whatever they were looking for downstairs or in the master bedroom.

The pictures?

He left Jane behind to dash down the steps to the living room. The pictures had been on the fireplace mantel this morning. He'd noticed them before he left and had meant to tuck them away somewhere. The space where they had been was bare.

At the sound of sirens Reid headed around the corner of the house and arrived at the front as Jane came rushing from the front door to meet up with Jackson and the paramedics.

"I'll take you to Rebecca," Jane said. "Any sign of Olivia?" she asked Reid.

"Not yet. I'm going to check out back." He went through the house to the back deck. "Olivia!"

A sound barely registered off to his right behind the shed. Was that a cry or just a bird?

He jogged across the grass and rounded the corner of the shed where he spied movement over by the river. Olivia's wheelchair had sunk into the mud, nearly in the water. The water lapped against her legs and into her lap.

He raced to grab the wheelchair handles, but he couldn't budge it out of the muck with her in it. "I've got you." He splashed into the water and reached one arm under her knees. "Grab hold of my neck." He lifted her out of the chair and struggled up the muddy bank to practically collapse onto his knees on the grass. "You okay?"

"Yes. Those men. They wanted the pictures."

"Did you recognize them?"

"They wore masks," she said.

"How long ago did this happen?"

"A couple of hours. I tried to call Jane when I heard the noise at the door, but I didn't get her."

He remembered the call just before the tornado hit. "How'd you get out here?"

"One of the men brought me out." Her lip trembled. "He was going to drown me if I didn't tell him where to find the pictures. Is Rebecca all right?"

"She's unconscious but alive." He pulled out his phone and called Jane. "I've got Olivia. I think she's okay, but you might have a paramedic check her out. We're out back by the river."

"Be right there."

"Let me get your chair now." Reid left Olivia on the grass and tugged her wheelchair out of the muddy river. It would need a bath.

Jane and a paramedic ran out the back door to join them. Jane hurried to Olivia's side. "Olivia, what happened?" She moved out of the way as the paramedic knelt beside Olivia.

"Two men broke in while I was napping. They wanted the pictures. I think they took them."

Jane flinched and looked at Reid. "Did you search for the pictures?"

He nodded. "They're gone. Good thing you already scanned them. And they took your laptop. I'm sure they'll want that to make sure you hadn't copied them in some way. You'd better get the pictures uploaded to the Cloud to make sure you have access to copies. There's more going on here than we know."

She nodded. "My entire computer automatically backs up to the Cloud so it's all safe." Her phone rang and she grabbed it. "It's Captain Andreakos." She put the call on speakerphone before she stepped closer to Reid. "Chief Hardy."

"I found it," the captain said without any preliminary greeting. "But someone else got there first, and there was only an open hole. It's recent too. We had rain last night, and fresh footprints marked up the mud." He sounded disappointed. "We might have seen the person who dug it up. A truck pulled away from the pullout in the forest as we were approaching. I didn't think anything of it with all the hunting around here or I would have gotten the license plate number."

Jane sagged against Reid. "Where could it be? Has a bomb like that been detonated in the area?"

"Not that I know of. It's clear there was something in the hole. I'll poke around and see if I can find any other clues. I'll be in touch."

She thanked him and ended the call. "No device."

"Someone has it somewhere." Reid clenched his hands into fists and bit back a groan. The realization was terrifying.

The air was heavy with silence and loss, and even the river's scent felt foreboding. Jane watched Parker, ears up, as he lay by the railing watching bugs buzzing around the deck light.

The sun threw out its brilliance as it sank into the water, and Jane held Reid's hand as they sat on the back deck of his house. They'd had little time to themselves and even less space to catch their breath from the day's events. Rebecca was in the hospital overnight for observation, but Olivia seemed fine.

Olivia and Megan had wanted to hear all about the tornado. Megan cried when she heard their house had damage. But Olivia sat with a stoic silence at first.

"At least we weren't there," she'd said finally before she and Megan went to the bedroom to watch a movie and rest.

Jane and Reid had escaped after dinner. She *would* figure out who was behind this. There was simply no other choice. They'd both been silent with internal sorrow after seeing Will. It was hard to articulate what she felt, and she knew Reid had the same difficulty. What did they do with this?

And this missing nuclear material was horrifying. Had she provided the missing clue to a madman? She shuddered and hugged herself.

"It's not your fault." He gave her hand a tug, and she went with his need for closeness, especially since she craved it too.

"It's hard to say when the device was taken, but it's so disappointing."

Bullfrogs croaked from the river, and the cicadas tried to overpower the sound. She was content to let Reid's steady heartbeat under her ear soothe her as it drowned out the cacophony of the night creatures.

He pressed a kiss against her hair. "What are you thinking?"

"I don't feel much like a chief. I can't even get justice for our son. I'm a fraud. I don't like being helpless."

He hugged her tight. "Me neither. I always thought I had the power to change my life, to carve out a space in the world for Will and myself. This is the hardest thing I've ever done."

She let a few tears leak against his chest. "I'm so tired, and I need to sleep, but ever since Will was arrested, every time I close my eyes, I see the anguish on his face. Sleep won't come."

"Same here. If I had a sleeping pill, I might take it."

"It's so hard right now with the mud of despair sucking me down. I have to find out who is behind this. It's all on me."

"Hang on, honey. When this is over, we'll grab our boy and go on a trip."

She sat up. "Where?"

"What about Maine?"

She scowled at him. "I see what you're trying to do, mister. My mother doesn't want to see me. She doesn't want me to destroy her perfect little life. And she doesn't deserve to even know her grandson. Not after what she's done."

"That's all true, but since when are we only supposed to be good to others when they deserve it? It might bring healing to both of you."

"Oh sure, play the Christian card. I don't want to have anything to do with Kim. I know now where I stand with her, and I don't see any kind of relationship developing between us. I have you and Will. I realized today that's enough."

"I understand. I won't push. But if you want to go at some point, we can. How about going back to Indiana to see my grandparents? We could meet my uncles."

She loved the light of hope and anticipation in his eyes. "I could get on board with that, and so will our boy. I think it's a good idea to get him out of town for a while, let the rumors die down. Even when he's exonerated, people will stare and ask questions. They always do."

"That's what I thought too. I have to start that documentary on Rome, but I can put it off for a few weeks. I'll be starting a new one after that on what sudden stardom does to teens."

"That sounds interesting."

"I thought so when the producer approached me. I have to get going on it in about two months."

His calm optimism raised her spirits. "I guess a lot will depend on Olivia. We won't be able to be gone for longer than a couple of days, and even then, we'd need to arrange night care for her."

"True. I wasn't thinking about her. We have to juggle a lot of balls right now. Maybe Olivia's sister could come stay with her for a while. I know she would have loved to have taken her in, but she didn't have room in her apartment."

"She'd probably do that then. We'll figure it out."

Her team was working hard. There had to be a break in the case soon. She could feel they were on the verge of something, and she hadn't sensed that before.

She palmed the rough stubble on his cheek. "You're so good for me. You know just what to say to encourage me."

He kissed her, and his warm lips jump-started her heart. "How did I live for fifteen years without you?" she asked.

"The good news is, you don't have to be without us ever again. You're stuck with me." He cupped her face in his hands and kissed her thoroughly before he raised his head, staring into her eyes. "One of these days when we can relax, I'll have an important question to ask you."

She flushed all over. "The answer will be yes."

THIRTY-THREE

Jane's team turned expectant faces her way when she entered the war room. While she was letting Augusta run the investigation into Lauren's death, this was still her team, her job.

She set down a tray of coffee and a box of beignets from Pelican Brews on the table. "Good morning. We have a lot to go over, so I brought sustenance."

The murmurs of joy made her smile, and she stepped out of the way with Parker so they could snatch coffee cups and beignets. She knew what they all liked so the drink tops held names.

Nora lifted her caramel macchiato in salute. "Thanks, boss." She went back to her chair at the front table where she'd left her laptop and reports.

Augusta and Jackson echoed their thanks and slid back into their chairs as well. Jane ordered Parker to the corner where he settled on the floor with his head on his paws.

She gathered her thoughts and went to the whiteboard. "Good work yesterday. Most of the debris from the tornado was gone from the streets when I came in."

Jackson nodded. "Everyone in town turned out to help."

"Anyone hospitalized?"

"No, just minor cuts and scrapes. I think about five businesses are totaled and a few more have things like roof damage and broken windows. Several houses were damaged, including Olivia's."

"I saw it and took pictures. Olivia took it in stride." Jane turned to the whiteboard. "I have a lot to report on my investigation into Gail Briscoe's death. It may or may not be related to Lauren's death, but the information is interesting."

With the marker she jotted down the things she'd uncovered, including Gail's attempted blackmailing of Lauren. "You know most of this, but I also talked to the state health board. I received the details of their investigation this morning, and I've uploaded those documents into our system."

Jackson leaned forward and studied the listed points. "We still haven't discovered who Lauren's lover was. He might be the key to all this."

"That's what I think too. Maybe there's some connection we're missing." Jane glanced at Augusta. "Any thoughts?"

Augusta set down her coffee. "I've been thinking about this obsessively. Someone wants Will to seem guilty. What could be the reason for that? Why would Lauren's secret lover want to make a kid look like a murderer? It's nutty."

Jackson snapped his fingers. "Distraction or disruption. It's accomplished both. The chief had to step away from the investigation, plus it's distracting her from any other case in the department."

Jane stared at him. "You're right, Jackson. What would the perp want to distract me from investigating into if I'm focused on clearing Will?"

"Gail's death," Augusta said. "It's the only other major case on our docket right now. So we're missing something. If we figure it out, we figure out who's behind this."

The detective rose and went to stand by the whiteboard. "Gail was under investigation. Her lab was in dire financial straits—serious enough for her to attempt blackmailing a friend. Do we know anything about her business?"

Jane hadn't looked into how long she'd owned it or anything about the actual lab. "Not really. I stopped by and questioned an employee, but he didn't shed any light. I didn't ask him how the business was structured or how long it had been in operation."

Nora looked up from her laptop. "I found it. Been in business fifteen years, but she got a new loan two months ago, and there was paperwork filed to change to a partnership entity. The partner is Falls Trust. It seems to be a shell corporation."

Jane wanted to slap her forehead. Such an elementary piece to overlook. "I should have looked there first. Two months ago. Could Lauren have given her the money after all? Maybe she was the partner."

"If so, she would have taken over the business on Gail's death," Augusta said.

"But now she's dead too, so it doesn't seem likely." Jane studied the board. "I wonder if the partner knew the lab was about to receive an injunction? With Gail dead, the investigation stopped because she was the guilty party."

"You think the partner might have killed her?"

"Or had her killed. What's the address on that shell corporation?"

"The Bahamas," Nora said.

Fishier and fishier. A flash of hope shot up her spine. Maybe this would lead somewhere.

"Augusta, see if you can find out who is behind Falls Trust."

"I can try, but those are often hard to open up."

"If the lab was going under, the partner wouldn't have much left. Unless he or she thought they could revive it before it went under."

"Or maybe they didn't want to be dragged into the limelight when Gail was arrested," Nora said.

Jane flashed back to the things she'd discussed with Reid. "I know this is a crazy idea, but I wonder if it could have been Lauren's lover? He's someone who has maintained major secrecy about his identity. Reid and I ran through the type of people who might be irreparably hurt by scandal."

"Interesting idea," Augusta said. "But no proof."

"No." Jane glanced at Nora. "Any update on Lauren's murder? No footprints or any other evidence along the riverbank?"

"Too many searchers tramping along the water so that's a dead end."

Jane had expected as much. "Anything else at all?" She hated revealing the desperation in her voice, but she couldn't quite contain it.

Jane glanced around at the rest of the team. "Will is up for bail on Wednesday. We have two days to come up with a good reason for him to be released. Or to completely exonerate him and get the charges dropped."

"I vote for the second option." Augusta got up and hugged Jane.

A lump formed in Jane's throat as she accepted the embrace and clutched her tightly. "Thank you, Augusta. Thank you all for your help and belief. It's been a rough few days." She called Parker to her and turned to exit.

"How is Will?" Nora asked as they left the room together.

"We saw him yesterday. He's hanging in there but depressed and hurting. I want him home."

"So do we." Jackson touched her arm on the way out. "We're all praying for him and pulling for a quick release."

Her team's support was heartwarming and much needed after so many obstacles to overcome.

Reid pressed on the intercom at the gate to Charles's place. "Good morning, Charles. You wanted to see me?" Birds chirped in the woods around the compound, and the air smelled fresh after the storm.

"Come on in." While the tinny voice was still speaking, the gate began to open.

Reid drove through and opened the other manual gates along the way to the house. He'd been shocked at the text asking him to come. At best he and Charles were guarded with one another. And he'd asked him to come without Jane, which felt sneaky.

There hadn't been time to talk to her anyway. She'd been out of the house this morning by daybreak for an early consultation with her team. Reid had been praying constantly that something new would be discovered today.

Charles met him at the door, his shaggy white hair combed straight back and dressed in his shorts and tee. "That was fast. Coffee?"

"I wouldn't say no."

Reid followed him into the aroma of bacon and coffee in the kitchen. He accepted the mug the older man offered and took a fortifying sip. He'd tried to figure out what Charles could possibly want but had come up empty.

Charles indicated the stools at the island. "Have a seat. Breakfast?"

"No thanks. Coffee is fine. We saw Will yesterday. He seems to be dealing with it all okay."

Charles poured coffee into a to-go cup and slid it to him. "We need to head out. I made a call to juvie and arranged to see Will. I have to bring you along though. I hope you're okay with it."

Reid blinked. "That's fine. I wouldn't turn down any opportunity to see Will."

"Let's go then."

Reid took the cup of coffee and followed Charles outside. What had just happened? Charles seldom asked for anything, and he hadn't this morning either. He'd just made arrangements and expected Reid to fall in line. It was going to take a while to figure the man out.

For the first part of the drive to Bay Minette, Reid tried to make small talk, but Charles replied with one-word answers and stared out the window at the passing scenery until Reid gave up. When they were ten minutes from the juvenile center, Charles finally turned to Reid.

"You're good for Jane, Reid. I want you to know that."

"Thank you. She's good for me and Will."

"Jane and I have always had a . . . difficult relationship. My fault, not hers. She wanted what I couldn't give her. I'm not the warm sort of dad most girls need. Just who I am. Sometimes I look at her and can see she wants me to tell her I love her. I open my mouth and nothing comes out. Of course I love her. That's why I dragged her out of that hellhole. That's why I lied in the first place."

The tension left Reid's shoulders. "I think you should tell Jane all this, Charles. She'd listen, and it would warm her heart."

"I don't think I can. I've tried so many times. It's not in me. I know what she sees in you. You're everything I'm not—caring, warm, fiercely loving. I put food on the table and took care of things. It's not enough for her though. I can see that, but I can't fix it. I'm glad she has you."

He reached over and gripped Charles's shoulder in a quick squeeze, then released it. "I know Jane loves you, Charles. It would go a long way with her if you'd talk to her. She has so many questions about her mother. Why you really left her. Why she didn't want to see Jane. I think you have more answers than you're willing to admit."

Charles looked at the road ahead. "I'd like to keep those memories sealed away. They're more painful than you can imagine."

"Not any more painful than mine. I had to face looking at pictures of my father murdering my mom in cold blood. I did it for Jane. For Will. If you reach down inside yourself to where you say you love Jane, you can summon the strength to talk to her too. You can work past all that."

Charles nodded and put his hands in the pockets of his shorts. "I'll think about it."

"You could write her a letter if you can't say the words. It might open up the dam."

"I'm not the eloquent sort on paper or with words."

"Plain truth doesn't have to be eloquent."

"I suppose not."

Reid parked in the lot at juvie hall. "Does Will know you're coming?"

"I didn't talk to him, but I'm sure he knows by now. He should be waiting for us in a room."

Reid wanted to know why Charles had arranged this meeting without Jane, but he kept his questions locked behind his teeth. After a few minutes of good-old-boy talk with Charles's acquaintances, they were at the door to the same room as yesterday.

Will jumped up when he saw them. "Grandpa!" His voice wobbled, and he practically fell into Charles's arms.

Reid's heart squeezed to see the special bond between the two. Charles might have trouble sharing his feelings with Jane, but Will had no problem seeing right into his grandfather's heart.

Reid took his turn hugging his son before they settled around the table.

"I didn't expect to get to see you, Grandpa."

"I pulled a few strings." Charles stared at Will with a pensive expression. "False accusations like this are particularly hard to deal with. Being arrested is bad enough when you know you were in the wrong, but this isn't your fault, Will. Not in any way."

Will's head lowered. "I shouldn't have left her. It wasn't gentlemanly. I should have stayed there until I was sure she was out of the water." His chin trembled, and he swiped at tears tracking down his face.

Reid stared at Charles. How had he known Will was wrestling with this?

"It wasn't that long ago Elizabeth tried to frame me. I thought she loved me. I trusted her. I still wake up in the night mad about it. Betrayal is hard to get over."

Will clenched his fists. "It's so unfair, Grandpa! Why would anyone try to frame me? I don't understand."

"I don't know, son. But I want you to hold your head high. Don't take on the guilt people will want you to feel. This is not your fault. Hold the course. Your mom will figure this out."

Will's nod was shaky, but at least it was agreement. The guard came to the door and their conversation was over, but Reid could tell by the light in Will's eyes that the visit had done him a lot of good.

Now they had to solve this like they'd promised.

THIRTY-FOUR

R eid had sounded reserved when Jane called him to meet for a picnic lunch by the dock, but she hadn't asked any questions. She sat at a picnic table under a large water oak tree overlooking the water. Pete had already eaten all the fish she'd brought while she waited for Reid, and the big bird sat on a piling, watching her with an intent expression.

"All gone." She rinsed her hands in the water and dried them on a napkin.

Reid's SUV pulled into the parking lot, and she waved before unpacking the bag of sub sandwiches, chips, beignets, and sweet tea.

She drank in the sight of him in khaki shorts and a red tee. His straight black hair stood up on end from the salt-laden breeze. His smile surfaced when he saw her, and he hurried to join her.

He dropped a kiss on her lips. "Did you get my text about the new aide for Olivia? She's coming this afternoon so Megan can go to cheerleading practice."

"That's great. I got a text from her a little while ago, and she's doing fine. Rebecca's getting out of the hospital this afternoon. Mild concussion and she'll need to rest, but she will be fine too."

"Any more thoughts on that nuclear device? I'm worried who has it."

She handed him a meatball sub. "Me too. I sent Jackson out to the island to talk to Gabriel. Even though it's unlikely he has it—not when he wanted those pictures."

"What did you do all morning?" His lids came down, and she could tell he didn't want to talk about it. "What?"

"Your dad wanted me to go with him to see Will. I had to accompany him because of regulations."

She couldn't help the stab of jealousy. Why hadn't her dad called her? "What was that all about?"

"He wanted to tell Will he knew how hard it was to be accused unjustly. Your dad feels more things than he ever reveals."

"And he couldn't open up in front of me. I get it. He's like a clam protecting its pearl." She shouldn't let it bother her, but it hurt that her dad never seemed able to talk to her.

"Anyway, I think it helped Will, and that's the important thing."

"It is. Did you tell him about the radioactive material?"

Reid shook his head. "There wasn't time."

"I should talk to Dad about it. Maybe he knows something."

"And what about calling your mom? She has to know about it. Kim should have told us about it when we were there."

Jane felt a little sick, but she knew it was necessary. "I'll give her a call."

She wrapped her sub sandwich back up to keep it from drying out. A squirrel ran along the grass, taunting Parker, who went over to investigate. The breeze wafting up from the water cooled her forehead.

She called her mother's number. "I'm not sure she'll answer."

"She's already talked to you, so maybe she'll quit avoiding you."

"Hello?"

The answer in Jane's ear surprised her, and she couldn't choke out any words at first. "Mom? I-It's Jane. Something has happened here, and I need to ask you a couple more questions."

"I told you no good would come of those pictures." Her mother's voice was terse. "What's happened?"

"Where do I start? My son is being charged with a murder he didn't commit, and someone stole the pictures before I could give them to Gabriel. I know about the radioactive material, but it's missing. Someone took it just yesterday. Who else knows about it?"

Her mother gasped. "Are you remembering more from the three days in the woods?"

"Only part of it. Tell me everything that happened, Mom. And who is behind this."

"I-I can't. It's for your own good, Jane. He's too powerful. He'll destroy you. I didn't step out of your life fifteen years ago to protect you only to have him undo all my sacrifice."

"You sound scared. Who *is* he, Mom? He can't be that scary. Not when we lived with Moses."

"Moses was a two-bit wannabe. You have no idea of how ruthless this guy is. He could snap his fingers and you'd disappear. No one would have any idea where you went."

"Gabriel?"

Her mom barked out a bitter laugh. "Gabriel is a bumbling clown. He only wants to be tough."

"He knew about the safe-deposit key though. I could see him breaking in to steal the pictures and the map."

"Have you talked to him to see if he stole them?"

"Not yet. And why did you make the map? If you were helping Moses run guns, wouldn't he already know where they were? Why were they hidden all these years?"

"Moses bought the radioactive material and had Gabriel hide

it along with the bricks of plastic explosives. But neither of them knew I saw what they'd buried. I overheard them talking about how much money they could make, but they planned to hold on to it for a while and sell it to the highest bidder. I couldn't have that on my conscience. You and I moved it and the guns that night, and I made a map of where I buried it.

"I had a little time, but I knew once they went to get it, they'd know I had to have taken it. I saw Gabriel go back to the woods a couple of years later, and I knew my time at Liberty's Children was up. The group had mostly dispersed anyway. I hightailed it out of there that same night. I'd heard later that Gabriel had gone to Kentucky, and I hoped that meant he'd forget all about me."

There was no mistaking her mom's fear of the mastermind, but Jane couldn't summon any pity for her. She could have called the cops as soon as she'd found it. There were so many other ways this could have played out.

"If it's gone, who took it?" her mother asked.

"I guess I'll have to figure that out." Jane ended the call and told Reid what her mother had said. "She doesn't see Gabriel as a threat, but I'm not convinced yet."

Reid touched her arm. "I just got a text from Elliot. He wants to talk to us."

"What about?"

"Something about Lauren's investigation, but he wanted us to come by."

"We're at a dead end until Jackson reports in anyway. Let's go."

The task in front of her seemed hopeless. Was she going to fail Will?

The breeze had died and the sun was hot on Reid's face when he got out of the SUV at Elliot's houseboat. The water was choppy today after the storm, and the ropes holding the boat in place creaked against the pilings.

Elliot rose from his deck chair when Reid and Jane reached the gangway. He seemed steady, and his eyes were alert as he came to meet them. "You got here fast."

Reid let Jane and Parker board first. "You said it was important."

"Come on in, and I'll show you. I found some emails and a contract in a weird folder that I hadn't seen before."

They followed him into the houseboat. Reid looked around. "You must be feeling better. You cleaned the place up."

"I'm going stir-crazy. I want to get back to work, and the doctor just released me. When are we starting another documentary?"

"As soon as Will is cleared."

"It's definitely interesting." Elliot gestured to the sofa. "Have a seat. I made two copies, one for each of you. The names and emails have been stripped out, and these were saved in a hidden folder on the Cloud drive I hacked into."

Reid took the paper Elliot handed him and scanned it. Parker lay down at Jane's feet.

Elliot handed a sheet of paper to Jane. "Let's cover the contract first. There's a shell company I located in the Bahamas that invested money in the Briscoe lab."

"Nora, my forensic tech, discovered the corporation's name, but that's all she found out so far. This is the contract?"

"Yes, and it says if Gail reveals the partner's name, the contract is null and void and all monies invested would need to be returned within thirty days."

"The guy was majorly paranoid," Reid said.

The language was a little hard to follow, so he was glad Elliot was condensing it for them. "This was dated two months ago."

"Yes, and Gail was about to go under when the money came through."

"Why would this guy fund her I wonder?"

"Hard to say. There's nothing mentioned about that."

So this wasn't any more than Nora had discovered, but Reid didn't want to burst his bubble. "Okay."

"That's the least of the information." Elliot passed over more papers. "Gail had evidence about a plan to kill someone. The emails are vague, but there's enough there to scare the guy, I'm sure."

Reid looked over the paperwork and noticed the word *bomb*. "Jane, look at page three. Dated a week before Gail died." He studied the paragraph, then read it aloud. "'Lauren let slip what you're planning, and I think it's brilliant. Scary but brilliant. I plan to be far away when it happens though, and I'll need money to live. I'm sorry to say our lab is going to be shut down, so I need to disappear if you don't want your name revealed.'"

Jane touched a finger to the page. "She says something on down about a bomb. Did you see that? Two paragraphs down past her talking about her trouble with the lab."

Reid jumped down a couple of paragraphs. "'Everything you're planning will go up in smoke with that bomb.'"

He looked up at Elliot. "We've discovered someone is after some radioactive material in a lead box. This might be the guy." He returned his attention to the paper. "'I already have a letter ready to go if you don't see your way to helping me out. Two hundred thousand will set me up somewhere in South America, and I'll never say a word about your dirty bomb. You'll never hear from me again, and I'm sure that's the way you'd prefer to keep it. So would I.'"

Elliot winced. "A dirty bomb. That's been a big fear for a long time. Why would anyone want to use one?"

Reid had no answer to that question. No sane person would even think of it. He gazed at the paper again. "Looks like the guy is agreeing. He says he'll put the money in a Swiss bank account on June 1."

"Two days after she's killed," Jane said. "That can hardly be coincidence."

"No," Reid agreed.

Jane's face paled. "Stolen radioactive material was bad enough. But actual nuclear contamination? Inconceivable."

"Let's talk to your dad. If anyone knows what went on out in that compound, he does. The man who keeps more secrets than the CIA may be the only one who can give us some direction."

THIRTY-FIVE

Jane couldn't get the thought of a towering mushroom cloud on US soil out of her head. She clung to Reid's hand as they walked toward the SUV with Parker at her other side. She let him in and got behind the wheel.

"I think Dad would have told me about something like a nuclear device if he knew anything," she said.

Reid buckled his seat belt. "When has your dad ever been forthcoming?"

"But this is truly important. He'd want me to find it, to warn people."

"Like the stuff in the safe-deposit box was minor? Or your mother's whereabouts? Every time we talk to him about this case, we find out something important."

She started to reply but her phone rang. "It's Jackson," she said as she answered the call through the vehicle's speakers. "What did you find?"

"No trace of them, Chief. Tents are gone, no boats or inflatables."

"Did you check the other side of the island in case they moved after the storm?"

"Yep. Walked around the whole thing, which is why it took so long. They aren't there. I'll ask around when I get to town and see if anyone saw them. Alfie might have some idea. He knows everything else that's going on in town."

"Okay, thanks for looking." She ended the call and exhaled. "I didn't realize until now how much I was counting on being able to find and talk to Gabriel."

"They only had small boats. He would have had to come to the harbor."

"Unless he arranged for a larger boat to pick them up. There are plenty of captains out there looking for charters."

"True. So we're back to checking with your dad."

"I guess so, but I think it's a dead end too." She wanted to pound on the steering wheel and scream. "Gabriel must have gotten off the island before he broke into your place."

"He would have known you'd look there first. Are there any other remote places to hide?"

"A thousand. I have no idea where to check next." Jane started the engine and drove away from Elliot's houseboat.

People were out picking up tree limbs in their yards from the tornado yesterday, and the sounds of saws and hammers penetrated the police radio chatter. Several people waved and she waved back. And a few turned their heads, which hurt.

"What do you make of Elliot's findings?" she asked.

"I was concerned to know of the dirty bomb's existence, but the thought of someone using it here in the US? Terrifying. What could be their reason for it?"

"A terrorist group could want to cause fear."

He nodded. "Or an assassination. Anyone big coming to the country in the next few weeks? Heads of state?"

"I don't keep up on politics much." She gestured toward his phone. "You might look it up and see who's coming."

He bent his head over his phone to read news stories. After a few minutes he huffed.

"What?"

"There will be a meeting of heads of state at the UN to discuss climate change. Nearly a hundred of them."

"When?"

"The end of June. Two weeks." He looked up. "Which would explain the hard push to get that weapon if this is where they're planning to use it."

"No way to know who is the target."

"Could be all of them."

Jane smacked her palm on the steering wheel. "My mom knows who it is. I wish I had a way to make her tell me."

"Maybe you do." He held her gaze. "A little blackmail of your own?"

"Maybe Dad could get it out of her."

Jane didn't hold out much hope on that front. As much as her mother hadn't wanted Jane to show up on her doorstep, she would want to hear from her dad even less. "I can ask him to call though. It's worth a shot. We have to do something. But he'll say no. He's the hardest man in the world to convince to do something for me."

She caught his sideways glance in her peripheral vision, and the speculation in his eyes caught her by surprise. "What?"

"Your dad and I had a talk this morning on the way to see Will. He mentioned how hard it is for him to tell you he loves you."

She turned her head a moment and gaped before refocusing on the road. "I don't believe you."

"I encouraged him to talk to you. He's not the kind who wears his heart on his sleeve."

"That's an understatement." She couldn't even fathom hearing those words from her dad. Her mother never told her she loved her while growing up either. Jane cut her gaze to Reid again. He'd been the first one to ever say he loved her. Will often told her now too. They'd soothed her hurting heart in so many ways.

She hadn't realized that until now.

———

Reid's phone rang as they reached the first gate at her dad's compound, and he pulled it out to stare at the screen. "Unknown caller."

"Answer it. It could be Gabriel."

Reid swiped it on and waited to hear the demands he was sure were forthcoming. He punched on the speakerphone.

"Where's the cute little sheriff?" Gabriel's voice demanded.

Reid snapped his gaze to Jane. She'd been right. "If you wanted to talk to her, why call me?"

"Because you don't want her hurt. And she's going to be hurt if I don't have what I want."

"I thought you took what you wanted. The pictures are gone."

"What are you talking about?"

Her mouth set and her eyes shadowed, Jane made no move to punch in the code for her dad's gate. She pulled out her phone and began recording the conversation.

"You didn't break into my house and take the pictures?"

"You've lost the map?" A string of profanity spewed from the phone. "How could you be so stupid?"

So it *was* the map he'd wanted. The pictures were just a smoke screen. "We'd like to know who took them too. Jane assumed you had them. She sent the Michigan state police to the site, and everything is gone."

"She did *what*?"

"You heard me. Someone took the map and dug up the weapons. If you didn't take the pictures, who did? Did someone in your group double-cross you?"

"No one would dare. It had to be someone you told about it."

"We told no one."

Gabriel sputtered more curse words and hung up.

Jane lowered her window and punched in the gate code. "If it wasn't Gabriel who broke in, who was it?"

"One of his cohorts? Or is this bigger than we realize? Who else could have known about the bomb material?"

Jane chewed on her lip. "After we talk to Dad, let's head for my office so I'm in the hub of what's happening as it's happening."

The gate began to open. She drove in and parked in front of her dad's house. When she opened the back door, Parker ran off to chase squirrels.

Reid took her hand. "You doing okay? All this hitting at once has to be hard. Remember anything else?"

She shook her head. "I think it has to be someone close to Gabriel though. Maybe he told someone about it." Who? Edward hated her dad, but wouldn't Gabriel know if his boss was doing something on his own? It didn't make sense.

Jane saw her dad by the bunker. The older man waved at her and Reid as they got out of her SUV. This visit felt like she was grasping at straws. Her dad wouldn't tell them anything.

He opened the second gate and headed their way. The air was heavy with humidity and smelled of rain and mud left over from last night.

"Just putting my drone away." He took one glance at Jane's face. "What's wrong?"

"Do you know anything about a dirty bomb Moses and Gabriel planned to sell to the highest bidder?"

She launched into what her mother had told her and everything that had happened. His eyes widened when she said she'd had the Michigan state police dig up the location.

His eyes narrowed when she mentioned the dirty bomb. "Why are you just now telling me you remember all that?"

"Wait, what?" Jane eyed him. "You *knew* about the nuclear material and the explosives?"

He mopped his red, wet face with a handkerchief he pulled from the back pocket of his overalls. "Come inside out of the heat, and I'll tell you what I know. I'd hoped it would never come to this."

Frowning, Jane glanced at Reid as they followed Charles into the cool wash of the air-conditioning. She was met by the scent of some kind of Mexican dish from his dinner, maybe enchiladas.

Her dad went straight to the pristine gray kitchen and poured them all a glass of sweet tea. He handed them glasses beaded with moisture, then took a big gulp. "Hot out there today." He motioned for them to come with him to the living room where he sank into his recliner. "I've known about the bomb for years."

Jane shuddered and closed her eyes. Her dad simply didn't know how to be open and honest with her. Or anyone.

Beside her on the sofa, Reid set a calming hand on Jane's shoulder. "How did you know about it? Did Kim tell you?"

Charles glanced at her. "Actually, Jane told me."

She gasped. "That's not true! I just remembered it when I saw the picture of it."

"Remember when you had some sleepwalking bouts when you were about seventeen?"

She nodded. "So you said. I never woke up to realize what I was doing."

It had been during a period when she was anxious about where to go to college and what she wanted to do with her life.

"I was leading you back to your bedroom, and you said something like, 'It's buried but it will explode.' I asked what you meant, and you said, 'It's that dirty bomb, Dad. The one Mom and I buried. When is it going to explode? We need to be far away.'"

Jane shook her head. "I have no recollection of that."

"You were asleep. I asked where it was, and you said, 'Under the twisted tree by Mom's cabin.' I knew exactly what cabin you meant, and at first I dismissed it as a nightmare. But I was uneasy since I knew your mom was buying and selling all kinds of weapons for Moses. I wanted to go look for it, but I was always so busy here and tried to convince myself it was long gone anyway. I should have checked to be sure."

Jane sagged against the back of the sofa. "And you never said anything?"

"What was there to say?" He took another gulp of tea. "Did you look at the pictures?"

"We did," Jane said. "It contained pictures of the murder. But why all the interest now, after all these years? I mean, of course there's no statute of limitations on murder, but no one was looking into Reid's mother's disappearance. No one really knew she had

276

been killed. It seems out of place. I think it was all about getting that bomb."

Jane's stomach churned. They were no closer to finding out who had killed Lauren so they could get Will out. And that was the most important thing to her.

THIRTY-SIX

A distant alarm blared and Charles whipped around to race to his control room. "There's an intruder!"

Reid and Jane followed, though Reid didn't think it was likely to be anything serious. Maybe a deer had wandered into the compound and brushed up against sensors. It could even have been Parker nosing around outside.

They followed Charles to the small control room, and he called up screen footage. The bank of computer monitors showed various parts of the land around the compound, and Reid saw nothing amiss until Charles went to the one on the far right and fiddled with the settings. The video displayed three men dressed in black with face masks, manipulating electronic equipment in their hands before they entered the bunker on the west side.

"Someone's breached the bunker," Charles said. "That's impossible."

The camera showed the men moving noiselessly through the interior. One man held a box of plastic explosives with wires, and another man carried the cylinder with the ominous black-and-yellow radiation symbol.

Jane gasped. "That's the lead box with the nuclear material!"

Charles opened a safe and extracted an AK-47 as well as a pistol.

"Call ATF and then get off the property. I don't want you in harm's way."

Jane drew her gun. "I'm going with you."

"Me too," Reid said.

Charles shook his head. "You are responsible for Will. You can't run the risk of leaving the boy on his own."

Jane shook her head. "Dad, there are three of them! You can't take them on alone. Reid can get Parker and leave the property."

"I'm not leaving you." How could she even think he would? She was strong and capable, but those guys meant business. Even now he kept glancing back at the screen to see what they were doing. Time was running out to stop them.

She put her hand on his arm. "Will has lived most of his life without me. If I die down there, he would still have you. What if that bomb detonates and all three of us die? Who would take care of Will? He'd never survive the trauma of losing us all. You have to go, Reid. You have to."

He was shaking his head as she spoke even though he realized like a punch to his gut that she was right. Will meant everything to both of them. Sometimes you made sacrifices for your kids, and this was one of those times. Their boy was locked up and in trouble. No one would get him out if the three of them died today.

He swallowed past the knot in his throat. "I think we should all leave and let ATF handle this."

Charles moved toward the door. "I'm not walking away from my property, but you and Jane should go. I don't have time to argue. You two figure it out."

Jane reached up and brushed a kiss across his cheek before following her dad. Reid had a contact at the ATF from a previous documentary, and he placed a call and told the agent everything he knew. Once he was certain help was on the way, he forced himself to move toward the front door, though his legs felt wooden and weak.

He wanted to grab a gun and join Jane and her dad. He loved her with every fiber of his being, and the danger down in that bunker was terrifying.

He could only pray and place her safety in God's hands.

The air smelled musty and damp as Jane descended into the bunker. She paused at the metal door.

"Let me go first." Charles brushed past her to unlock the door.

The metal door on the east side scraped open and lights in the bunker automatically went on. "I wish we had some idea where they are," Jane said.

Her dad held up his phone to show her the video still running. "They're in the food storage room." He held a finger to his lips. "Quietly and quickly."

The world had been worried about terrorists setting off a dirty bomb for years, but as far as she knew, no one had ever done it in the US. Its main effect was to cause fear, but it also would render her father's property and much of the surrounding area unusable for years. If the blast didn't kill them, they would likely get sick from the radiation. She didn't want to leave Will and Reid, so they had to be smart about this.

She was so lost in thought she bumped into her dad and knocked him against a steel shelf. It clattered and several paint cans fell to the floor with an even louder racket. She grabbed her dad's arm and drew him back into a side room.

A man's alarmed voice echoed, and she heard footsteps. She shouted, "Police, drop your weapons!"

The man swore, and the slap of boots against concrete bounced off the walls. She darted past her dad into the main area and leaped over the fallen paint cans to give chase. Her dad's heavy footsteps thundered after her, and she pointed toward the pantry for him to check for the bomb while she followed the escaping men. She could only pray they hadn't had time to put the bomb together.

Light illuminated the darkness as the men flung open the door and raced outside with Jane in pursuit. They disappeared into the canopy of green forest, and she plunged into the bushes where she'd last seen them and paused to listen. The leaves and vegetation muffled their location, and she couldn't tell where to head.

There. A sound came from her right, and she went that way. And promptly bumped into Reid.

She shouldn't have been so glad to see him, but his presence always gave her more courage and stability. "Reid. You were supposed to be off the property."

"I can't find Parker. I've been calling for him, but he's not coming. Did you find the bomb?"

"No, the men got away. I'm not sure if they have the bomb or left it behind."

Her father emerged from the barn over the bunker. "No bomb. They took it with them, probably because they didn't have time to set it. Which way did the men go?"

"I'm not sure," Jane said. "They vanished into the woods that way." She pointed to her right. "That area is covered with dead leaves, and I'm not the best tracker in the world. And Parker is missing. I'm going to look for him."

Her dad nodded. "I'll call ATF and have them organize a road-block. Maybe we can still catch them."

She watched him disappear into the barn before she took Reid's arm. "Let's find my dog."

———

Reid studied the ground as he trailed Jane. "I see dog tracks along the creek this way."

Jane turned and followed him along the gurgling brook that led deeper into the thick woods. It was cooler here with the leaves blocking out the brutal Alabama sun. They picked their way past rocks and shrubs, berry bushes, and tiny waterfalls.

"He can't have gone this far, can he?"

"Those have to be his tracks. What can he be after? He never roams this far from you."

"I know. I don't get it." She cupped her hands, but he grabbed her wrist.

"Don't call him," he whispered. "I hear voices. He's a smart dog. What if he heard those men in masks? This direction is the road, and the fence was probably breached here. There's that trail running from the road for ATVs too."

She nodded. "Look, Parker's tracks veer here. Right toward that ATV track."

Once before someone had sat out here watching Will. The place was a fortress, but Charles's land eventually ran out. That's where the danger lay.

Twigs snapped under Reid's feet, and tree branches caught at his clothing. His shoes kept sinking into the mud. The break in the trees ahead revealed a glimpse of the road and a white SUV sitting there.

Reid grabbed her hand and pulled her down behind a thick shrub. "I saw movement," he whispered in her ear.

She crouched beside him and struggled to slow her raspy breathing. He did the same. His pulse pounding in his ears sounded loud enough to be heard clear to town, though he knew he was the only one hearing it.

He peered up around the edge of the shrubs and saw a quick swish of a red tail. *Parker*, he mouthed to Jane. The dog was following the men. Reid held his position and saw another man with his back to them. There was no mistaking the three men dressed in black he'd seen on the video.

"We need to follow them."

"But how? We don't have a vehicle. They'll be gone by the time we can get my SUV."

The drone. Her dad just had it out. "Text your dad to launch his drone. We'll follow by air and see where the SUV goes."

She nodded and pulled out her phone. Now he could only pray the men didn't make a move until Charles got here.

They crept closer and peered at the SUV. The men took off their masks, but they were too far for him to recognize any of them. Jane snapped several pictures with her phone and ran some video as well as they watched the guys.

She gave a soft whistle as the engine started on the SUV, and Parker came running back to them. "Good dog," she said quietly.

"Let's circle back and get to the SUV," he whispered in her ear. "Your dad has had enough time to get the drone launched. I'm sure he has it already trained on that SUV."

She nodded, and they rushed as fast as they could back to the driveway.

THIRTY-SEVEN

Jane's dad sat beside her in the SUV with his military-grade laptop tracking his state-of-the-art Newham drone. Reid sat in the back so her dad could direct Jane. ATF hadn't arrived yet, and there had been no roadblocks set up between her dad's compound and Pelican Harbor.

She'd left Parker shut in her dad's house for now. She might not be able to protect anyone else, but she could protect her dog.

Charles peered at the screen. "They're still on Bon Secour Highway. About four miles ahead of us."

"Stay with them." Jane's biggest fear was they'd make it to I-59 and disappear in the heavy summer traffic. A white vehicle wasn't the easiest to track. Gulf Shores would be teeming with white cars today.

"Let's think ahead," Reid said by her ear. "What would be the easiest way to escape?"

She thought for a minute. "Out on Fort Morgan Road. There are a lot of private docks. They could slip into a driveway and escape by boat if it was preplanned."

"I hope that's not the plan," her father said. "The drone won't be able to see the vehicle through the trees. Some of those places are heavily wooded."

"If they go that way, we could take the drone out past the trees to Mobile Bay where we could watch for boats." She tossed her phone to Reid in the backseat. "Please text Augusta and Jackson and ask them to bring a boat out to the Mobile Bay side of the peninsula."

"I'm on it."

Her father never lifted his gaze from the computer screen. "As long as there aren't multiple boat launches occurring, we might track them. If the boat we're following doesn't dock in two hours, I'll have to bring back my drone so there's juice for it to land."

She turned on the lights and siren, pressed hard on the accelerator, and maneuvered around cars that pulled over ahead. "Let's just get to them and take them into custody."

"There are three of them, and they are professionals," her dad pointed out. "And we don't want that dirty bomb detonating. We have no idea if they had time to arm it or not."

"And there are three of us, and two of us are law enforcement," Jane snapped. "If you're afraid, I can let you out."

Her dad shot her a searing look that made her close her mouth. "Sorry, Dad. But we can do this."

"I'm not saying we can't, but we might need backup. They could have automatic weapons for all we know."

"We sure don't want a shoot-out," Reid said. "And I think if they'd armed the bomb, they would have left it in your bunker."

Cars still moved to the right and let her pass. "How far ahead now?"

Her dad hadn't taken his gaze from the laptop. "They're merging into traffic on 59 and going south. I suspect you're right, and Fort Morgan Road is their destination. We have to be careful we don't push them into doing something stupid that might kill people. Stay far enough behind that they don't hear your siren. There are a lot of vacationers out here. We don't want any of them harmed."

While Jane knew the counsel was wise, she wanted to slam into that vehicle and force the men off the road. Her cooler head prevailed though.

"Where's the ATF?" Reid asked. "Have we heard any more from them?"

"I haven't," Jane said. "Didn't they tell you they'd be right out?"

"Yeah," Reid said. "But their idea of right away must not be the same as ours."

"The men will be to Fort Morgan Road before the ATF could arrange a roadblock," her dad said. "If we can overtake them on the peninsula, we've got them. Traffic is light out there, and Jane can force them to stop."

Jane drummed her fingers on the steering wheel as traffic in front of her didn't seem to notice her bubble light. When the clueless driver still didn't move, she "yelped" the siren a moment until he moved over.

She zoomed past. "Now how far?"

"About two miles ahead of us."

It felt an eternity as the minutes ticked by with her dad giving occasional updates. She had to get that bomb back.

"They're on Fort Morgan Road. Go get 'em!"

Jane accelerated as fast as the vehicles ahead would let her. Once she got close enough for them to hear the siren, they'd speed up too. She prayed she could make up some of the distance before they realized they were being pursued.

"They're speeding up. They've heard us back here," her dad said.

She nodded and gripped the steering wheel with both hands as her SUV careened around a curve. Where was the white SUV? The curvy road blocked her view of the other vehicles up ahead.

"Where are they?"

"About half a mile ahead. Oh, wait, the vehicle disappeared!" Her father made some adjustments. "I still don't see it. The trees overhang the road, and there are several tracks they could have taken out to the water. Let me see which ones have boat launches." He messed with the computer some more. "All three have boat launches, and all three have boats moored at the docks."

"Keep watching and see where the SUV breaks through the trees."

"We'll have to make a decision to turn down one of the tracks." Her father stared ahead, then back to the screen. "Nothing yet. Take the first driveway up ahead."

She nodded and did what he suggested. The drive was barely wide enough to get down. "I don't think this is it."

"You're right. Back out and try the next one."

Brush scraped at the sides of her SUV as she maneuvered back to the road. Several cars delayed her swerving onto the road, but she was finally able to go forward and turned into the next lane. This one was wider and looked well used.

"I see it! We're on the wrong track. Turn around. It's the next driveway." Her father ran his finger over the trackpad. "They're getting on the boat."

She turned her siren to the yelp sound as she reached the end of the drive. But the sinking sensation in her stomach told her they were going to be too late.

Reid hung on to the door as Jane turned the SUV into the narrow gravel drive. She was a maniac behind the wheel. Thick brush scraped by the side of the vehicle, and large water oak trees blotted out the sunshine. She gripped the wheel and maneuvered around a big pothole.

"I think they're heading for Dauphin Island," her dad said. "I'll have to bring back my drone or it will be lost at sea."

"It's only money, Dad! We have to get that bomb."

"I don't care about the money, but my drone doesn't have enough power to continue to track them to Dauphin Island. It will fail no matter what. I'll take the drone down to just above the boat to see if I can find the name so we can track it on the island."

They broke through the brush into clear blue skies by a dock. The white SUV was parked there.

She parked her SUV, and Reid got out to rush to the dock and stare out over the whitecaps at the boat zooming away from them. Jane and her dad joined him. In the distance the escaping boat kicked up foam. Farther out were oil platforms and barges carrying coal. The drone was a black dot that zoomed down to hover over the boat.

Reid tipped his head to one side. What was that noise on the wind? The other two hadn't reacted, so maybe the sound was his imagination.

He put his hand on her shoulder. "Was that a gunshot?"

"I didn't hear it."

The retort of a gun repeated, and the drone plunged from the sky and dove into the waves.

"They shot my drone!" Her dad slammed his laptop shut. "We're helpless."

Jane clutched her hands together and went to the end of the

pier where she stared at the disappearing boat. "They're getting away!"

Reid's phone vibrated in his hand. He glanced at the message from Augusta, then handed Jane the phone. "You got a text from Augusta. They're on their way, but ETA isn't for about thirty minutes."

"Oh man. Not good. That's plenty of time for the men in black to disappear." She glanced back toward the white SUV. "Maybe there's something inside the vehicle to help us know where they're heading."

She ran back along the dock to the grass and tried to open the door. "It's locked. I'll get my Slim Jim."

Stepping to the back liftgate, she got inside her vehicle and returned with the unlocking tool. Within moments she had the door open and was inside. She unlocked all the doors with the button on the driver's side.

"Reid, you look in the backseat. I'll see what I can find in the passenger seat."

Reid ducked inside the back and felt under the seat and along the side of the door. Nothing. He looked in the pocket on the far side and found an assortment of pens and paper along with napkins and a few receipts. Nothing helpful.

"Nothing in the glove box but vehicle registration and the owner's manual." Jane flipped down the visor, but it held only the mirror.

Her dad approached the car with his laptop. "I got a snapshot of the name of the boat before he shot the drone down. It's the *Westwind*."

"That's Gabriel's boat. I'll tell Augusta." So maybe her mother had been wrong and Gabriel was more of a threat than she'd realized. Jane activated her phone and placed the call to Augusta. *Voice mail*, she mouthed. She left a detailed message. "Call me back when you get this."

Reid lay on his side and looked under the seat. A wooden object caught his eye, and he pulled out a hand-carved pipe. It still held traces of tobacco. Something about it felt familiar, but he couldn't place it.

He got out when Jane did and saw the droop of her shoulders. He started toward her to show her the pipe, but her dad got there first.

Charles put his arm around her. "You did everything right, Jane. The guys had a plan. I wish I'd gotten a look at their faces."

"I did snap some pictures." She opened her phone and called up the pictures she'd taken in the woods. "Have a look."

He took the phone and swiped through the pictures, pausing at the last one. "Something about that guy . . ."

Reid peered over Charles's shoulder at the burly figure. Something about his stance triggered a sense of familiarity. It took a second for it to register. "He walks like you."

Edward.

Jane stared at her dad. "I'd suspected Edward, but why wouldn't he tell Gabriel about all he was doing? I've been trying to figure out why on earth you would be the target of a dirty bomb. It seems extreme, but Edward hates you."

Charles pressed his lips together and stared at the photo. "Let me enlarge this last picture." He used his thumb and forefinger to blow up the image of the man's face, and though the picture was blurry, Reid inhaled at how much it looked like Edward.

"It's my brother." Charles rubbed his head. "And it makes a twisted kind of sense. I destroyed his family, so he plans to destroy mine. That's why he implicated Will in Lauren's death. He wants to punish me through Will."

"How did you destroy his family?" Jane asked.

"I sent his boy to jail. Colton. You might remember him, Jane. The two of you used to be inseparable."

She wished she could remember.

"He ended up just as bad as his dad. You were in college, and I'd decided to go see my brother. Try to connect again." He shrugged. "Stupid idea. When I arrived in town, I spotted a punk with a gun shaking down an old woman. I intervened, but the poor old lady was shot before I could stop him. I tackled him and called the police. My testimony sent him to prison. It was Edward's boy, Colton. He died in prison during a yard fight."

"And Edward never forgave you," she said.

Reid looked down at the pipe in his hand, and the sudden realization of where he'd seen one like it hit him. At the compound in Kentucky. "Look here, guys. I found this under the SUV's backseat. Edward had one like it that nearly fell out of his pocket when we spoke to him."

Charles took it and turned it over in his hands. "He started carving these when he was fifteen."

"Any idea where he might go in this area?" Jane asked.

Charles shook his head. "I haven't spoken to him in years."

Reid ran his fingers through his sweaty hair. There was something just out of the grasp of his memory. His eyes widened, and he put his hand on Jane's shoulder. "Didn't Edward say something about Fairhope when we saw him? Remember? He told you to go back to Fairhope."

She nodded. "I'd thought it was a slip of the tongue, but maybe it's more than that. It's the only lead we have. Let's head there."

The three of them ran to the SUV and buckled up.

"It's normally an hour to get there from here, but I'll use my siren and lights." Jane flipped on both, and Reid saw the speedometer hit seventy by the time she was a mile out on the road back to town.

"Where might they go in Fairhope?" Reid asked. "Does Gabriel have any known contacts there? All I know about Fairhope is that lots of artists live there. And it's cute." Its reputation as the cutest town in the South was well deserved.

"Maybe just a change of vehicles," Jane said. "If we can get the police out there, they might find someone waiting in the parking lot by the pier."

"Lots of well-known people have homes there," her dad said. "Ball players, authors."

Jane hunched over the steering wheel, and the speedometer zoomed higher. At times she was doing ninety on open stretches on I-98 when traffic was light.

Her phone sounded, and she glanced down at the console where it lay faceup. "It's Augusta." She touched a button on her steering wheel to answer. "Any news?"

"I got someone down to the Fairhope marina, Chief. He found the boat, but no one was there. We were too late."

"Thanks for trying."

Jane pulled to the side of the road and beat on the steering wheel. "Too late! Now what?" Her phone dinged, and she glanced at it. "Nora just sent over the picture of the man in the backyard of Lauren's house. Let me take a look at it before we go."

"Okay."

He watched as she opened the file and enlarged the picture.

The color drained from her face, and she handed her phone to Reid without a word.

He stared at it. "That looks like . . ."

"Edward," she whispered. "Dad, look at this."

Confirmation Edward was in this up to his white hairline.

THIRTY-EIGHT

Jane's SUV rolled into Fairhope, and she glanced around with a rising sense of helplessness. "I have no idea where to look. Or even if Edward's here."

"I wish I had my drone," her dad grumbled. "I might be able to see something from the air."

She ran through a drive-through and got them all a sweet tea before she parked in the lot. She lowered the windows. "Let's go over what we know."

She ticked off the points with a finger as she made them. "One— Edward knew Lauren, and it's likely he was the mysterious lover. Two—Edward wants revenge on Dad for his part in sending Colton to prison. Three—he's likely the one who framed Will for revenge."

"One other thing," her dad put in. "Gabriel didn't seem to know about some of this. Edward was always one to hold back his thoughts. He's likely been planning this a long time, and Gabriel was his patsy."

"A family resemblance," Jane said under her breath. Her dad was the pot calling the kettle black.

"I'm calling Mom," she said.

"I don't know what good that will do," her dad mumbled.

She ignored him and placed the call. Her mom answered on the second ring. "I was about to call you, Jane."

The woman who'd avoided her for fifteen years actually sounded eager to talk. Jane tried to squelch the hope that sprang up like a seed left dry too long. It meant nothing.

"Why were you about to call me?"

"I felt bad that I didn't tell you everything. You deserve that much. I don't want to live in fear anymore. The one you're looking for is your uncle. Edward Hardy."

Verification at least. "He's got the dirty bomb in his possession, Mom. He broke into Dad's bunker with it and we interrupted him before he could set it off. We're trying to find him now. Do you have any idea where he might have gone?"

"He got away again with the bomb?"

"Yes. Do you know if he's got any contacts down here? Maybe in Fairhope?"

"I don't know of any place like that, but what I do know is that Edward is a trickster. He's good at making you think he's doing something and then doing exactly the opposite. I can't tell you how many times he made me cry when we were living at his compound. So if you think he's gone to Fairhope, chances are he's gone in the other direction."

Jane shuddered at the word picture. "He doesn't sound like someone I'd like to be around."

"I hope that helps. I'm sorry it took so long for me to tell you."

Jane thanked her and didn't mention she'd already figured out Edward's role in this. At least her mom had wanted to help. That had to mean something.

"Mom says he will do the exact opposite of what we expect."

Her dad took a slurp of his sweet tea and mopped the perspiration from his forehead with a napkin. "She's right. So he's not here in Fairhope. It was a trick to lure us away from his real plan."

What might he be trying to hide? Gabriel claimed not to have known the map had been taken, which meant that Edward didn't even trust his second-in-command.

Reid leaned forward from the backseat. "His main goal is revenge. He nearly had that bomb planted in the bunker, but we chased him off in time. What could be his fallback position? You know him best, Charles. Any ideas?"

"In his mind I killed his son. He framed Will. He wanted to turn my entire compound into a useless mess of radioactive dirt, which would have been just revenge too. The three things I care about are Jane, Will, and my compound. What else is there for him to target?"

Jane caught her breath and struggled to make sense of her thoughts. "What if he led us away from the compound but plans to circle back there?"

He'd probably been laughing his head off as they raced after him, only to find him zooming over the water in the ultimate wild-goose chase to Dauphin Island. If she had followed through with her original plan to get a boat and follow him there, they'd be looking all over the island. At least they'd figured out to check Fairhope, and sure enough, his boat was here.

"Let's get back to Dad's place. He could already be there."

And probably *was* already there. Gabriel or one of his other minions had probably picked him up and immediately headed back to Pelican Harbor. That bomb could already be armed and ready to go off the minute they came through the gates.

"Let's get ATF out there."

"Already on it," Reid said. "I just got a text, and they're thirty minutes away."

"We should get there about the same time." She tossed her

phone back to Reid. "Would you text Augusta and have her head that way too?"

He nodded and began tapping away at her screen.

She rolled up the window and started the engine. All she could do was pray they got there in time.

———

Jane had the siren blaring and lights flashing all the way back to Pelican Harbor. When she reached the edge of her dad's property, Augusta and Jackson were parked at the gate waiting on them.

The gate was wide open and Jane gasped. "He's already in there."

Jane had considered sending Augusta the code to get in, but she didn't want her officers going in by themselves. Though there had been three men in her dad's bunker, Edward could have gathered Gabriel and his men here as well. A dozen men or more could be lying in wait to ambush anyone entering the property.

She parked her SUV behind the squad car and got out. "Brazen, isn't he? He didn't even sneak in another way but came right through the front gate. And left it open as if to brag about it."

"I got here a few minutes ago, but I wanted to wait on you and the ATF. We don't know what we're facing here."

Jane got out binoculars and went to stand beside Augusta at the fence. "Exactly right."

Though she knew her detective was brave, Augusta had a family waiting on her to come home too. That had to be in the back of her mind just like it was nagging at Jane. She glanced at Reid, who followed her, and knew he would want to be able to hug Will again, just like she did.

This situation couldn't be overstated.

The house came into sudden view as she adjusted the binoculars. There was a figure in the rocker on the porch, and his white hair gave away his identity. Her dad's chickens pecked in the dirt in front of him, and she thought she saw Parker lying on the porch in the shade, but dusk was coming fast, and it was hard to make out the shadows.

She handed the binoculars to her dad. "Edward is sitting in the rocker waiting on us."

She couldn't figure out his angle. Wouldn't he want to arm the bomb and get out of there? He wouldn't want to die in a blast from that bomb any more than the rest of them did. Did he want to taunt his brother?

When her dad handed the binoculars back to her, his mouth was in a grim line. "Grandstander. He always thinks he has to make a statement. I'm going in alone. He wants to gloat and taunt me, and I'll let him have his say."

She grabbed at his hand. "Dad, no! He might be suicidal and blow up the place while you're there. I can't lose you."

Her dad's other hand came down on hers. He showed her his phone. "I'm calling you right now, and we'll leave the connection open so you can hear what's happening. I'll be fine, Button."

The slip of the tongue caught at her heart, but her dad walked through the open gate before she could reply. His long legs ate up the distance, and she watched him pause and open the second gate. In a few minutes he was a speck in the distance, so she focused the binoculars on the scene, veering between her father and her uncle.

She turned to Jackson. "You have a long-range rifle in the trunk?"

"Yes, ma'am."

"Get it and circle around through the woods until you're close enough. Keep it trained on Edward Hardy. If he looks like he's going to blow up something or pulls out a gun, protect my dad."

Jackson nodded and got the rifle out of the trunk. Her hands were too shaky to try to stop an ambush herself.

She turned on the speakerphone and turned on a recording app, then perched her phone on the fence. She brought up the binoculars again. Reid had found the other pair and stood watching with her.

"Edward," her dad said. "I hardly expected to see you after all this time. Implicating my grandson in a murder wasn't enough for you? You had to bring a bomb here too? Where is it?"

Her uncle rose and smiled. "I've been dreaming of this day for years, Charles. You killed my boy, and you're about to discover how it feels to have everything you care about stripped away. I don't care what happens to me anymore. Doc says I only have a few months anyway, so if I was going to get justice for Colton, I knew it had to be soon."

So that was why this had all come up so suddenly. Edward was dying. Her dad would be alone. No, not alone. He still had Will and her.

"I'm sorry," her dad said. "No matter what went down between us, you were always my brother, Ed."

"Don't try to talk your way out of this, Charles. Retribution is at hand."

"You never even let me explain. I didn't even know it was Colton when I took him down for the murder of that old woman."

"If you'd known, would it have mattered?"

A question Jane could answer. No, it wouldn't have mattered. Justice ran through her dad's veins even stronger than his blood.

"No," her dad said. "What he did was wrong."

"And it should have been up to me to punish him, not you! You didn't have the right."

Her dad propped a boot on the first step to the porch. "When did you hear about the dirty bomb?"

"Gabriel mentioned it about five years ago. I didn't think much about it until my diagnosis a few months ago. Then I realized I had a powerful weapon to bring you down. When Lauren told me where you were finally—and even better, that you had a grandson—I started making plans."

"You've known Lauren a while?"

"She came to camp looking for Gabriel. She thought he might know how to find Reid Dixon since they were roommates when he was at Liberty's Children. I thought maybe if we found Reid, we'd find you since he'd been married to Button. She turned into quite the lawman, by the way. Plucky little thing."

"Leave Jane out of it. This is between you and me."

"That it is." Edward nodded.

"How did Gabriel know where to find Reid?"

"He didn't, and he sent Lauren off. But I liked her looks, and she liked my money. We got along for a while until I got tired of her constant demands for money. The house I bought wasn't good enough, the car wasn't fancy enough."

Her dad grabbed a porch post and walked up a step. Jane glanced at Reid. "He's trying to get close enough to strike."

Edward pulled a hand out of his pocket, and Jane saw a remote in his palm. Her pulse stuttered in her chest. "That's the detonator," she whispered.

Her uncle seemed relaxed and happy to talk. "I cut her loose and thought that was the end of it until she showed up with news of where to find you. I fed her some more money to keep me posted, and that was working well until she shot off her mouth to her friend. I had to buy Gail off too, but I figured it was worth it. I was going to be dead and I couldn't take the money with me. But she threatened me, and that's not something I could let slide."

"Then Lauren figured out you killed her. She was going to tell Jane."

"Worse than that. She wanted more money, and I was tired of giving it to her. And I saw the perfect way to wreck your life."

When she saw his hand twitch with the remote, Jane screamed, "No!"

THIRTY-NINE

Reid reached for Jane when she screamed, and she buried her face in his chest. Burying his face in her hair, he closed his eyes, and in that moment before death could take them, he prayed for God to help their boy get through this.

A retort echoed in the treetops, and Reid lifted his head. That wasn't a bomb blast—it was a rifle.

Reid brought the binoculars up and looked toward the house. Edward lay crumpled on the porch with his arm out flung. The remote lay next to him, and Charles reached down to pick it up as Parker bounded out of the dusky shadows to nose at his knee.

"Edward is down," Reid said. "I can't believe it."

Jane released him and took off running for the house. The SUV would have been faster, but he needed to release the pent-up energy as much as she did, and he loped along beside her. Winded and sweating, they reached the porch in time to see Jackson and several ATF officers burst from the trees brandishing weapons.

Charles had the detonator in his hand and gave it to the first ATF agent he saw. "I don't know where the bomb is, but I expect it's in the bunker somewhere. He would have wanted to destroy everything important to me. Check the entrance in the barn. It's probably open. And Edward is alive. He'll need a medic."

"I called for one, and we'll find the bomb," the agent said. The men got out equipment and went toward the barn.

Jane ran to her father and embraced him. After an awkward moment, Charles's arms came down around her. His eyes looked moist, and he backed away.

"I need to tend to Edward." He turned and knelt beside his brother.

Edward's eyes fluttered open, and he stared up into Charles's face. "So you won after all, Charles. You always did. I hated being younger."

"I know, Edward. Did you kill Lauren yourself?"

Reid exchanged a glance with Jane and brought out his phone. He began to record the conversation.

"Gabriel. He always followed instructions well." Edward coughed, and a bubble of blood oozed from his lips. "He arranged to get that firefighter out of the way too. I didn't want him to continue to plague the lab and uncover the money I gave Gail. It was all turning out so well. You always ruined things. I hate you."

A long sigh eased from Edward's mouth, and he turned his head. The light of life went out of his eyes.

"Found it!" an agent called from the door to the barn. "Stay back while we remove the bomb."

Jane waved to show she understood, and Reid draped an arm around her. He didn't know what to say to Charles, and he knew she didn't either. He was so private.

Charles rose and went to lean against the door. His shoulders shook, and Reid took a step toward him, then stopped and turned off the video. Charles wouldn't welcome any kind of comfort from him. He glanced at Jane and inclined his head toward her dad.

Don't be afraid, Reid mouthed.

She bit her lip and nodded, then went to her father's side and put her hand on his arm. "I heard what he told you. I'm sorry, Dad. His hatred has to hurt. Reid and I recorded both conversations. He confessed to killing Lauren and framing Will. We can get him out of jail now. Thanks to you."

Her father gave a long exhale and turned to face her with wet eyes. "How soon?"

"It will probably take until tomorrow. But I'll get right to work on it."

The joy in Reid's heart nearly exploded it. To have their son out of that terrible place and back home where he belonged was almost too much to believe. But Reid knew this day was bittersweet for Charles, who had just lost a brother in the worst possible way.

―――――

Neither of them had slept all night. Reid had gotten Olivia settled while Jane had taken part in the interrogations. The police had picked up Gabriel in Mobile, and he'd chirped like a bird when he was offered a deal of life imprisonment if he gave the details of the murders. The dirty bomb had been all Edward's idea, and Gabriel hadn't been happy to hear he'd been cut out of a major part of the plan.

Reid parked in the lot outside juvenile hall. "Ready?"

Jane held up a sheaf of papers. "Let's do this."

They got out into a brilliantly blue day with the sun glaring down. He took her hand, and they strode into the correctional facility. Will didn't know he was about to be a free boy again. Reid's throat was thick, and he was struggling to keep all the emotion in his heart from incapacitating him.

He stood back while Jane took care of the details. It seemed an eternity before an officer brought Will out into the waiting room.

He looked paler and sadder than they'd seen him two days ago. His brown eyes went wide when he saw them. "Mom? Dad?"

Reid went to him and pulled him into his arms for a fierce hug, then released him, gripping him by the shoulders. "You're free, son. Totally exonerated. Your mom found the killer. He's been arrested, and there are no longer any charges against you."

"What?" Will glanced from Reid to his mother. "For sure?"

Jane was crying now, the tears tracking down her exhausted face. Her hair was a wreck, but Reid didn't think he'd ever seen her look so beautiful with raw love and joy on her face. She opened her arms, and Will ran into them.

"I knew you'd do it, Mom." Will's sobs shook his shoulders. "Thank you. Do I get to go home? Can I have pizza for dinner? Did you bring Parker?"

Reid met Jane's gaze, and a huge smile broke across his face, so big it threatened to crack open his face along with his heart. A heart could only stand so much joy.

Reid gripped Will's shoulder. "Yes to all those things. They're getting your belongings, and we're out of here. Megan and Parker are waiting at home, along with Olivia. Megan is baking chocolate chip cookies in celebration. I don't think she slept last night either. We'll tell you about the last twenty-four hours later."

He nodded to the officer who brought a bag of Will's clothes. "You want to change?"

"Can we just go? I want a shower and clothes that haven't seen the inside of a cell."

Jane linked her arm in Will's, and Reid did the same on the other side. They stepped outside into a light breeze. A songbird serenade from the trees added to the joy Reid felt.

Will sniffed. "That's the smell of freedom. I'll never take it for granted again." He broke down again and turned into Reid's arms to bury his face in his dad's chest. "I wanted to believe, but I was so scared, Dad. Scared we'd never go fishing again. Scared we'd never take off on one of our adventures again or play Monopoly. That I'd never sleep in my own bed. I can't believe it's really over."

Reid clutched his son and looked over at Jane, who was also crying. He held out a hand to her, and she stepped over to embrace Will too.

"Let's go home, son."

FORTY

Their borrowed boat sailed under a perfect full moon, and Jane sat on a chaise lounge with her feet up while Reid navigated the boat into a small cove, shimmering with light and fragrant with sea salt.

He dropped anchor and flipped on the running lights around the boat. They gave a romantic glow to the deck. He pulled out the picnic basket before giving Jane a long look followed by a wolf whistle. "You look stunning."

She stood and did a little twirl that made her tropical dress swirl around her knees. "Thank you, kind sir. This is the first time I've had on a fun dress in ages." She fluffed the tips of her hair. "Megan dolled me all up with makeup and a curling iron. I about didn't recognize myself in the mirror." She drank in his tall, dark handsomeness. "You don't clean up too badly yourself. A collared shirt and khakis." He looked good enough to eat, but she didn't say that.

The past four days had been packed to the brim. Olivia had been weak from her ordeal but was doing well today. Jane glanced over at Will, who was lounging next to her. He'd been having nightmares, and both she and Reid had rushed to him in the middle of the night. She'd arranged for some counseling next week.

Reid popped the bottle on some nonalcoholic wine and produced three glasses that he filled to the brim with the bubbly concoction. "I'm ready to celebrate and put this all behind us. Let's start a new life."

"I'm ready." She touched glasses with both of the men in her life and took a swig of her drink. "Perfect. What did you bring for dinner?"

Will sat up and frowned. "It's not time for dinner."

"What do you mean it's not time for dinner? I can smell seafood, and I'm starving. I barely ate while you were incarcerated, you know. I need to find the five pounds I lost."

Will looked up at his father. "Dad, tell her. I'm dying here."

Puzzled, Jane stared at Will. "What's going on? You're buying this boat instead of borrowing it? You're moving away? What's up?"

A tender smile lifted Reid's lips and lit his eyes with laughter. "Like we'd ever move away from you. Not happening, honey."

Will scrambled to his feet. "Dad, don't wimp out. Want me to do it?"

"I think I'm the man for the job, Will." Reid dropped to one knee and reached into his pocket.

Jane caught her breath, and her stomach took a dive with the next roll of the waves. She covered her mouth with her hand as he opened a black velvet box. Will dropped to both knees and put his hands up in a pleading gesture.

Reid took her hand and lifted the sparkling ring for her examination. "Will you marry me, Jane? For real this time?"

"Marry *us*. It's a package deal, Mom. Dad's had the ring forever. You're killing me—are you ever going to say yes?"

Jane couldn't tear her gaze away from both faces long enough to study the ring. It was enough to know she was wanted so badly. By both of them.

"You haven't answered," Reid said.

"Yes, of course! A thousand times yes." She was laughing and crying all at the same time.

"Yippee!" Will jumped to his feet and enveloped her in a hug before Reid managed to do it. "We're going to be a real family. When's the wedding?"

Reid rose and pulled Will away from her. "I think it's my turn. You'll be off to college before we can blink, but your mom's always going to be mine."

"Mine too," Will protested. "You both are. I won't forget my parents when I'm in college. Sheesh, what kind of son do you think I am?"

"The best kind," Jane said in unison with Reid. She leaned into her new fiancé's arms and inhaled the spicy scent of his soap and cologne.

"Put the ring on her, Dad. Do I have to tell you everything?"

"Evidently." Reid was laughing so hard he could barely pull the ring out of its slot and slip it on her finger.

She was intoxicated with happiness, totally spent with joy. Was this real?

She rose on her tiptoes and wrapped her arms around Reid's neck to pull his head down for a kiss. The love and devotion in his lips told of the family she'd always longed for. The perfect place to rest her heart.

EPILOGUE

The Michigan woods held so many familiar smells for Jane—childhood left behind, fear, longing, joy, despair all mingled with the rich aromas of loamy soil and fallen leaves. The leaves decorated the trees with shades of gold and red, and through a break in the vegetation she spied the old cabin.

She hung on to Reid's hand, more for his sake than for hers. Today was going to be traumatic when they found his mother and began the first trek to her final resting place, a cemetery near their home where Reid could visit often.

Philip and Gretchen Parks, Reid's maternal grandparents, huddled with Will near the rim of the hole several forensic techs were digging. Will brought them so much comfort. Her gaze went to Reid. Like father, like son.

He'd come through his ordeal, and there'd been no more nightmares for a couple of months now.

The techs with their gloves dug slowly and carefully, stopping to bag every item they found. This had to be done right so they had all the proof that would add to the charges against Gabriel. It wouldn't bring Denise back, but it would bring justice.

Finally.

Reid's fingers tightened on hers as the first gleam of bone

showed through the black loam. There she was. He gasped and closed his eyes.

"We can wait in the cabin," she said softly. "There's no shame in that."

"I want to be here. I want to know." His voice was low, and his grip on her hand tightened.

He released her hand and put his arm around her to pull her more tightly into an embrace. He brought her left hand to his lips and kissed the wedding ring set on her finger. Sometimes she still couldn't believe she was married to this wonderful man and had such a perfect life.

He trembled a little as they began to put his mother's remains in the coffin, and she hugged him when she saw the glimmer of moisture in his eyes. This moment had been a long time coming.

It seemed like eternity as they stood there in the October wind and chill before the techs stepped out of the hole.

Her father was to her right, and he stepped closer to her as the men closed the casket. "They're ready to take her back to Pelican Harbor. I'm sorry, Reid."

Reid smiled. "It's a good day, Charles. Mom's not in that assortment of bones anyway. She's laughing in heaven. There's a lot of closure today. I didn't think this day would ever come."

"I know." Her dad glanced down at Jane. "You did great, Jane. I'm really proud of all you've done as the new chief. You're a remarkable officer."

Had she heard him correctly? She stared at him to make sure he wasn't mocking her. There was seldom a hint of praise in the things he said to her growing up. Grades were never up to snuff. Learning to be a crack shot had been challenging. Even her cooking was critiqued.

He cleared his throat. "I know I haven't been the easiest parent.

I'm not good at it. Things I know I should say get stuck in my throat. But you're a good daughter, Jane. And a good person. I wish I could take the credit for how you turned out, but I think that was more you than me."

"I wouldn't say that," she said. "You taught me hard work and focus."

The wind lifted his bushy white hair and blew it into his eyes. He batted it away, and his gaze stayed intent as though there was more he wanted to say but didn't know how.

"I love you, Dad."

"I-I love you, Jane." His voice went gruff and hoarse.

That cost him, and his sacrifice to say something difficult brought moisture to her eyes. Of course, everything made her cry right now. She wanted to hug him, but it was such an unnatural gesture she couldn't make her arms move. Their locked gazes would have to be enough.

He put his hand on her shoulder and gave a light squeeze. "See you back home."

Reid tucked her into the warmth of his embrace again, out of the wind. "I knew he had it in him."

"I didn't." She nodded toward the cabin. "Did you ever see it?"

"Not the inside." He motioned to Will, who was standing alone as his grandparents walked alongside the casket as though they couldn't bear to be away from their daughter.

Will bounded over to meet them. "What's up, parental figures?"

"We were going to go check out the little cabin. Want to come?"

"Sure." He fell into step beside Jane.

Her heart was trying to jump right out of her throat. She'd hoped to have Will there when she made her announcement, and her dream came true.

Reid fiddled with the door and managed to get it open. Jane stepped inside out of the wind. The musty, closed-up smell made her wonder if anyone had been in here during the last fifteen years. Thick dust and debris flew up from under her feet as she moved, and she caught the scent of animal droppings.

She wrinkled her nose. Maybe this wasn't the best place to talk. "It's not as nice as I remember. Back then it felt cozy. Like a little hideaway."

"It might have been fifteen years ago." Reid wandered over to look in the fireplace. "Some half-burned paperbacks here. I remember your dad talking about burning your mom's books."

"Grandpa burned books?"

"He didn't want my mother getting any ideas above the place where he wanted her."

Will's eyes clouded. "That's messed up. I'd never do that to Megan."

The two were an established couple now, and Olivia had improved so much. She barely needed a walker now, and Jane rejoiced when she moved home last week. Not that Jane hadn't wanted her in the house, but she'd been so happy to see her friend's recovery.

Well, this place would have to do. Was there ever a perfect place and time for life-altering news? While this might not be the place she wanted to remember as the spot, it was also a time of renewal. For her, for Will, and especially for Reid.

Her gaze lingered on the curve of his jaw and the strong jut of his chin. His thick brows and those brown eyes that held so much warmth and approval. How did she get so lucky?

She reached her hand into her pocket and closed her fingers around the piece of plastic. "I have something I wanted to talk about."

"Okay." Reid's smile dimmed. "You look a little serious. Are we in trouble or just me?"

"It depends on what you mean by trouble. How hard will it be for me to talk both of you into changing diapers?" She brought the pregnancy stick out of her pocket and opened her palm to show it to the men in her life.

Reid stared at it, then his gaze lifted to hers before it darted over to make sure Will was handling the news all right. "A baby? You're saying we're having a baby?"

"Mom!" Will rushed to her and grabbed her by the shoulders. "Are you serious? I'm getting a baby brother or sister?"

"That's right, honey. I know it probably feels weird at your age."

"It feels *spectacular*! You'll have to teach me how to hold it and stuff. I've never been around a baby before." Tears leaked from Will's eyes, and he pulled her into a hug.

She clutched him tight and peeked past him to see Reid, who still looked wide-eyed and in shock. "I think I'd better talk to your dad."

"Oh, yeah, sorry." Will stepped back and motioned Reid forward. "Your turn, Dad."

"I think this was a little out of order. Again." But Reid's smile was as bright as lightning. He scooped Jane up and twirled her around the dusty old cabin where things had changed so much.

He set her down and kissed her, a warm approval that sent heat all the way through her, then leaned back, leaving her breathless. Jane took his hand, then reached for Will's.

"I think we have a nursery to get ready." Her heart was full to bursting.

This time she felt ready to take on caring for a baby. This time she was ready for anything that came their way. God had once taken everything, but then he'd given her back so much more.

A NOTE FROM THE AUTHOR

Dear Reader,

You've stayed with me through the whole series, and Jane has finally found her happily-ever-after with Reid and Will! It's been a long time coming, and I'm thankful you gave me the leeway to tell the story that needed three books to get to the end. I hope you've loved reading this series as much as I've loved writing it.

Life doesn't always turn out perfect, and I wanted to leave that final heartbreak of Jane's broken relationship with her mother. Sometimes life is like that, but God fills in the holes for us. He soothes the heartbreak and becomes mother, father, sister, brother, or friend for us. He's always comforting us when we need it most.

As always, I love to hear from you. I'm thankful every day for the blessing of having readers like you in my life. Thank you for being there!

Colleen Coble

ACKNOWLEDGMENTS

Eighteen years and counting as part of the amazing HarperCollins Christian Publishing team as of the summer of 2020! I have the best team in the industry (and I'm not a bit prejudiced), and I'm so grateful for all you've taught me and all you've done for me. My dear editor and publisher, Amanda Bostic, makes sure I'm taken care of in every way. My marketing and publicity team is fabulous (thank you, Paul Fisher, Kerri Potts, and Margaret Kercher!). I'm truly blessed by all your hard work. My entire team works so hard, and I wish there was a way to reward you all for what you do for me.

Julee Schwarzburg is my freelance editor, and she has such fabulous expertise with suspense and story. She smooths out all my rough spots and makes me look better than I am. I learn something from you and Amanda with every book, so thank you!

My agent, Karen Solem, and I have been together for twenty-one years now. She has helped shape my career in many ways, and that includes kicking an idea to the curb when necessary. She and a bevy of wonderful authors helped brainstorm this new series. Thank you, Denise Hunter, Kristin Billerbeck, Robin Caroll, Carrie Stuart Parks, Lynette Eason, Voni Harris, and Pam Hillman!

My critique partner and dear friend of over twenty-two years, Denise Hunter, is the best sounding board ever. Together we've created so many works of fiction. She reads every line of my work, and I read every one of hers. It's truly been a blessed partnership.

I'm so grateful for my husband, Dave, who carts me around from city to city, washes towels, and chases down dinner without complaint. My family is everything to me, and my three grandchildren make life wonderful. We try to split our time between Indiana and Arizona to be with them, but I'm constantly missing someone. ☹ Most important, I give my thanks to God, who has opened such amazing doors for me and makes the journey a golden one.

DISCUSSION QUESTIONS

1. Which lies have you found to be most painful? Blatant lies or lies of omission?
2. We sometimes block out painful or traumatic memories. How do you deal with those?
3. What do you think drives a person to care only about money like Lauren did?
4. How easy do you find it to forgive someone who hurts you? Or someone who hurts someone you love?
5. Do you think Reid should have paid off Lauren or fought her grab for money?
6. Jane's relationships with both her parents are complicated. What do you do with complicated relationships?
7. Revenge drove Edward's actions. What do you do to keep from seeking revenge?
8. What do you think Jane should do now about her mother and half sisters? Is there always hope or should she give up?

Don't miss the gripping new stand-alone novel from

USA TODAY bestselling romantic suspense author Colleen Coble.

A STRANGER'S GAME

COMING JANUARY 2022

Available in print, e-book, and audio.

THOMAS NELSON
Since 1798

THE HOPE BEACH SERIES

Welcome to Hope Beach. A place of intoxicating beauty
. . . where trouble hits with the force of a hurricane.

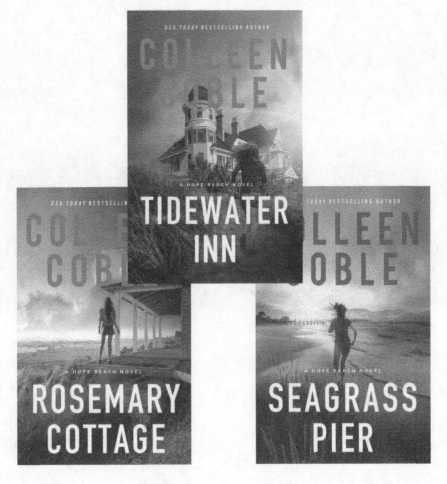

Available in print, e-book, and audio.

THOMAS NELSON
Since 1798

PLEASE ENJOY THIS EXCERPT
FROM *STRANDS OF TRUTH*

"Coble wows with this suspense-filled [novel]."
—*Publishers Weekly*

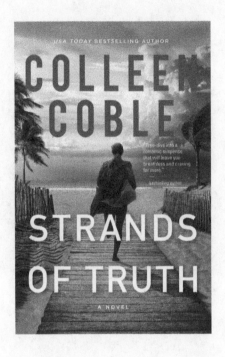

AVAILABLE IN PRINT, E-BOOK, AND AUDIO

THOMAS NELSON
Since 1798

PROLOGUE

JANUARY 1990
ST. PETERSBURG, FLORIDA

Lisa ran to her Datsun Bluebird and jerked open the yellow door. Her pulse strummed in her neck, and she glanced behind her to make sure she wasn't being followed. She'd tried not to show fear during the confrontation, but it was all she could do not to cry. She couldn't face life without him.

She'd been on edge ever since yesterday.

Twilight backlit the treetops and highlighted the hanging moss. Instead of finding it beautiful, she saw frightening shadows and shuddered. She slid under the wheel and started the engine, then pulled out of her driveway onto the road.

She turned toward the Gulf. The water always calmed her when she was upset—and she had crossed upset moments ago and swerved into the scared zone.

Her belly barely fit under the wheel, but this baby would be born soon, and then she'd have her figure back. She accelerated away from her home, a dilapidated one-story house with peeling white paint, and switched on her headlights.

The radio blared full of the news about the Berlin Wall coming down, but Lisa didn't care about that, not now. She switched channels until she found Tom Petty's "Free Fallin'" playing, but even her favorite tune failed to sooth her shattered nerves. Could she seriously be murdered over this? She'd glimpsed madness in those eyes.

She pressed the brakes as she came to a four-way stop, but the brake pedal went clear to the floor. She gasped and pumped the pedal again. No response. The car shot through the intersection, barely missing the tail end of another vehicle that had entered it before her.

Hands gripping the steering wheel, she struggled to keep the car on the road as she frantically thought of a way to bring it to a stop that didn't involve hitting another car or a tree. The baby in her belly kicked as if he or she knew their lives hung suspended in time.

"We're going to make it, little one. We have to. I can't leave you alone." No one would love her baby if she died. Her mother couldn't care for her child. She cared more about her drugs than anything else.

Lisa tried to tamp down her rising emotions, but she'd never been so frightened. The car fishtailed on the sandy road as she forced it back from the shoulder. Huge trees lined the pavement in a dense formation. Where could she drive off into relative safety? A field sprawled over on the right, just past the four-way stop ahead. If she made it through, it seemed the only place where they might survive.

Had the brakes been cut? What else could it be? She'd just had the car serviced.

Lisa approached the stop sign much too fast. The slight downhill slope had only accelerated the speed that hovered at nearly seventy. Her mouth went bone dry.

Her future with her child and the love of her life depended on the next few moments.

She could do it—she had to.

The tires squealed as the car barely held on to the road through the slight turn at high speed. Before Lisa could breathe a sigh of relief, a lumbering truck approached from the right side, and she laid on her horn with all her strength. She unleashed a scream as the car hurtled toward the big dump truck.

The violent impact robbed her lungs of air, and she blacked out. When she came to, she was in an ambulance. She fought back the darkness long enough to tell the paramedic, "Save my baby. Please . . ."

She whispered a final prayer for God to take care of her child before a darker night claimed her.

CHAPTER 1

The examination table was cold and hard under her back as Harper Taylor looked around the room. She focused on the picture of a familiar Florida beach, which helped block out the doctor's movements and the smell of antiseptic. She'd been on the beach at Honeymoon Island yesterday, and she could still smell the briny scent of the bay and hear the call of the gulls. The ocean always sang a siren song she found impossible to resist.

Calm. Peace. The smell of a newborn baby's head.

"All done." Dr. Cox's face came to her side, and she was smiling. "Lie here for about fifteen minutes, and then you can get dressed and go home." She tugged the paper sheet down over Harper's legs.

"How soon will I know if the embryo transfer was successful?" Though she'd researched the process to death, she wanted some assurance.

"Two weeks. I know right now it seems like an eternity, but those days will pass before you know it. I've already submitted the lab requisition for a beta-HCG test. If we get a positive, we'll track the counts every few days to make sure they are increasing properly."

Dr. Cox patted her hand. "Hang in there." She exited the room, leaving Harper alone to stare at the ceiling.

Her longing for a child brought tears to her eyes. She'd felt empty for so long. Alone. And she'd be a good mom—she knew she would. All the kids in the church nursery loved her, and she babysat for friends every chance she got. She had a wealth of patience, and she'd do everything in her power to make sure her child knew she or he was wanted.

She slipped her hand to her stomach. The gender didn't matter to her at all. She could love either a boy or a girl. It didn't matter that this baby wasn't her own blood. The little one would grow inside her, and the two of them would be inseparable.

Once the fifteen minutes were up, she was finally able to go to the bathroom and get dressed. She already felt different. Was that a good sign, or was it all in her head? She slipped her feet into flip-flops, then headed toward the reception area.

The tension she'd held inside melted when she saw her business partner, Oliver Jackson, in the waiting room, engrossed in conversation with an attractive woman in her fifties. She hadn't been sure he'd be here. He'd dropped her off, then gone to practice his bagpipes with the band for the Scottish Highland Games in April. He said he'd be back, but he often got caught up in what he was doing and lost track of time. It wouldn't have been the first time he'd stood her up.

Oliver was a big man, well over six feet tall, with broad shoulders and a firm stomach from the hours spent in his elaborate home gym. She'd always wondered if he colored his still-dark hair or if he was one of those lucky people who didn't gray early.

Even here in a fertility clinic, this man in his sixties turned women's heads. She'd watched them fawn over him for years, and he'd had his share of relationships over the fifteen years since his divorce. But Oliver never stuck with one woman for long. Was there even such a thing as a forever love? She hadn't seen any evidence of it, and it felt much safer to build her life without expecting that kind of faithfulness from any man. Having a child could fill that hole in her heart without the need to be on her guard around a man.

He saw her and ended his conversation, then joined her at the door. His dark-brown eyes held concern. "You changed your mind?"

She shook her head. "Not a chance."

"It seems an extreme way to go about having a family. You're only thirty. There's plenty of time to have children in the traditional way."

"Only thirty? There's not even a boyfriend in the wings. Besides, you don't know what it's like to long for a family all your life and never even have so much as a cousin to turn to." She knew better than to try to explain her reasons. No one could understand the guard she'd placed around her heart unless they'd lived her life.

His brow creased in a frown. "I tried to find your family."

"I know you did."

All he'd discovered was her mother, Lisa Taylor, had died moments after Harper's birth. Oliver had never been able to discover her father's name. Harper still had unpleasant memories of her grandmother, who had cared for Harper until she was eight before dying of a drug overdose at fifty. Hard as those years were, her grandmother's neglect had been better than the foster homes where Harper had landed.

This embryo adoption was going to change her life.

"I'll get the car."

She nodded and stepped outside into a beautiful February day that lacked the usual Florida humidity. Oliver drove under the porte cochere, and she climbed into his white Mercedes convertible. He'd put the top down, and the sound of the wind deterred further conversation as he drove her home.

He parked along the road by the inlet where she'd anchored her houseboat. "Want me to stay awhile?"

She shook her head. "I'm going to lie on the top deck in the sunshine and read a book. I'll think happy thoughts and try not to worry."

His white teeth flashed in an approving smile. "Sounds like a great idea."

She held his gaze. "You've always been there for me, Oliver. From the first moment Ridge dragged me out of the garage with his new sleeping bag in my hands. How did you see past the angry kid I was at fifteen?"

He shrugged and stared at the ground. "I'd just given my kids everything they could possibly want for Christmas, and they'd looked at the gifts with a cursory thank-you that didn't feel genuine. Willow was pouting about not getting a car. Then there you were. I looked in your eyes and saw the determination I'd felt myself when I was growing up poor in Alabama. I knew in that moment I had to help you or regret it for the rest of my life."

Tears burned her eyes. "You've done so much—making sure I had counseling, tutoring, a job, college. All of it would have been out of reach if not for you."

He touched her cheek. "You did me proud, Harper. Now go rest. Call me if you need me."

She blinked back the tears and waggled her fingers at him in a cheery good-bye, then got out and walked down the pier to where the *Sea Silk* bobbed in the waves. A pelican tipped its head to gawk at her, then flapped off on big wings. When she got closer to her houseboat, she slowed to a stop. The door to the cabin had been wrenched off. Someone had broken in.

She opened her purse to grab her phone to call the police, and then her gut clenched. She'd left her phone in the boat cabin. She'd have to go aboard to report the break-in. Could the intruder still be there?

She looked around and listened to the wind through the mangroves. There was no other sound, but she felt an ominous presence, and fear rippled down her back. She reversed course and went to her SUV parked in a small pull-off nearby. She'd drive into Dunedin and report it.

Ridge Jackson drove through downtown Dunedin at twilight to meet his father. His dad was usually straightforward and direct, but when Dad had called for a meeting, he'd been vague and distracted. Ridge couldn't still a niggle of uneasiness—it was as if Dad knew Ridge would be a hard sell on whatever new idea he'd come up with.

He had no doubt it was a new business scheme. Oliver Jackson had his finger in more pies of business enterprises than Ridge could count, but his dad's main company was Jackson Pharmaceuticals. The juggernaut business had grown immensely in the last ten years. He had the Midas touch. Everyone expected Ridge to be like his dad—charismatic and business oriented—but what Ridge wanted to do was pursue his work of studying mollusks in peace.

He smiled at the thought of telling his dad the great news about his new job. The offer had come through yesterday, and he still couldn't take it all in. Dad's distraction couldn't have come at a worse time. Ridge had to sell his place in Gainesville and find somewhere to live on Sanibel Island.

He parked and exited, ready to be out of the vehicle after the long drive from Gainesville. He went into The Dunedin Smokehouse, his favorite restaurant. The tangy aroma of beef brisket teased his nose and made his mouth water. They had the best brisket and pecan pie in the state.

He wound his way around the wooden tables until he found Dad chatting up a server in the back corner. He had never figured out how his dad could uncover someone's life story in thirty seconds flat. Ridge liked people, but he felt intrusive when he asked someone how their day was going.

Dad's grin split his genial face. "There you are, Ridge. I've already ordered our usual brisket nachos to share. How was your trip?"

"Good. Ran into some traffic in Tampa, but it wasn't too bad."

"Uh-huh." His dad stared off into the distance. "I've got a new project for you, son."

Ridge squared his shoulders and steeled himself for the coming battle. "Before you even get started, Dad, I've got a new job. I'm leaving the Florida Museum, and I'll be working at Bailey-Matthews Shell Museum on Sanibel Island. I'll get to work with one of the best malacologists in the country. I'm pretty stoked about it."

Most people heard the term *malacologist* and their eyes glazed over. He'd been fascinated with mollusks ever since he found his first shell at age two. It was a dream come true to work for the shell museum. He'd be in charge of shell exhibits from around the world.

His dad's mouth grew pinched. "I, ah, I'm sure it's a good job, son, but I've got something bigger in mind for you. It's a chance to use your knowledge of mollusks for something to benefit mankind. This isn't just growing collections, but something really valuable."

Dad always managed to get in his jabs. Preserving mollusks had its own kind of nobility. Ridge narrowed his eyes at his dad and shut up for a moment as the server brought their drinks. When she left, he leaned forward. "Okay, what is it?"

"I've bought a lab for you. You'll be able to study mollusks and snails to see if they hold any promise for medicinal uses. I'd like you to concentrate on curing dementia first. I don't want you or Willow to end up like my dad."

Ridge's grandfather had died of Alzheimer's last year, and it hit Dad hard.

Ridge held back his flicker of interest. His dad knew exactly which buttons to push, and Ridge didn't want to encourage him. Ridge had long believed the sea held treasures that would help mankind. Researchers thought mollusks might contain major neurological and antibiotic uses. "That sounds—interesting."

"I've already put out the call for lab assistants and researchers. You'll just oversee it and direct the research. I've even created a collection room for you to fully explore the different mollusks." His dad took a sip of his tea. "It will be a few weeks before we're up and running, but in the meantime, you can comb through research and see where you want to start."

"You're just now telling me about it?"

His dad shrugged. "I wanted you to see the lab in all its glory first. We can go take a look when we leave here. There's only one caveat."

Ah, finally the truth. Story of his life. Dad always held back the full truth about anything. He should be called the master manipulator.

Ridge took a swig of his drink. "What is it?"

"I want you to start with pen shells. They're already so versatile, and I believe there's more of their magic yet to be discovered."

White-hot anger shot up Ridge's spine. "This is about Harper instead of me, isn't it? It's been that way since you first saw her camping out in our backyard as a teenager. You're such a sucker for a sob story. I overheard you on the phone the other day, you know. You were telling her you'd be there for her and the baby. She used to get into trouble wherever she went, and I doubt that's changed. And you're still the same patsy." He spat out the last words with a sneer.

Dad's brows drew together in a dark frown. "I've never understood your hostility toward her. And she's long outgrown any kind of reckless behavior."

They'd had this discussion on many occasions, and he wasn't going to change his dad's mind about her. From the moment she'd shown up in Dad's life, Ridge had resented her and the way his father catered to her. Ridge had gone off to his freshman year of college when Dad took Harper under his wing. She'd been a runaway from the foster care system, and he'd done more for her than for his own kids. He'd gotten his secretary to agree to foster the girl. She hadn't had to work during her high school years like he and Willow had. Dad had hired tutors to help her catch up while they'd been expected to figure out their studies by themselves.

The woman had been a thorn in his side for fifteen years. No part of him wanted to have anything to do with her. "What's Harper have to say about it?"

"I haven't told her yet."

Ridge stared at his dad. Typical. Only reveal half of what you know and keep the other half for negotiation. He was sick of his father's half-truths.

But what if in working with Harper, he was able to find definitive proof that she was only hanging around Dad because of his money? Ridge knew it was true. His dad hated being used, and it wasn't often someone managed to get the best of him. Harper was that one exception.

He wanted to get to the bottom of whatever clever plan she'd hatched.

He reached for a nacho laden with smoked brisket and jalapeños. "Tell me more about the lab."

His resolve helped him walk through the lab after dinner. He would enjoy working with the impressive equipment and facilities, and it almost superseded his goal of bringing down Harper. Almost.

ABOUT THE AUTHOR

Photo by Amber Zimmerman

Colleen Coble is a *USA TODAY* bestselling author and RITA finalist best known for her coastal romantic suspense novels, including *The Inn at Ocean's Edge*, *Twilight at Blueberry Barrens*, and the Lavender Tides, Sunset Cove, Hope Beach, and Rock Harbor series.

Connect with Colleen online at colleencoble.com
Facebook: @colleencoblebooks
Twitter: @colleencoble
Pinterest: @ColleenCoble